A Rayne of Terror publication

Becoming...and excerpt of *The Lazarus Contagion*

Copyright © Saul Bainbridge (writing as Jacob Rayne) 2013

Cover art created by Stephen Bryant of SRB productions

Dedicated to Michelle, for absolutely everything.

Becoming…

There are places in this world which are magnets to evil and violence. Peth Vale, the large, secluded house on the hill at the edge of Marshton town, is one such place.

There is probably a similar place in most towns, a place that parents forbid their children from visiting, where those same children will cower, yet dare each other to enter.

Peth Vale is variously known as: 'A portal of evil,' 'Hell's gates,' and 'The Murder House,' depending on which of the superstitious locals you were to ask.

Rumours say that the house is haunted, and it may well be: enough lives have ended here to justify that claim. Others say that blood taints the land the house stands upon, a curse forever to be repeated.

Some of the more imaginative locals have reported hearing screams and depraved laughter from Peth Vale during Marshton's long nights.

You may dismiss this as urban myths, bogey man stories, but, on the days before today, their ears have not deceived them: the screams and laughter have been real.

This is not the first time in Peth Vale's short history that the house has been a site of horrific violence. It will doubtless be the last too, but those are stories for another day, for it is with one particular spate of horrors that we are concerned.

Peth Vale, which sits in expansive gardens, is currently ablaze; the fires illuminating its many windows making them look like blazing, infernal eyes. The air is thick with petrol fumes and smoke, which rise from Peth Vale's roof in a huge black column.

The house continues to burn, the flames which crackle and consume its frame helped by a light southward breeze.

The air soon fills with sirens, as the police arrive at the scene and cut the hefty chains that secure Peth Vale's iron gates. The gates creak open, allowing the crime scene team to flood into the grounds of the burning house.

What they find there brings more than one meal up and out of the stomach of its host, to lie, steaming, in the damp grass. Peth Vale's paved side yard is awash with blood, some of it mere hours old. Two trails lead across the patio, ending near a row of dirty white tiles.

A fingerless, decomposing hand sits in the corner of the patio, among the dried blood. A severed noose hangs from one of the trees, the loop from it lies a few feet away in the grass, blood drying on the thick strands of rope.

One of the officers follows the twin trails of blood, past fresh blood splatters, towards the swimming pool. The water is filthy, with a red tinge to it.

Just visible through the murk are black cylindrical forms at the bottom of the pool. The smell from the stagnant, bloody water causes the policeman to gag and lose his supper.

The police drain the water from the pool and start to drag the black, weighted tarpaulins out, storing them on the poolside before they are unwrapped.

There is a corpse inside each one, most of them horrifically mutilated. They all look as though they have died very recently.

By this time, the fire brigade has reached the scene. They are too late; the house is beyond salvation.

'Best thing for it,' states one officer, who is in the midst of discovering his second Peth Vale crime scene.

Two firemen venture into the burning building and drag out one more body. This is the worst of all. Although badly burnt, the body is still recognisable as being female. The head has been severed and the skin removed. Arguably, it is this body that has the most significance to this tale.

It will take the police all night to catalogue the crime scene, then transport and identify the bodies.

By the time this is done, they will already have apprehended their main suspect, allegedly a death-masked, merciless killer seeking bloody revenge on all who have wronged him.

But there is more to this tale than first meets the eye.

And that is the end of the story, years after this all began.

Instead of observing the police's brutal interrogation of their suspect, let's hear the events which led to this bloodbath.

Let's hear about the real killer and his becoming…

Part One – Hunted

Becoming: To come, change or grow to be

Chapter 1

The dying October sun was shedding the last of its blood onto the dark clouds above Marshton town as Rhonda Williams pulled her car onto the driveway of her detached home.

Cursing, she realised that the bin men had recklessly left the bin across the bottom of the drive, in such a way that she'd have to get out and move it before she could park up. Raindrops spattered the windscreen as she opened the door.

'Just great,' she hissed, putting one of her work files over her head to shield it from the concussive force of the falling rain while she hauled the bin back to its usual position by the back door.

As she dusted the stale dirt from her hands, she noticed that the kitchen light was on. 'Lazy little bastards,' she hissed, realising that her son, Mark, and her sixteen year old daughter, Hannah, were home and hadn't been arsed to put the bin back. 'How many goddamned times do I have to tell them?' she muttered as she got back into the car.

She parked the car in front of the garage and got out, again sheltering under the file as she used the light from the boot to search for the correct key.

With it in hand, she pulled the bag of shopping from the boot and moved to the door.

She inserted the key and turned it, feeling a strange sense of something being wrong.

The bottle of sparkling wine in the shopping bag clinked against the door as she fumbled and dropped the key.

Then it struck her what was wrong: eyes were crawling over her skin like dozens of tiny spiders. She looked round and saw no one.

Muttering angry words beneath her breath, she put the bag down and bent to pick up the keys.

As she concentrated on the key, a gloved hand lifted the lid of the wheelie bin next to the one she'd dragged back along the drive.

She heard gurgling laughter then the bin lid slamming shut.

She jolted and spun to face the source of the noise. Her entire body shaking with the fear that pulsed through her, she grabbed the lid of the bin.

Pulled it up.

A white-painted face stared up at her. The eyes were painted with black crosses, the nose was a black circle and the mouth a dark grin that seemed to stretch from ear to ear. A shock of fuzzy black hair sat atop the leering face.

She froze in her confusion.

Rhonda's heart leapt into her throat as the clown let out a low, disturbing chuckle then stood up from the bin. Her eyes were drawn to the cleaver in the clown's hand. It was dripping with blood that looked black in the fading light.

The clown's first step towards her shocked her into action. She picked up the bag of shopping and turned the door handle. The hinges squealed as the door opened. She pulled the key out of the lock and forced her trembling body through the doorway.

She slammed the door on the clown's arm which was reaching through the doorway.

Tried to force the door shut but the meaty limb blocked its path.

She screamed as the clown barged the door with his shoulder. His black- and white-painted face appeared in the open door. Thinking fast, she pulled the wine bottle out and swung it at his head.

The bottle exploded, showering glass and fizzing wine everywhere. The clown stumbled back just enough to allow her to get the door shut.

At first, her shaking hand missed the keyhole but finally the key sunk in. She lifted the handle and turned the key, just as the clown hurled himself against the glass.

To her relief the glass held, but she knew that it wouldn't last forever.

The clown's face pressed against the window, distorted by the pressure he was exerting on the glass. His wounds left small slicks of blood down the window. He let out an insane laugh that would stay with her as long as she lived.

She rushed away from the door, eager to take her eyes from the hideous spectacle. She let out a low groan as the strip light in the kitchen flickered and went out, plunging the room into darkness.

A bang on the kitchen window made her jump. She could picture the clown braying his fists against the glass, trying to force his way inside.

Putting him out of her mind, she instead concentrated on reaching her kids and making sure they were safe.

The next blow on the window went right through her.

She let out a panicked sob and made her way through the darkened house.

The hallway carpet was wet and sticky, but she couldn't see why. She called out to her children.

Silence greeted her calls.

A clinking sound came from above her.

'Mark, is that you?' she cried out. The noise came again, startlingly loud in the silent house. 'Hannah?'

The braying on the kitchen window had ceased. The absence of the noise should have been a relief, but it wasn't; at least with the noise she had known where the clown was.

She flicked the light switch at the bottom of the stairs. It didn't come on. Her shaking legs carried her to the telephone stand near the front door.

The house was eerily silent, the only noise the occasional clinking sound from above her head.

Her nostrils picked up a smell that was familiar but hard to place. She ignored this for now, as the jumble of her thoughts had more important things on which to concentrate than working out the origin of a strange smell.

Her shin slammed into the telephone stand. Cursing, she reached under it for the small torch kept there for emergencies. Shook her head in disbelief when the torch failed to work.

Another brief rummage in the telephone stand produced a small candle which was held onto a plate with melted wax.

She found the match box on top of the plate and flicked a match against the scratch pad. The match flickered into life, offering a brief respite against the oppressive darkness. She lit the wick on the candle and turned to face the stairs.

The scream tore from her gut as she saw the body swinging from a chain attached to the bannister. At first she thought it was Mark, but then she realised that the body was thicker and longer.

It was the body of Alan, her husband.

The chain was fastened around his ankles, suspending him upside down from the bannister. He moved a little, creating the metallic noise that she had heard earlier.

Alan's throat bore a ragged wound which was choked with clotted blood which left trails from his throat, over his head and onto the carpet. Dark blood was congealing on his forehead and in his hair. Thick trails of it were matted into the carpet, leading down the stairs to the corridor.

She realised that the heavy coppery smell was what she had smelt earlier.

She stared at her husband's blood-spattered corpse for what felt like hours. Finally she tore her eyes from his body, but everywhere she looked she was reminded of his fate. The carpet, walls and even the ceiling were splashed with thick blood spray.

Her heart sank when she realised she was going to have to pass him to see what fate had befallen her kids.

Alan's corpse swayed a little as she set foot on the stairs. It seemed like he was trying to get her to acknowledge his death.

She blotted it out as best she could, keeping her eyes glued to the blood-drenched carpet. It was hard to believe that a body could contain so much blood.

As she moved level with him, the chain again clinked with his movement. The candle light cast everything in a dim glow, making the everyday abnormal and macabre.

She found her gaze drawn to him and the whites of his eyes that bulged out of the crimson mass that was now his face.

Looking away, she forced her shaking legs to move past him, crying out when his body nudged against her. The cold, sticky feel of his lifeless flesh both saddened and sickened her.

Finally she was past him, and she ran up the stairs to prevent herself from looking at him again.

On the landing the candle flickered in the draught from the open bathroom window. She felt a sense of utter dread at the realisation that the window was open as it meant the clown had had access to the house while she was fucking around trying to find a candle.

She rushed into the bathroom, slamming the window shut. The noise was reassuring and unsettling at the same time.

The dim light from the candle revealed a shadowy form behind the shower curtain.

Oh, God, it's him, he got in while I was downstairs, she thought.

But the shape seemed smaller than the clown had been.

Her left hand held the plate with a white knuckle grip. A chill ran through her, in spite of the heat that the candle provided.

Her palsied right hand gripped the shower curtain.

Without waiting to prepare herself for the scene behind it, she yanked it back.

Chapter 2

Mark slumped back against the edge of the bath, surrounded by a pool of blood. The crimson fluid was splattered up the cream tiles that surrounded the bath, like Jackson Pollock rendered in blood.

Unable to resist, she moved closer and examined her son's body. His arms and legs had been hacked off and were stacked next to him like kindling. A deep stab wound in his chest seemed to have been the fatal blow.

She sobbed as she remembered holding Mark as a child, thinking what a bright life he had to look forward to. Instead he had barely made the threshold of manhood before he'd been butchered.

She back-handed tears from her eyes and resolved to find her daughter.

Hannah's bedroom door was shut, but the idea of her escaping the clown's rampage did not occur to Rhonda. She felt certain he'd killed all of them.

She gripped the handle, her stomach churning at the sticky feel of dried blood on the brass.

This time she did hesitate, her mind struggling to cope with the reality of already finding two of her family brutally murdered.

She closed her eyes, took in a deep breath then turned the door handle. Shoved hard. The door flew open, slamming into the wall behind.

As she moved in, the plate upon which the candle sat shook, throwing moving shadows over the darkened room.

The curtains were drawn, but they billowed slightly in the wind.

A pool of blood was slowly spreading across the floor towards her. Hannah's body slumped in the middle of the growing sea of crimson. Her white pyjamas were drenched in blood and clung to her crumpled frame.

Rhonda couldn't see her daughter's face and would soon come to wish it had stayed that way. She approached quickly to get the horrid spectacle that awaited her out of the way.

She stood looking down on her daughter's body, her eyes seeming to take in the grisly details for an eternity.

Hannah's head had been pounded into a bloody pulp, revealing gleaming shards of skull and small chunks of brain through her blood-soaked blonde hair.

Rhonda retched and her dinner came flooding out of her, mingling with the blood on the floor.

Rhonda again started to cry until a noise from outside the room thrust her out of her sorrow.

Her eyes scanned for a suitable weapon, landing upon the small baseball bat that Alan had bought Hannah on their last holiday in America.

She hefted the heavy wooden bat in her hands, feeling confident it would do some damage provided she could get a hit in with it.

The bat shook in her hands as she turned away from her daughter's ruined face and started back towards the landing.

It was as she set foot on the landing that she first heard the menacing laughter from above.

She looked up to see the clown falling towards her. He seemed to move in slow motion, but this was still too quick for her to react. His weight slammed onto her, pinning her facedown on the floor.

While she tried to pull air into her lungs, he got to his knees.

His hands gripped her hair and yanked her head back. She smelt blood and greasepaint. Her bulging eyes stared up at the clown as he rolled her onto her back.

The black- and white-painted face leered down at her. The white paint contained specks of blood from where she'd hit him with the wine bottle.

His grin seemed to widen further as he raised the cleaver above his head. A single drop of blood rolled down the blade and landed on her belly.

Then the cleaver came down.

Her arms rose to stop the blow. The blade bit deep into her forearm, sending white hot pain flashing through her entire body. The clown pulled hard, wrenching her arm up. The blade was still wedged in the bone.

Rhonda cried out and tried to roll to her side, but the clown's blood-smeared fist crashed into the side of her face, sending transparent specks flying across her vision. She tasted blood in the back of her throat.

The clown yanked the blade again, this time pulling it loose. Agony tore through Rhonda's body.

The blade came down again, this time hitting her in the throat. She felt the blade slice through the muscle of her neck and wedge against the bone.

Blood welled up out of the wound. The crimson liquid filled her mouth too and she feared it was going to choke her.

The clown pulled the blade loose, smiling as he brought it down again, further widening the severe wound that he had created. Warm blood sprayed her face and chest.

One by one, Rhonda's senses shut down. Her smell was first to go, the scent of blood suddenly disappearing.

Her touch was next, it felt like she was floating, numb.

The taste of blood faded, shortly followed by her hearing. The clown's mouth moved in a silent laugh.

She saw the black crosses around his eyes, saw the immense black grin, then she saw nothing at all.

Chapter 3

The man known as Alfred Wright (soon to be dubbed Mr Chuckles the Psychotic Clown by the press) woke the next morning with a sense of calm.

He showered – somewhat reluctantly as he enjoyed the feel of dried blood against his skin – then dressed. While he ate breakfast he relived the events of the previous evening.

The man, woman and teenaged boy had been a welcome bonus. All he'd really cared about was getting to the Williams' snotty daughter and teaching her a lesson. She and her friend had had it coming.

Alfred had loved working as a teaching assistant in Marshton's combined primary and secondary school. The money wasn't great, but Alfred felt that doing something he enjoyed was indeed a rare thing, so he'd cherished his job.

He had loved being around the kids. Not in a creepy way, just he identified more with them than he did the adults who shunned and mocked him.

He'd never liked life as an adult; life as a kid was much better, they were encouraged to free their imaginations and chase their dreams instead of doing jobs they hated just to earn a living.

So when Hannah and that little bitch Jane Miller had accused him of touching them in the toilets after school, his world had fallen apart.

The headmaster had been supportive, but couldn't be seen to be taking a soft approach to such a serious accusation.

After a few weeks of humiliating questions, Alfred was told that unfortunately he wouldn't be kept on at the school.

At first Alfred had been philosophical, reasoning that it had all happened to teach him a lesson, but then the abuse had started. His home had been broken into and 'Kiddy fiddler' had been spray-painted on his wall. His possessions had been trashed and dog shit rubbed into his bed and clothes.

His beloved wife told him that she could no longer tolerate the stigma of being married to the man who had been branded a pervert and a clown.

If the cap fits, he'd thought with a grin the night before he decided to break into the Williams' home.

He had lost everything because of a vindictive lie two snot-nosed little kids had told. He'd shown Hannah. Smashed her head right in with a claw hammer.

Jane would get the same treatment, once the hysteria had died down a little.

He couldn't wait to get his hands on the little bitch and teach her the lesson she sorely needed.

A smile crossed his face as he thought of Hannah's splintered, bleeding skull. He was going to make even more of a mess of Jane's head. He couldn't wait to shut her smart mouth once and for all.

Chapter 4

Mike Miller laid on his horn as the driver in front ground to a halt for no apparent reason.

'Come on,' Mike shouted, waving his arms in an attempt to communicate the urgency of the situation.

The man in front got out of the car, showing a complete lack of embarrassment for his shit driving. He ignored Mike and resumed chatting on his mobile phone.

'Are you fucking kidding me?' Mike shouted, slamming his hand into the horn.

The man ignored him.

Mike looked for a gap in the traffic but it seemed none of the bastards were going to let him out.

He felt suddenly, irrationally, terrified. He had to pick up his son, Luke, from school, and didn't want to be late, especially given the recent murders in town. Mike's daughter, Jane, was going straight to a friend's house, so he didn't need to pick her up.

He couldn't bear the thought of the killer getting his vile hands on Luke.

No fucking way was he going to let that happen.

He slammed his foot on the gas. Steered hard right onto the other side of the road.

The prick on the phone leapt out of the way, a comical expression on his face. Mike took his wing mirror off as he drove past.

A car on the other side of the road brayed his horn. Mike returned the horn and flashed a middle finger.

'Asshole,' the other driver shouted.

'Fuck you,' Mike roared, pulling onto the correct side of the road once he'd passed the arsehole on the phone.

He checked the clock.

Five minutes to cross town in rush hour.

He groaned as he realised he had no chance of making it.

Chapter 5

Alfred approached Marshton's school on foot. As it was almost Halloween, he found he could get away with wearing his fiendish clown makeup. Some of the other parents were dressed up too, clearly picking up their children for Halloween parties.

The school bell sounded just as he reached the school where he'd spent so many happy working hours.

He strolled up to the gates, marvelling at the laziness of some of the parents who couldn't even be bothered to get out of their cars.

He nodded a greeting to a man dressed up as an undead Michael Jackson and waited by the gates.

His heart thudded against his ribs, partly at the fear of being discovered, but mostly through excitement of what he was going to do to Jane when he had her to himself.

Alfred smiled at the parents as they took their kids. Within a few minutes most of them had gone. It became clear that the three remaining kids weren't going to be picked up any time soon.

None of the trio was Jane, but one was her younger brother, Luke. He would have to do for now until Jane showed up. Hell, maybe he could hurt the little boy and send photos to Jane, really fuck with her mind.

His grin widened as he explored this possibility.

He went over to the three kids and smiled. Luke was the smallest of the three, probably eight at the very oldest.

'Hi, there, Luke,' he said, flashing his big clown's smile.

The boy smiled back.

'I'm a friend of your daddy's,' Alfred continued.

'Don't listen to him, Luke,' said Melanie, a sullen and much less trusting little girl who was also waiting to be picked up.

'I don't have to listen to you,' Luke told her.

'That's right, you don't,' Alfred said. 'Don't listen to her. Your dad said I was to take you to a Halloween party. He said we were to go and get you a costume first. Then we'll go and get ice cream and head off to the party.'

'Don't listen to him,' Melanie said.

'You're just jealous cos I'm going to the party,' Luke said, sticking out his tongue.

He walked off hand in hand with the man that he believed was his father's friend. He didn't see anything wrong with this; after all, clowns were happy people who always made other people smile.

Melanie ran back into the school to tell a teacher about the scary clown who had taken Luke.

Chapter 6

Mike pulled up outside the school and saw one small boy waiting. He wondered why there wasn't a teacher with him, especially with things the way they were in Marshton.

Where was Luke?

His heart picked up a little when he realised that his son wasn't waiting outside.

He dived out of the car and ran over to the kid.

'Where's Luke?' he asked.

While Mike waited for the boy to answer, the school doors burst open and a teacher ran out with a little girl.

'They went that way,' Melanie told the teacher, pointing to the path that led onto the estate.

'What's going on?' Mike asked, fear already starting to consume him.

'We're not sure,' the teacher said.

'The scary clown took Luke,' Melanie said.

'Shit,' Mike shouted, making both Melanie and the teacher jump. 'Why was no one watching him?'

The teacher shifted from foot to foot, staring at the floor.

'What did he look like?' Mike asked Melanie.

'A clown,' she said. 'He had black crosses over his eyes and a big black grin.'

'If he hurts my son…' Mike said, glaring at the guilty-looking teacher.

The teacher was still staring at the floor when Mike ran in the direction that Melanie had pointed.

Frantic, Mike scanned the estate. He couldn't think straight. Shit, they could be anywhere by now.

Why hadn't Luke listened when he'd warned him about strangers?

He ran farther into the estate, unable to escape the growing feeling that he may never see his son again.

Mike spent the next half an hour in sheer despair. The realisation that the stranger could have taken his son anywhere by now had begun to sink in.

The cops had made an appearance and were assisting in the search, knocking on doors with photos of Luke and an artist's impression of the clown based on Melanie's description.

They were getting nowhere.

No one wanted to be the one to tell Mike the bad news, but, by his broken expression, it was clear that he already knew.

Unless they had a miracle there was no way they would find his son.

Chapter 7

Alfred flinched as there was a knock on his door. He locked the kid in the bedroom, made sure he had washed off all of the face-paint with a quick look in the mirror then answered the door.

'Hello, Sir, we're investigating the disappearance of a child from the local school,' the well-dressed man who was obviously a plain-clothes policeman said.

'Oh, how terrible. I'll do whatever I can to help.'

'Thank you, Sir. This is the child,' he said, flashing Luke's photo.

Alfred's brow furrowed as he considered the picture carefully. He paused for a few seconds then shook his head. 'Nope. Can't say I've seen him, officer. Sorry.'

'What about this guy?' he asked, holding up the artist's impression of the clown.

Alfred stared at the inaccurate picture and frowned in concentration. 'Yeah, I think that's Eddie,' he said.

'Eddie?'

'Yeah, Eddie. Don't know his surname. He lives out by the edge of town.'

'Thank you.'

'Not at all. And I hope you find the missing kiddie.'

As he started to close the door, a knocking sound came from upstairs.

Luke had been a bit scared when he'd seen the huge, forbidding house where the clown was leading him, but he hadn't been too frightened until he'd been locked in the bedroom.

For the first time he began to suspect that the clown wasn't who he said he was. He'd remembered what his dad had told him about the man who had been killing people in town.

Another warning from his father flashed into his head – something about not going near this house because bad things had happened here.

The photo of the clown holding a meat cleaver on the bedside table led him to the conclusion that he had been taken by the killer.

Screaming, he beat his fists against the locked door.

Chapter 8

The cop put his hand in the door to stop it from closing.

'You mind if I take a look inside, Sir?' he said, suspicion obvious on his face.

Alfred mentally cursed.

'Course not,' he said. 'My kid's a fucking nightmare at the moment.' He tried on a smile but it didn't quite fit.

The cop seemed to sense his deception.

Alfred looked down at the cop's belt. No gun, just a cosh. Nothing he couldn't handle.

'Please, come in,' he said, shutting the door behind the cop. 'He's upstairs. Second door on the right.'

Alfred tried to remain calm but he had a feeling that he was in deep shit. He decided to wait before he made his move.

The cop moved upstairs. Alfred followed a few steps behind. The braying and screaming became louder.

'He's got ADD or something,' Alfred said.

The cop couldn't have looked more suspicious if he'd tried.

They reached the landing.

Almost time, Alfred thought. *Soon as he notices the key, it's time.*

'You make a habit of locking your kid up?' the cop said, pointing to the key in the lock.

The words were barely out of his mouth when Alfred's fist smashed into his ear hard enough to knock him back into the wall. For a second he didn't know where he was.

His vision cleared to see Alfred waving a meat cleaver above his head.

He went for his cosh, but the blade bit into his bicep, cutting him to the bone. Blood poured from the wound. His arm dangled, limp and useless, by his side.

He had time to let out a cry of pain before the cleaver slammed into the side of his neck.

The pain barely registered. He realised he was falling.

Realised he was dying.

Then he saw the man leading a wide-eyed child out of the locked room. Officer Kent had time to recognise the fact that it was the kid from the photo then life ebbed away from him in a crimson tide.

Chapter 9

Mike was across the road from Peth Vale, spinning aimlessly, hoping for the miracle that would bring his son back into his life.

Halfway round his second spin, he saw a man rushing down the house's long drive.

It took him a few seconds to register that the man had a child with him.

After another second he noticed that the kid was Luke.

'Hey,' he shouted.

The man looked at him and picked up his pace.

'That man's got my son,' Mike announced to anyone listening.

He ran after the man who had taken Luke.

Alfred cursed as he realised that he'd been spotted. Trust his car to be out of action too. Damn his luck. He'd have to steal the first one he saw and get out of town.

Dragging the boy by the arm, he ran. The little bastard was trying to be awkward by resisting. He was screaming and crying fit to raise hell too.

Alfred thought about it. Weighed up his options. He'd be much faster without the kid. He could always find him again. Or not, he was a fucking nightmare.

'Fuck it,' he muttered, slashing the cleaver across the child's belly.

Alfred shoved the screaming kid away, taking a brief second to admire the blood which was already soaking into the boy's white t-shirt.

Then he ran.

Mike let out a cry of rage when he saw the blade dig into Luke's belly. His son's scream tore through him.

The man took off, faster without his struggling, screaming burden.

Mike reached his son and started screaming for help. Blood was pissing out of the wound.

Mike pressed his hand to the wound, trying to stem the bleeding.

He called for help again, praying that his son wouldn't die.

Chapter 10

Alfred grinned as he ran. He'd known hurting the kid would stop the dad in his tracks, no matter how intent on retribution he'd been.

Now he just had to escape the cops and get out of town. After that, he'd be home free.

He had a friend in the next town who'd let him crash on the settee until the shit storm blew over.

He ducked into a back yard as he saw a cop running down the alley towards him. Pressed himself against the wall until the cop had passed. Then he snuck out of the yard and set off for his friend's place.

The first cop to reach Mike called for an ambulance. He tried to keep his expression neutral but he figured the kid's wound was fatal. He'd seen blood like that before and it had resulted in a one way ticket to the morgue.

He hoped his face didn't communicate this to the kid's father. Poor fucker had been through enough today without his son dying.

It didn't seem like the dad had seen him anyway; he was just staring at the kid.

The kid looked pale and weak. He'd be lucky to survive.

Chapter 11

Alfred saw a group of cops by the edge of the estate. He felt sure they'd see him if he tried to pass them, so instead he looked for a hiding place. He saw a house with an open back door and darted inside.

The blare of a TV came from the living room and he looked in to see an old woman reclined on the settee, her eyes closed, a paperback tented on her lap.

He passed the doorway and moved upstairs, searching for a hiding place. There was a big wardrobe in one of the bedrooms.

He'd hide in there later, but he decided he may as well be comfortable while he waited and lay on the bed, planning to move when he heard the old woman come upstairs.

The ambulance took Mike and Luke to the hospital. Mike was beside himself at the thought of losing his son. He'd lost his wife, Laura, in a car crash the previous year. Luke and Jane were all he had.

He paced back and forth in the waiting room, impatient to hear back on his son's condition.

Over an hour passed before Mike stopped his nervous pacing and sat down. A cop came in to see him.

'How is he?' the cop said.

'Not good. He was bleeding really badly.'

'He'll be fine. If he hung on this long…'

'I hope you're right.'

The cop gave him a smile that was meant to console. 'I'm Sergeant James Hirst,' he said, offering his hand.

'Mike Miller. Good to meet you. You caught this freak yet?'

Hirst tutted then shook his head. 'Fucker's disappeared. Don't worry. We will catch him. He took out a cop earlier. Just before he left the house.' Hirst sniffed.

'You ok?'

'Yeah. He was a good friend of mine. Saved my ass a few times. Feel bad I couldn't return the favour.'

'Not your fault.'

'I know. But believe me, we'll get everyone we can onto this. I've got a kid the same age as Luke. I understand how you're feeling.'

Mike nodded. 'I reckon I can help with the investigation. I got a good look at him. Don't think I'll ever forget that face.'

'Good news for us. When you find out your boy's ok – which you will do, I assure you – we'll take a statement.'

'Yeah, of course.'

'I'll leave you to it.'

'Thanks, Sergeant Hirst.'

Chapter 12

Alfred jolted awake, startled by his unfamiliar surroundings.

He looked around, trying to place where he was. He heard knocking and realised that this was what had woken him. Voices followed the knocking.

Finally he remembered that he was hiding from the cops.

Being careful not to be spotted, he peered out of the window and saw the old woman talking to a cop at the front door.

Most of the words were muffled by the glass but he could make out the cop advising her to lock her doors as there was a lunatic on the loose. This brought a smile to his lips.

The old lady nodded and thanked him for his concern.

The cop looked up.

Alfred ducked away from the window, feeling sure he'd been spotted. His heart started to race.

A tense few minutes passed. The cop didn't come upstairs. Alfred blew air through his pursed lips. This was all turning out to be a hassle.

But it would all be worth it when he got his hands on that little bitch Jane.

Chapter 13

Finally the doctor came in to see Mike. By his closed-book expression Mike couldn't tell whether he was the bearer of good or bad news.

The seconds dragged out like hours between the doctor's entrance and him opening his mouth.

'He's stable,' he finally said.

Mike burst into tears of relief and joy then rushed the doctor and hugged him hard enough to hurt his ribs.

'Thank you. Thank you,' he sobbed.

'It's fine, Mr Miller. I'm just doing my job.'

'You're amazing. I can't ever thank you enough.'

He let go of the blushing surgeon and apologised for making a scene.

'I understand,' he smiled. 'Now, Luke is sleeping at the moment, but as soon as he wakes up I'll come and get you.'

'Is he going to be ok?'

'I'm not going to lie to you; we almost lost him. But he's fine now. He'll have a nasty scar, and, no doubt, even nastier nightmares, but he'll live.'

'What do you drink, Doctor?'

'Oh, you needn't worry about that.'

'I insist.'

'No, really. It's a pleasure to give a little boy the gift of life. It saddens me that I need to do such things but I'm glad that I can help. Now, I'll come and get you when he wakes up. Try and relax.'

'I can now that I know he's alright. Thanks again, Doctor.'

Alfred decided that it was time he headed out from the old woman's house and hoped he could just sneak out without her noticing.

As he set foot on the stairs there was a crash against the door.

It's a SWAT team coming to take me in, his panicking mind told him.

But the door crashed again and a large youth came flying into the house as the lock busted open. The big youth caught his balance just before he landed in a heap on the floor. A metal bar glinted in his hand.

Alfred froze on the stairs, hoping to avoid being spotted by this new intruder.

He felt certain he'd been seen and time seemed to stand still until the youth finally moved into the front room.

Briefly, he thought about stopping the intruder before he attacked the old lady.

But he knew that the lad's appearance would help him. It saved him hurting the old lady as he made his escape and would distract the police from the search for him.

He heard, 'Stay in your seat,' from the lad in the front room.

'What are you doing?' came the woman's shrill cry. 'If you don't leave right now I'm going to call the police.'

Alfred moved down the stairs and towards the front door.

'Tell me where you keep your money and I won't hurt you,' the youth said.

Alfred left the house quickly, fearing the old woman was about to start screaming. He heard a strangled cry then a flat, wet sound, and figured the old woman had been introduced to the metal bar.

Alfred felt bad for letting her die – she reminded him of his late mother – but it meant he was less likely to get caught.

He moved off into the darkness, trying not to picture what had happened to the old dear.

Chapter 14

Sergeant Hirst and his superior, Jason Brent, shook their heads as they took in the scene of the old woman's death. A metal bar sat beside her on the settee, pieces of brain and skull still clinging to the weapon which sat in a small pool of blood on the dark green leather.

'What sort of coward could do such a thing?' Hirst pondered aloud.

'Probably won't be too long till we find out,' Brent said, 'since the stupid bastard left the murder weapon here.'

'Probably hasn't even bothered wiping it clean.'

They watched as the crime scene guys came in and did their thing. Took in the streaks of blood up the wall behind the settee. It was Hirst who first noticed the splintered lock on the tea cabinet.

Handprints in the dust showed that something had been taken from the cabinet. On the floor next to the tea cabinet was the old lady's pension book.

'So all this for the sake of a hundred quid,' Hirst said.

'For fuck's sake,' Brent muttered, appalled at the depths to which some of the town's scumbags would sink in order to get their drug money.

The crime scene guy looked up, a blank expression on his face. 'Sorry, Sir. What was that?'

'Just that all of this,' Brent said, pointing to the sorry remains of the old lady, 'was for her pension money.'

'Fucking wankers round here,' Hirst chipped in.

'You can say that again,' the crime scene guy said. 'We've got some good prints here in the dust. Fucker may as well have written his name on the wall.'

'Let me know when you have the results,' Hirst said, turning and heading out to the car.

Chapter 15

A few hours after hearing that Luke was going to be ok, Mike finally got to see his son. He held him carefully as if afraid he might break.

'I don't think I'll ever forget this,' Luke said.

'You will, son. Don't worry. They'll find him and he'll get what he deserves.'

'I hope they cut him like he cut me.'

'I do too. Now you get some sleep.'

'I don't want to. He will be in my dreams.'

'I'll be here. I'll wake you up if it looks like you're having a bad dream.'

'Promise?'

'Promise.'

Mike kissed his son's forehead and stroked his hair until he settled down to sleep.

Chapter 16

The crime scene guy had finished with the prints from the scene and he announced that they belonged to Johnny Taylor, a member of a local gang who were forever causing trouble in Marshton. The gang had been busy, robbing most of the street where the old lady had been killed.

Hirst's eyes lit up. He'd been looking forward to finally getting something concrete on Johnny T. The little prick belonged behind bars.

He called Brent and told him the news.

Ten minutes later, Hirst kicked in Johnny T's front door. A handful of armed police accompanied him and Brent as they made their way inside.

The twat was asleep, not even a hint of guilt over the death of the old dear. Hirst kicked some remorse into him until Brent and the armed cops pulled him away.

Johnny T was bloody and battered and, for a change, speechless. Usually you couldn't shut him up.

The cops cuffed him and dragged him off to the station.

The gang that Johnny T led were known locally as the Marshton Eight. Johnny T and his seven friends – Scotty, Dave, Otis, Tommy, Billy, Olly and Pete – were infamous in Marshton. Each of them had a string of convictions as long as the average arm.

One of Sergeant Hirst's favourite phrases springs to mind, and it sums up the Marshton Eight perfectly: 'If they had half a brain, they'd be dangerous.'

They felt that they were above the law, as the police had long given up trying to convict the gang, as they were repeatedly sprung from jail by their slimy lawyer, who grew fat and rich from their drug money. Consequently, the gang's behaviour got worse.

There are pricks like this in every town. You'll have seen them, the lads who shout abuse at everyone from the safety of their gang, but the moment they are alone, they are suddenly quiet as church mice; the lads who belittle anyone who does not follow the crowd; the gangs who beat people up, but baulk at the idea of a one on one fight; the lads who drive around town all night, trying to intimidate people by over-revving their souped-up cars.

Johnny T is the leader of the gang because he is the only one of them who has done time for murder (well, for a few months until his lawyer bribed the judge).

The others all look up to him as he is 'A Respected Badass Killer', to borrow Otis's words. After all, how 'badass' it is to break into an old woman's house and bludgeon her to death for her pension money.

The fact that the other seven are in awe of this spineless act should speak volumes.

Johnny T likes to brag that he 'owned that jail,' when in fact he cried himself to sleep every night, giving out drugs, money and blow-jobs to avoid being beaten by the real 'badasses' in prison.

Scotty and Olly are brothers from the McCain family, a long line of unemployables. They both hold the standard drug possession charge that seems to be mandatory to join the Marshton Eight.

Both have a long history of breaking and entering, and have logged jail time for assault in the past. Both brothers have a boxing background – in fact Scotty once held an amateur title – but neither of them is as hard as they claim to be.

Pete is the youngest of the gang, sometimes nick-named 'Baby face.' The nickname is partly due to his youth and partly because of the legion of bastard children he has fathered and then neglected.

He is the only one of the gang not to have a conviction for violence, but it should not be assumed that he's a decent guy; he has attacked plenty of people, he has just never been caught.

Dave is a violent man, the oldest of the gang at twenty, with a string of robbery convictions (both armed and unarmed).

His longest stretch in jail came as a result of a shambolic attempt to rob Marshton post office. He carries a knife with him at all times, for opportune muggings, and is one of two of the Marshton Eight who are genuinely dangerous.

Luckily for the general public, he chooses to water down his sly criminal mind with copious amounts of cheap beer.

Tommy also has a string of convictions for violence, but he is not as brave, or as fearsome, as he would, no doubt, like everyone to believe. More often than not, he waits until the gang has their victim on the floor before he mercilessly puts the boot in.

Billy was also convicted with Dave in their ill-advised armed robbery of the post office. He used to go burgling with Dave, tying up and beating any occupants of the house.

On 'special occasions,' as he put it, he would set fire to the house and watch the flames from a safe distance. He almost killed a father and his two children during one of these incidents.

Otis is the other member of the gang who walks the walk. He possesses the standard drug dealing, possession and assault charges.

He has spent the longest time in jail too, serving two years for blinding a police woman with a Phillips head screwdriver. It should have been longer, but the Marshton Eight's corrupt lawyer got his sentence reduced.

Otis also enjoys prank-calling the emergency services, particularly the fire brigade. A building collapsed, killing a teenage girl, while fire-fighters sped to one of Otis's fake calls.

As a result, all incoming calls are compared to the tapes of Otis's prank calls to avoid any precious time being wasted.

Chapter 17

Alfred woke up in the field where he'd spent the night. His friend hadn't been home and Alfred's clumsy attempts to break in had been met with an ultrasonic alarm.

After fleeing the scene, he'd hidden behind a hedgerow where sleep had claimed him. He groaned as something landed on his lap and opened his bleary eyes to see a few scruffy kids throwing stones at him.

As a second stone landed in his lap he rolled over and glared at them.

'Piss off before I gut the pair of you,' he growled.

The kids bolted, shocked by his sudden fury.

He groaned, realising that they would tell their parents. After parents came cops. Best get moving.

His house was out of bounds as it was under police surveillance.

Also, which Alfred found more worrying, the kid's dad knew where he lived.

An encounter with the lad's pissed-off father was not high on Alfred's list of things to do.

The answer to the problem hit him like a bolt of lightning.

The old lady's house. She was dead. No one had known he'd been there. The cops would probably have finished their checks by now. He'd lie low in the house for a few days then he'd go for Jane.

Trying his best not to look suspicious, he made his way back into town.

His muddy clothes drew attention to him but not as much as he'd feared.

At the old lady's house, he did a lap of the block to make sure there were no lurking cops. Satisfied that the place seemed clear, he peered in through the window and flinched back as he saw a man in the front room.

A few minutes later the man left. He didn't look around as he stepped out of the front door and so didn't see Alfred.

Alfred recognised him from photos he'd seen in the paper. He was a cop, and a good one at that.

It was fortunate that the youth had killed the old woman. That had taken a lot of heat off him.

Alfred ducked under the crime scene tape and pushed open the front door.

Once inside, he took a look in the front room. The old dear's corpse was gone, but the splashes of blood remained on the walls.

Shaking his head at the youth's cowardice, he climbed the stairs and headed for the old woman's bed.

Chapter 18

Three days later, Luke was discharged from the hospital. The wound in his belly was still agonising but it was healing well with no signs of infection.

The pain on Luke's face saddened and angered Mike. He found himself wishing that he could lay his hands on the asshole clown and vent his frustration.

Luke was coping relatively well, but he had terrifying nightmares which made him wake, screaming.

Feeling sorry for her younger brother, Jane told him that he could sleep in her room if he wanted. He took her up on the offer, hiding himself beneath the bed with his back against the wall. That way the clown couldn't sneak up on him.

He hauled a duvet over himself and slept peacefully. Under the bed the nightmares didn't seem to be able to reach him.

Alfred woke with a start after a nightmare in which the old woman with the busted skull had come back to life and tried to make amends for him not saving her.

Rubbing his eyes, he sat up. His breathing gradually slowed. All this inactivity was no good for him. It was time to get out into the world and start scaring people again.

He decided to get some face-paint from the joke shop in town. The killer clown was ready to make another appearance.

Chapter 19

Later that night, Luke was asleep in his usual spot under his sister's single bed. Above him, Jane was snoring gently. The house was quiet and still. The only other sounds were the sigh of the wind and the gentle pattering of rain hitting the windows.

Luke was woken by the distinctive squeak of the front door opening. He remained under the bed, his mind full of panicked thoughts, unable to think straight. The idea to call for help didn't occur to him.

Chapter 20

Alfred smiled at himself as he caught a glimpse of his sinister face-paint in the hallway mirror. That little bitch Jane was going to shit herself when she saw him.

He let out a chuckle at the thought of the horror he was about to inspire in her and made his way through the silent house to the stairs. The hammer in his left hand was ready to taste blood. His cleaver was tucked into the back of his clown costume.

He carefully made his way up the stairs, nervous excitement making his heart race, making his breath come in fast, ragged bursts. His smile grew as he reached the upstairs landing without being discovered.

A floorboard creaked beneath his foot as he stepped towards the doors to his right.

He crouched, his ears straining for noises from the rooms. He felt certain he'd been discovered, but no one came.

After a long moment he moved down the corridor again.

One of the doors bore an ornate sign that spelt out Jane's name. Smiling, he turned the handle. The door creaked open, revealing his sleeping target.

After a second's debate he decided to take out the parents first. That way he and Jane could have some quality time together without being disturbed.

There was the little lad to take care of too, but he could wait until Jane had suffered his wrath.

He stepped across to the parent's room, wincing as the floorboards creaked. The open door invited him into the bedroom where the man was snoring on the bed.

Alfred grinned and pulled out the cleaver. He would finish Daddy quickly so he could get to Jane. He was eager to get his hands on the little bitch.

His pulse starting to skyrocket at the thought of what he was about to do, he moved closer to the bed.

He lifted the cleaver above his head and brought it down hard. The heavy blade sunk into the man's throat.

Blood sprayed out, hitting the ceiling and raining down onto Alfred. He relished the feel of it on his painted face.

The man convulsed, already dying. The last of his blood jetted out of the wound in his throat.

Alfred could wait no longer. He turned away from the body, which was already starting to fall still, and approached Jane's room.

The room was dark and silent as he made his way across to the sleeping form in the bed. A pale foot poked out from beneath the bed covers.

Alfred grinned at the thought of his murderous fantasies becoming reality.

He pushed the dripping cleaver back into the waistband of his pants, intending to smash Jane's body with the hammer.

The hammer in his trembling hand, he crept over to the bed. His breathing sped up at the thought of his next actions. He paused for a long second, his eyes glued to the girl who had caused him such pain and anguish.

Then he brought the hammer down hard on her exposed head.

The blow gave him greater pleasure than any orgasm he'd ever had. A thin ribbon of blood flowed out from the dent in her skull.

She awoke, screaming, panic hewn into her young features.

Smiling, he brought the hammer down again.

Chapter 21

Under the bed, Luke froze. He knew that there was nothing he could do against the clown. All he could do was wait and pray that he wasn't discovered.

His sister's screams pierced through him but he was too scared to do anything. The wet smacking noises that had started off the nightmare scene had stopped for the time being, but the sounds that now came from above were arguably worse.

The bedsprings creaked beneath the clown's weight. It sounded like he was jumping up and down on the bed. Accompanying the creaking bedsprings were liquid slurping sounds and muffled cries from his sister.

Luke was too young to know what the noises meant but he knew that it wasn't good.

He lay, his hands clamped over his ears, his eyes tight shut, praying for an end to the noises that threatened to obliterate his innocence.

Alfred leant back when he was finished, grinning as he took in Jane's blood-spattered body and horrified face. Then he raised the hammer. Her eyes widened and he felt himself growing hard again.

The hammer smashed into her forehead, drawing a splash of blood from the circular indentation in her skull.

Laughing, he brought the hammer down again and again. Bone splintered beneath the merciless assault.

Dripping gore covered the walls, the ceiling, the bed and the grinning clown. When her head was a bloody husk with the occasional gleaming shard of bone poking through, he stopped hitting her with the hammer.

He stood over her, admiring his handiwork. For the first time, he registered a blaring noise from outside the window.

Sirens.

Some fucker must have called the cops.

'Bastard,' he hissed, realising that he was caught red-handed.

Annoyed that his fun had been interrupted, he dragged the limp body by the arm. The corpse made a wet thud as it hit the floor.

He shoved it under the bed with his foot, grimacing as he saw the lake of blood which was starting to spread from the shattered skull.

He shoved the body in as far as it would go, then pulled the bed covers down so it hid the space beneath the bed.

It wasn't perfect but it would have to do.

Leaving a trail of bloody footprints, he ran to the bathroom and picked a hooded dressing gown off the hook on the door. He slung it on over his blood-soaked clothes, pulled the hood up to hide his face and raced out of the house.

Chapter 22

Luke found himself pinned against the wall by his sister's body. Her dead eyes stared into his. One of them bulged out of her skull like a bloody boiled egg. The mangled remains of her head were still pumping out blood which was slowly creeping towards him. He tried to inch away from it but had nowhere to go.

The fluid felt warm and sticky against his bare arms. He pulled in fast, panicked breaths, trying to remain calm. The feel of Jane's blood on his skin made him puke. He cried out as the blood soaked into his pyjama bottoms, making them cling to his skin.

He screamed and tried to push her away, but he was pinned against the wall and had no leverage. All he could do was close his eyes and hope that he would wake up from this nightmare.

Chapter 23

Alfred saw a yard with a broken gate to his left and snuck inside.

Just as he did so a couple of armed cops ran past. Breathing a sigh of relief, he crawled into the shadows. He'd give it a little while then make his escape.

Hirst groaned as he saw the broken lock on the Miller family's front door. He didn't like where this was leading. The trail of bloody footprints along the corridor deepened his dread.

He moved cautiously inside, his gun drawn. If this asshole was still here he was going home in a body bag, consequences be damned.

His mind was a jumble of thoughts as he traced the footprints back to the stairs. He feared what he was going to find.

There would be no survivors, of that he was sure. This psycho was nothing if not thorough.

He stepped to the door marked with Jane's name plate. The door was slightly open, a bloody handprint adorning the white glossed wood.

He shoved it open, moving his gun around in case the killer was still lurking inside.

A glistening pool of blood was spreading from beneath the bed.

A low moaning sound came from under the bed, accompanied by frantic breathing.

This is it, Sergeant Hirst, he thought. *Show time.*

He approached the bed in a crouch, his gun trained on the space between the mattress and the floor.

He grabbed the bed covers and pulled them up. The sight of the girl's limp body made him blanch. Her pale skin was in sharp contrast to the blood which seemed to coat every inch of her.

The low moan became louder, the breathing faster and more ragged than before.

Hirst grabbed the girl's leg with one hand, keeping the gun trained under the bed with the other. He paused for a second and pulled the body back.

His finger almost pulled the trigger, but he saw how young the blood-smeared face that stared out from under the bed looked and he dropped the weapon.

'Jesus Christ, Luke, are you ok?' he asked, pulling the bed up.

Luke didn't say anything, he just stared straight ahead, saucer-eyed.

Then he shook his head and burst into tears.

Chapter 24

Hirst cradled the boy in his arms for what seemed like hours. The poor bastard had already been through enough without this happening.

Luke cried so much that Hirst was surprised he had any tears left. Hirst stroked his hair and did his best to comfort the boy until finally he stopped crying and fell asleep.

Footsteps from the hallway made Hirst dart for his gun.

'Fucking hell,' Brent said as he took in the scene.

Hirst dropped the gun. 'Poor bastard was hiding under the bed the whole time,' he said. 'God only knows what he has seen and heard.'

Brent shook his head at the thought. 'There's blood all over the ceiling in there too,' he said, pointing down the corridor to the master bedroom.

'I haven't been in there yet. I didn't want to leave the boy.'

Brent nodded. 'Fair enough. The father's in there. Throat cut. He probably suffered less than the two kids. Jesus, how old was she? Twelve?'

'Sixteen. Luke's only ten.'

'Poor fucker.'

They both watched the sleeping, blood-covered child then took him to the station.

Luke woke with a start. The mattress beneath him was hard and cold. He flinched when he saw someone standing over him.

'It's ok,' Hirst said. 'I'm here to help you, Luke.'

Luke relaxed when he recognised the kind-faced policeman. Then he tensed up as the memory of what had happened resurfaced.

'It's ok, Luke. Let it out. Let it all out.'

Luke curled up in a ball and sobbed until his eyes were dry. Hirst watched him the whole time, feeling anger and sorrow for his loss.

'Do you have any family who can look after you?' Hirst asked when Luke had finished crying.

'A grandma, but I hardly ever see her.' Luke sniffed and wiped away the last of his tears.

'Do you know her phone number?'

Luke shook his head.

'I'll find it and give her a call. She'll need to look after you. You can stay here until we get in touch with her.'

Luke didn't react. He was staring at Hirst, but it was like he was looking through him.

'I don't want to rush you, Luke, but I would like to take a statement from you when you're ready to talk about what happened.'

Luke nodded and resumed staring at the wall.

'I'll leave you to it.'

Luke let out a low moan and shook his head emphatically.

'Ok, I'll stay.'

Chapter 25

Alfred found himself in the old woman's bed with no recollection of how he had gotten there. The journey from the kid's house to the old woman's was a total blur.

His memory of the night stopped with the flashing blue lights ruining his fun. He smiled at the thought of what he'd done to the little whore. She'd lived just long enough to regret her actions.

Alfred chuckled as he pictured her terrified face. The memory was going to keep him smiling for a long time. The only thing he regretted – apart from his time with the girl coming to a premature end – was that he hadn't found the boy.

Alfred was tempted to go and check the hospital, tie up that particular loose end, but he knew that the police would be highly suspicious of anyone approaching the boy and decided to leave it for now. No sense in getting himself locked up.

He drifted back to sleep, eager to relive last night's fun in his dreams.

Hirst was furious that Luke's grandmother still wasn't answering the phone. He'd left her half a dozen messages but it seemed he was wasting his time.

'Is there anyone else who could look after you for a while?' he asked.

Luke thought about it and nodded slowly. 'Bryony, my friend from school,' he said.

Bryony and her mother had heard all about what had happened to Luke and his family and they were only too willing to take him in until he'd found his feet again.

'Hey, don't worry, they'll catch him,' Bryony said.

Luke didn't say anything but smiled at his friend's concern.

'We'll look after you, Luke,' Norma, Bryony's mother, said. 'Are you ok?'

Luke shook his head without lifting his eyes from the floor.

The sounds of his sister's torment were on a loop in his head.

Nothing seemed to shift them.

Chapter 26

A week later the police were no closer to catching the lunatic responsible for the deaths of the Williams and Miller families.

Luke was settling into life at Bryony's house, but he was becoming increasingly withdrawn. The incidents had destroyed his confidence and his trust in strangers.

Norma was deeply concerned about her young lodger, and did her best to make sure he had an outlet for his anger and sorrow.

She bought him a guitar as a present. He was touched by her kindness and it became one of his favourite pastimes. He and Bryony would jam on their guitars long into the night.

Norma also enrolled him in a kickboxing class to give him a way to get rid of the latent aggression he displayed with the vast majority of people.

Despite his new hobbies and the time he spent with his best friend, Luke found it impossible to forget the incidents with the clown.

The time he had spent trapped under the bed with his sister's bulging-eyed corpse seemed to have sucked the fun out of his life. He found that he still saw her wild, staring eyes both in his nightmares and in reality. They didn't go away no matter what he did.

Soon he would come to the conclusion that his sister wanted company.

Chapter 27

Everyone bar Luke seemed to forget about the incidents that had caused such terror in Marshton town.

He became depressed and withdrawn, only talking to Bryony and Norma, and Hirst when he made his weekly visit to check up on his young charge.

The kids at school didn't know that he was one of the clown's victims, and for that he was grateful. But the gap between him and his peers – already large because of his mother's untimely demise – became a gulf after his two run-ins with the killer clown.

He found it hard to make friends and avoided the other kids as much as possible.

Instead, he found he spent most of his waking hours thinking about death.

He came out of one of his trances to find he was walking on the waste ground near Peth Vale, the huge house on the hill that overlooked Marshton town like a malevolent sentinel, with a stray dog in tow.

The animal had been in the back lane outside his new home and he'd teased it with a stale piece of beef from the Sunday roast, leading it onto the outskirts of the land.

Deep down, he'd known it would work – the dog's ribs were on the verge of poking through its skin – but he'd still been surprised and elated when the dog had followed him towards the ominous house.

Luke jolted as if coming awake, and let out a cry of dismay as he stared down at the dog which lay at his feet.

The animal's head was a raw, bleeding mess. One of its eyes bulged out of the shattered, blood-clogged eye socket.

He looked around himself, unable to remember anything about coming out here with the dog.

He glanced down to see that there was a blood-covered half of a brick at his feet. His hands and clothes were covered with thick smears of gore.

After bringing up his breakfast, he stared at the body for a few moments, feeling a strange mixture of fascination and disgust, then hid it in the binbag he'd brought with him and hurried home.

As he tried to get to sleep that night, he thought about what he'd done, smiled as he pictured the dog's dead-eyed stare.

That night, Jane's sightless eyes stayed out of his dreams.

Chapter 28

Alfred had grown bored of the town in which he had spent the last few months. The scruffy, foul-mouthed women were no fun. He had attacked a few of them, but hadn't felt the thrill of his previous attacks.

He'd even come close to being arrested while with one of the hags. That would've been disastrous in more ways than one. Getting nicked was embarrassing enough, but he would never have lived down being caught with a munter like her.

He shook his head at the thought.

It was time to find a new home, somewhere where the women didn't look like they'd had their faces slammed repeatedly in car doors.

Pulling a map out of the glove box of his car, he turned to a page that showed the north east of England and closed his eyes. His finger circled over the map for a time then came down.

Where it landed he would go. Opening his eyes, he saw the town's name. It was a place he'd never heard of, but it had to be better than his current haunt. He turned on the ignition and set off for the town.

Chapter 29

Luke found that if he kept looking at the dead dog it kept the nightmares away. It was as if his sister was happy at the pet he'd provided for her. He became upset when the body began to putrefy as it stunk to high heaven.

He could not risk being discovered, so he reluctantly took the body up to the woods and buried it. Without it to look at, he feared that his sister's dead eyes would return to torment his sleep.

The nightmares stayed away for a few months but the gulf between Luke and his classmates had further widened.

They all called him weird behind his back, but none of them would dare say anything to his face. They'd seen his temper in action when he'd given a good kicking to Rory Simmonds from the year above.

Rory had been taken straight to hospital, with suspected brain damage. After that, no one dared say anything to him, derogatory or otherwise.

This was fine with Luke, he had nothing to say to them either.

Things were going well for Luke. He and Bryony were becoming close. He had an intense crush on her, but he wasn't sure how she felt about him. They were more than friends, that much was clear, but they weren't going out.

Bryony felt the same way about him but neither of them was bold enough to risk ruining their friendship.

The nightmares stopped until the anniversary of his family's deaths rolled around, when the dead eyes returned in his dreams. Sometimes he'd be awake when they appeared, seeming to stare into him from beyond the grave.

He knew there was only one way to get rid of them.

Chapter 30

Over the next few years Luke's obsession deepened. He found plenty of worthy subjects. The feeling of killing the animals was addictive and it added to the thrill of having the dead bodies to play with.

He found that he enjoyed inflicting pain more and more. It was a way of banishing his sister's dead eyes from his thoughts and dreams and it helped to free the pain he still bore from his two encounters with the clown.

He kept the animals alive longer and longer so he could extend their exquisite agonies as much as possible.

His collection grew. But the urge to play with something larger was impossible to ignore.

Luke was sixteen when Kate, one of the girls from the year above, began flirting with him. She was pretty with long blonde hair and curves like a porn star.

Luke was painfully shy around girls (other than Bryony) and at first didn't react to her advances.

He fantasised about Kate in his spare time, in between his macabre games with the stray animals of Marshton and his and Bryony's new favourite pastime of breaking into cars and taking them for joyrides.

As Kate's flirtations became more and more obvious he finally relented. He was getting nowhere with Bryony, so he decided to give it a go. As far as he could see, he had nothing to lose.

'Hey,' she winked at him as they passed on the corridor. Luke felt himself growing hard when he saw the miniskirt that almost showed off her pert arse. Upon seeing where his eyes had gone, she smiled and lifted the skirt a little, revealing a black lacy thong and an inch of perfect tanned buttock. She winked again. 'Were you going to say anything?' she asked, a naughty smile on her lips. Her pink lip-gloss sparkled in the light.

'Y-yes,' he said. 'I was g-going to ask if you wanted to go on a d-date.'

She smiled. 'Bless you, stuttering like that. Are you nervous?'

Luke kneaded the bottom of his t-shirt and stared at his shoes.

'Hey, sorry, I didn't mean to embarrass you.'

'It's ok,' he said, his voice barely more than a whisper.

'I'd love to go on a date with you. Why don't we go and check out the Murder House?'

'Um… I,' Luke began but couldn't voice his thoughts on visiting the house that was the scene of the beginning of his hellish childhood experiences.

'You aren't scared are you?' she smiled. It was a kind smile, but there was a challenge in it too.

'No, well, I…'

She leant in close. Her breath smelt of mint and stale cigarettes and the scent of a delicious perfume teased his nostrils. 'I'm scared too,' she confided. 'But it's good to be scared sometimes.' She moved her mouth to his ear. Her breath was warm against his neck and gave him a tingle in his groin. 'Besides, if we go up there we'll be all alone. I might even let you fuck me.'

Luke couldn't believe what he was hearing. She stared him in the eye and nodded, as if to show she meant her promise. Then she planted a kiss on his lips. 'I'll meet you outside here at nine tonight.' Before he could reply, she had turned and walked away, giving him a naughty wink over her shoulder.

He had to pinch himself as this all seemed like a dream come true. He watched her walk up the corridor, picturing the feel of her naked in his arms. The throbbing in his groin intensified so much that he had to turn and face the wall to hide his erection.

There was no way he was going to turn down this opportunity, even if it did mean revisiting the terrifying house on the hill.

Chapter 31

Darkness had descended upon Marshton when Luke snuck out of his bedroom window at half past eight.

Everyone knew that Peth Vale was no place to be going, especially after dark, so he dressed in black to make sure any lurking psychos found it as hard as possible to spot him.

He had doused himself in expensive aftershave and had gone to the trouble of buying a single red rose for Kate.

His heart slammed against his ribs, as hard as if he was running from the murderous clown who had brought a premature end to his childhood. His voice felt weak and tremulous, and he spoke aloud in an attempt to get used to talking with the butterflies he felt building in his belly.

He walked up to the school, chewing three sticks of gum on the way to make sure his breath was fresh. Kate was stunning and he didn't want the slightest thing to put her off him.

He felt on edge, partly due to the nervous anticipation of meeting up with Kate but mostly because he didn't like to be out after dark in his home town.

He moved into the grounds of the school. Checked his watch. Eight fifty. He could wait. Hell, he'd wait all night if he had to.

He smoked in an attempt to banish his nerves. It helped a little but not as much as he had hoped.

'Psst,' he heard from behind him.

If he hadn't recognised Kate's voice he would have jumped. He turned and saw her crouched down behind the low wall that surrounded the school.

'Oh, hi,' he said aloud.

'Fucking hell, ssh,' she hissed, beckoning him towards her.

He crouched and rushed over to meet her. Hid behind the wall with her.

'Are you trying to get us caught?' she whispered.

Luke looked puzzled, but followed her gaze to the security guard making his rounds towards the place where Luke had been stood not ten seconds ago.

'Oh, sorry,' he said, feeling like an idiot.

She planted a wet kiss on his lips in response. It was too short for Luke's liking, merely whetting his appetite for more.

'Come on,' she said. 'There's plenty of time for that later.'

They dodged over the wall, hugging the corner of the gym building as the security guard played his torch beam over the place where they'd been hid.

Luke's heart was beating at a frantic pace. Kate offered him her hand. It felt warm and fitted perfectly into his. He could feel that her heart was racing too.

'This is making me so horny,' she said with a naughty smile.

Luke was too nervous to feel the same way.

Kate dragged him to some bushes where they hid until the security guard had left.

'Let's go up to the field,' she said, leading him by the hand. They were both on edge in case the security guard made another appearance.

There were a few floodlights around the playing field for when the school's sports teams played late matches. Kate led him towards the solitary illuminated light.

They moved into the edge of the light, just so it was bright enough to see each other.

As Kate pressed her body into his he felt the warm curves of her breasts against him. His erection poked her in the belly. Embarrassed, he pulled his hips away.

'No, I like it,' she said, fixing him with a sultry stare. She grabbed his arse and pulled him forward so his erection pressed into her belly again. 'Mmm,' she moaned.

Luke was unsure of how to proceed, but he moved his face towards hers. They clashed noses and both pulled away, laughing nervously. Moving forward more tentatively, he kissed her.

They kissed softly at first, then harder. Her tongue probed in his mouth. He had been kissed before but never like this.

'Wait,' she said, pulling away.

Great, I've blown it already, he thought.

She saw the disappointment on his face and reassured him. 'No, I just want to get my dress off,' she smiled. Her eyes twinkled in the light from the floodlight. She slipped her dress off, letting it fall to the floor, and stepped out of it.

Her body was clad in lacy black underwear and looked amazing. He enjoyed the curves of her neck, savoured the swell of her breasts and the flat expanse of tanned flesh that was her stomach. The black panties showed enough skin to be pleasing but concealed enough to leave something to the imagination.

Luke pulled her in, relishing the smooth warmth of her buttocks in his hands.

'Not yet,' she said, pulling her hips away from him. 'You take your clothes off.'

He hesitated a moment, not wanting to reveal his pale, scarred body to her, but he reckoned the experience was going to be more than worth the momentary discomfort he would feel and fumbled his t-shirt off, getting his arm tangled behind him in his haste.

'Relax,' she laughed. It was a kind laugh and it put him at ease.

He self-consciously held the t-shirt over the broad scar on his stomach for a second then let it fall to the floor.

She looked him up and down. Saw the scar and winced. 'Jesus, Luke, that looks painful.'

Luke shrugged. He felt safe with her. She didn't want to pry. She said nothing for a moment that drew out for an eternity.

Once again, he thought that he'd blown it, that his gross, misshapen scar had ruined it for him.

Then Kate smiled. 'Hey, let's go to Peth Vale after all. There's a bed there. It'll be more comfortable than this hard ground. We'll be able to spend longer there too.'

This sounded good to Luke, despite the delay that this would present. Her perfect body disappeared from his adoring gaze, once again hidden under the black dress.

'Won't be long till you're seeing that again,' she winked. 'I'll take the lot off next time.'

Luke couldn't help but grin at the thought. She gave him a quick kiss on the lips then smacked him lightly on the butt. 'Are you going to get ready? I want to get there as soon as possible so I can ravage you.'

'Me too,' Luke said, throwing his t-shirt on as he walked away.

This was going to be sweet.

Chapter 32

After leaving the school grounds they took the shortcut through the woods, headed towards the outskirts of town, and thus Peth Vale. As they cut through the graveyard they heard raised voices coming from the other side of the small church.

'Just pissheads,' Kate said, noting the look of concern that had momentarily graced Luke's face. 'They'll probably not even see us.'

Luke nodded. Leaves covered the path like bodies on a battlefield. They crunched beneath their feet as they walked towards the small church.

The voices came louder, one of the youths snorting laughter.

'Fuckin' class,' one youth shouted and joined in the raucous laughter.

Luke and Kate drew level with the edge of the church. The path they needed to take lay off to the right. The youths were gathered around the gate they were planning on using.

Unconsciously, Luke started to guide them towards the unattended gate to the left.

'What are you doing?' Kate muttered. 'That's the long way round.'

Luke said nothing, just glanced towards the group of lads who were now looking at them.

'It's ok, Luke. They're just pissed. They'll be no trouble.'

Something about her voice reassured him and he changed his path so they were headed towards the gate on the right. Kate held his right hand.

The gang looked away from them and continued their conversation.

'See,' Kate whispered.

Luke smiled at her.

'Now let's go get laid,' Kate said, planting a kiss on the side of his face.

They drew to within fifteen feet of the gang. They were still continuing their conversation, not paying any attention whatsoever to Luke and Kate.

Luke counted six of them, all swigging from glass scrumpy bottles.

One of them looked up and met Luke's eye for a second then took a swig from his bottle and let out a belch.

Luke and Kate took a few steps forward. Luke was smiling, proud to be seen holding hands with the luscious Kate. The chavs still didn't seem interested in them.

Then Kate shouted, 'I was right. It is him,' and the group of youths ran at them.

Chapter 33

The whore Alfred had picked up on the outskirts of his new temporary home gasped and wheezed for air as he dug his thumbs into her trachea. Smiling, he thrust into her harder and harder, making the car's suspension springs creak beneath them.

As he emptied his balls into her, his grip on her throat relaxed. She smiled as she greedily gulped in air.

The smile disappeared when she saw the gleaming cleaver he pulled out from under the front seat.

The blood spray seemed to cover every surface in his car and he knew he was going to have to get it hosed down to avoid undue attention.

There'd been a twenty four hour garage on the road into town, so he'd go there once he'd finished with the hooker. He chopped her into fist-sized pieces, small enough that he could dispose of them without too much fuss.

The meaty feel of the cleaver digging into her lifeless flesh made him feel like a god. He bagged up the pieces of bloody corpse then used a shred of old shirt he found in his car to clean the blood off his face and arms.

At the twenty four hour garage he pulled into the car wash, opened the car doors and sprayed the inside of the vehicle until he was confident he'd removed all of the blood.

He turned the spray on himself, gritting his teeth against the intense cold of the water.

Then he dumped the bags of the hooker's remains in the bin behind the butcher's on the main street and set off back to his temporary abode.

On the way, he saw a road sign with a familiar place name.

Marshton. His home town.

Alfred smiled as he remembered his previous rampage in Marshton. That had been his finest hour, no doubt about it. It was fate that he was here, a mere hour's drive from the place where he had started his descent into madness.

Chapter 34

For a second, Luke failed to comprehend what was happening. Kate was grinning, but it was a cruel grin now.

The gang were already upon them. Luke tried to raise his right hand to punch the nearest youth, but Kate still held it.

He pulled his body round, swinging a left hook. The punch was off target, hitting the nearest lad in the eye and sending him stumbling back.

'The fucking prick's hit me,' he shouted, unable to believe it. 'You're gonna wish the clown had finished you by the time I'm done with ya.'

Luke pulled his hand free of Kate's and flung a hard right punch that connected heavily on the tall youth on his way in. His legs buckled, dropping him onto the tarmac.

The glass bottle flew from his hand but didn't break. Luke stooped and picked it up.

Jammed it into the face of the leering chav who was already throwing a wild haymaker at him. The glass shattered on the lad's face, sending a stream of blood running down from his eye.

He cried out and fell back, clutching the wound.

'You fucking bitch,' Luke shouted at Kate then he set off running.

'Did you seriously think I'd want to fuck a freak like you?' she shouted over her shoulder.

The gang ran after him.

Luke's heart was pounding fast now, but he was trying to think clearly. He knew his way out of the graveyard. Knew that there was an exit that led to a maze of alleys that ran towards his home. If he could get there he was confident he could lose them.

His confidence evaporated when he saw two big men flying towards him. They hit him hard, knocking him to the floor and making him cry out in frustration as one of his arms went dead.

One of the men pinned him down. Luke punched him in the eye, making enough room to squirm out from under him.

The second big man was pushing himself off the floor with his arms when he realised that Luke was escaping. Luke slammed his foot into his jaw as he ran past. The youth let out an angry cry and fell to the floor like he'd failed to do a press up.

Luke ran for all he was worth, headed for the exit that led to the back alleys.

Luke was a tough brawler. Since entering his teenage years, he had possessed a ferocious temper and refused to give up in a fight. However, he always did his best to avoid trouble.

He had a solid punch, and a hard kick, honed by long hours of training at the martial arts school Norma had signed him up for. He also had a well-practised chokehold which he had used to tap out pretty much everyone at his gym.

Still, everyone but the dumbest knew that fighting numbers was a good way to get your face rearranged. Two, maybe even three, he could have dealt with – on a normal night. But with his mind addled by panic, one arm hanging limp by his side and his legs aching and useless from the effort of running, he would be lucky to fight off one of the gang.

So Luke did the sensible thing: he carried on running as he reached the back alleys.

The gang pursued him. One caught up to him, but Luke shoved him to the floor, barely breaking stride.

Two of the gang gained on him. Luke pulled a bin down, so it lay across the alley as a barrier. The first of the two lads hit the bin and flew headfirst into a pile of bin bags. The second youth hurdled the bin and continued after Luke.

Luke rounded the corner and saw four of the gang at the far end of the alley. The other three came from behind him. The last member limped into the alley, completing the gang.

The two groups of four moved closer, trapping Luke between them.

'I will kill you all if you hurt me,' Luke said.

All of the gang laughed then one of them punched Luke in the face. The others laughed, harder than before. Fists clenched, they crowded round Luke, eager to have a go at him. Kate had caught up and she was watching now with interest.

He dropped the nearest one with a powerful right cross. Smashed the nose of the second under his clenched fist. Just as the gang moved in for the kill, Luke heard a booming voice over their taunts and jeers.

'Leave him alone, you bastards.'

The gang turned. Luke saw Tom, a lad from his year at school, next to one of the gates in the alley. A wooden baseball bat dangled by his side. He stood for a second that seemed to take an age to pass then the gang went for him.

Like Luke, Tom dropped the first youth to near him.

Though they fought bravely, there were too many of the gang. Luke was severely handicapped by his exhausted limbs. Everything seemed to happen too quickly for him to react.

One of the gang managed to wrench the bat from Tom's hands. It was downhill from there.

Luke took a punch to the jaw which made his brain move in his skull and nearly knocked him to the floor. He countered quickly, punching the culprit hard in the ribs. He felt them give way as he connected.

The youth fell, spluttering, but another took his place, swinging at Luke, who instinctively threw his arm up to cover his head.

Tom shrugged off a punch to the face and knocked his assailant down. Seconds later, another of the gang hit Tom in the gut and he fell to the floor, three of them surrounding him.

Luke's arms were gripped tightly by two of the gang members. He swung around, swinging the lad holding his left arm into one of the lads surrounding the fallen Tom.

One of the big men hit Luke hard in the face, mashing his lips into his teeth. Defiantly, Luke spat blood into the big lad's face screaming, 'You're all fucking dead!'

The big man wiped the blood from his face with his lime green sleeve. The two lads regained their grips on Luke's arms. Luke again struggled wildly, but a third member of the gang held him steady.

The big youth's fist sent a burst of pain shooting through his cheek. He stared his assailant straight in the eye and laughed at him.

'If you're so fucking hard, why does it take eight of you to beat up two of us?' Luke demanded.

The lad didn't reply, he just hit Luke in the face again. Three punches later, Luke still stood, his nose splattered across his face, mocking his assailant.

Another youth stepped in and began punching him. Luke watched three of the gang members putting the boot to Tom's limp, unconscious body.

Then one of the gang swung the baseball bat at Luke's head and he was sent crashing to the alley floor.

Chapter 35

He was still conscious, but everything seemed to swim around him. His senses were distorted like he was underwater.

He heard the gang move in, but barely felt their feet repeatedly slamming into his body. He wished for the sweet oblivion of unconsciousness but it never came.

'I think he's had enough,' he heard Kate say. She sounded concerned now.

'You sticking up for the little freak?' one of the gang said.

'No, I just…' There was a slap as one of the lads hit Kate across the face.

'Way to control your woman, Scotty,' the chav who'd called Luke a freak laughed.

Luke's vision was blurred, but he saw one of the youths grab Kate by the hair. 'What did you do with him anyway?' he growled.

'Nothing, Scotty,' she said, her voice wavering.

'She must have done something to make him grin like that,' one of the big lads said.

'Did you fuck him?' Scotty asked, giving Kate's hair a vicious pull.

'No.'

'She didn't,' Luke said.

'Who asked you, freak?' the biggest youth said. He stuck the boot into Luke's ribs. The breath whooshed out of him, but he still felt numb.

'We're gonna have to take this further,' one of the others said. Luke noticed that it was the big man who he had kicked in the face. 'We were gonna let you off with a good hiding, but you've cut Olly, and kicked me.'

'And you've fucked Scotty's girl,' the biggest youth chipped in.

'So you're gonna learn the 'ard way, son,' the oldest-looking member of the gang said.

They set upon him again, raining kicks on his broken body with renewed fury. He covered his face effectively, taking most of the kicks on his arms. The onslaught seemed to go on forever.

When, mercifully, they stopped, Luke felt like he was inside a washing machine.

'That's enough, really,' Kate said. 'You're going to kill him.'

'No, we're not,' said the biggest youth. 'But he's gonna wish we had.'

Suddenly Luke's world went black. For a terrifying moment he thought the gang's frenzied assault had dislodged his retinas and blinded him, but then he heard the swish of plastic and realised that they had just put a bin bag over his head.

One of them tied the bag round his neck, leaving him barely enough room to breathe.

They dragged him through the alley for a short time.

'You're fucking watching,' he heard Scotty say to Kate, punctuated by another slap.

He heard glass breaking, then the sound of a car door being opened.

'Take him to Scotty's,' a new voice said. 'We'll continue his education there.'

Chapter 36

Luke heard laughter then he was shoved into the boot of the car. The lid slammed down upon him, leaving him trapped in the darkness. His breath was warm and wet on his face. Petrol fumes penetrated the congealing blood that filled his nostrils. The driver's reckless driving style made the engine roar in his ears like manmade thunder.

A few minutes later they reached their destination. Luke was kept in the boot for a while, presumably until the rest of the gang had caught up.

Soon the gang's voices returned and the smell of cigarette smoke filtered in from outside the vehicle.

Luke tried to think now that he had a brief reprieve from the gang's attack. Short of fighting his way out, he couldn't think of an escape plan. He'd try, but he knew that the odds were severely stacked against him.

His hands scrabbled around in the boot, searching for a weapon. There was nothing he could use, but he did manage to get the bag off his head.

When the boot opened, he hurled himself up. His fist connected with the big man's nose, spraying blood onto his lime-green tracksuit. He grunted and staggered back, unprepared for the sudden ferocity of the attack.

In the blink of an eye, Luke was out of the boot. Two of the gang grabbed him and flung him against the car. The lad he'd punched pulled the bag back over his head.

'You're really gonna regret that,' he scowled.

They used some electrical cable to tie his wrists behind his back and marched him inside. Luke caught a strong whiff of curry just before he was pushed over a step into the house.

In an attempt to keep his panic at bay, he tried to figure out where he was. The answer was easy – there was only one curry house in Marshton and that was in one of the quieter streets. He'd walked past it dozens of times on his way to school. The curry house was a good half a mile from home, but if he could escape he would be able to find his way.

A foot slammed into the back of his knees, buckling them and throwing him to the floor. Dust rose from the bare floorboards, making him cough as it drifted up inside the bag. He could see a dim light through the plastic, and could make out the silhouettes of the gang.

A couple of them hauled him up and put him roughly onto a wooden dining chair. The binds around his wrists were adjusted so that he was tied to the chair.

'What are you doing? Leave the bag on,' one of them said as hands struggled with the ties around his neck.

'He's already seen our faces, Otis, man.'

'It was dark, you dumbass. He might not recognise us again.'

The bag lifted. Light stung his eyes as he looked around the room. He seemed to be in a front room, but it was in a state of disrepair.

The floorboards were bare, the walls the strange mixture of colours that only appear when they've been stripped of wallpaper. A bare light bulb blazed over the shithole room.

Luke took in each of the eight faces that watched him.

'Yeah, remember these faces,' the one who'd been called Otis said. 'We're the ones who're gonna teach you a valuable lesson.'

Kate looked on, a worried expression on her face.

From the kitchen, Luke heard the distinctive sound of a knife being pulled out of a knife block. Dave, the older, more hard-faced, one, came in clutching the weapon.

Luke's eyes widened when he saw the gleaming blade. So did Kate's.

Dave leant down in front of Luke and pressed the blade to his face. He grinned, exposing yellowing teeth, and ran the blade along Luke's jawline, drawing a single bead of blood at the tip of his chin.

'This has gone far enough, guys,' Kate said.

'Ah, fuck off home then,' Johnny T, the youth in the lime green tracksuit, snapped. 'I've had just about enough of your whining.'

'Don't fucking speak to her like that,' Scotty said, squaring up to Johnny T.

'You think you're fucking hard or something?'

'Lads, let's save it for the freak,' Otis said.

'He's right,' Dave said, pulling Scotty away by the arm.

'You wanna watch yourself,' Johnny T spat.

Scotty ignored him and turned to face Luke. His face contorted and he swung a wild punch that landed on Luke's forehead. The blow didn't hurt him, but he didn't like how close the knife was to his face.

'I reckon we should take it in turns to cut his face,' Dave said, again bringing the knife to Luke's cheek.

'Na, I've got a better idea,' Otis said.

'What? Better than cutting off his lips and making him eat them?' Dave grinned.

'Yeah,' Otis said. 'You'll like this, Dave. It's right up your alley.'

The rest of the group looked puzzled while Otis grinned.

'You gonna share?' Johnny T said.

'Billy, what did you get off your dad last Christmas?'

Billy's brow furrowed.

A wolfish grin slowly spread across Dave's face. 'I think I know where you're going with this, Otis, my man.' He bumped fists with his friend.

'Yeah, I think you're there,' Otis said. 'Billy go and get the gun.'

Chapter 37

Luke's face dropped even more at the g word. Whatever it was Otis had planned, a gun was going to significantly reduce his chances of getting out of here alive.

Kate had gone a little pale at the thought of it too, but she was still watching out of morbid curiosity.

The penny finally dropped for Billy and he disappeared upstairs with a grin on his face.

'This is gonna be fucking sick,' Otis beamed.

Luke's heart pounded in his ears but still he heard footsteps in the room above them as Billy moved around. A wardrobe door creaked open and the footsteps came back downstairs.

Billy held something in his hands that Luke couldn't see at first.

When Johnny T moved out of the way, Luke caught a glimpse of a small plastic carry case. He was puzzled, but relieved. It sure didn't look like a gun.

Billy opened the box and plugged the device into a socket on the wall. A few seconds later there was a harsh vibrating sound like that of an electric razor. Luke was still confused about what it was.

'Aah, I get yas now,' Johnny T said, hooting laughter.

'What colour?' Billy said.

'The clown's paint was black and white,' Dave said.

'I got black,' Billy said.

Luke tried to peer over the wall of thugs between him and the mystery vibrating object. He had a bad feeling about it, but he was glad it wasn't a firearm.

'I should get to do it,' Otis said. 'Since I came up with the idea.'

'I wanna go too,' Scotty whined.

'You can fuck off, Scotty,' Johnny T said. 'Otis gets the job.'

They crowded around Luke, still blocking his view of the contents of the box.

Otis came through the crowd, holding what looked like a hydraulic needle. He pulled the trigger for a second, as if to test the device. The sound went right through Luke like nails on a blackboard. It still wasn't clear what the object was.

'This will probably sting a bit,' Otis grinned. 'But don't worry, the lads will hold you still.'

Luke looked around at the swarm of grinning faces.

Otis came closer and set the tip of the device on Luke's right eyebrow. Then he pulled the trigger and moved it across Luke's brow. Luke screamed as fire raked a path across his face.

The gang hooted and cheered.

'We're just getting started, freak,' Otis grinned, bringing the needle of the tattoo gun down onto Luke's face again.

Kate stormed out of the house when she realised what they were doing to him.

The gang held Luke tight while Otis continued to tattoo his face. Mercifully, he blacked out after a few of the strokes.

Chapter 38

Alfred stopped on the outskirts of Marshton town to look up at Peth Vale. It was like a tumour that blighted the town, but he had always found it strangely appealing. He smiled at it and at the memories of the acts he'd committed the last time he was here.

He opened the gates and drove into the grounds of his old house. It was a good job he'd paid off the mortgage before he'd been sacked, or else he'd have lost the place. Now, it looked as though that piece of good planning was going to benefit him.

The house was musty but undeniably welcoming. He shut the door and kicked his way through the huge pile of letters that had massed beneath the letter box. He'd have a bonfire with those later.

For now, he'd lay up, wait until dark.

Then he'd go and relive his glory days.

When Luke awoke his face was burning. He smelt blood and ink. His arms and legs felt numb and heavy, but his face was alive with agony. His hazy vision revealed distorted images of the gang's faces as they laughed at him.

'Well, ain't you a looker?' Otis said. The tattoo gun in his hand dripped blood and ink onto the floor.

Luke wasn't sure what they'd done, but it felt like they'd covered his entire face in ink. He didn't know what was worse, the pain, or not knowing what they'd done to him.

He flexed his fingers behind him. The feeling was slowly returning to them and he felt the handle of the knife on the floor below his hand.

He looked around the gang members and none of them seemed to notice what he was doing. They were too busy laughing and admiring whatever they'd done to his face.

Moving carefully to avoid drawing attention to himself, he gripped the blade between his fingers. Checked that the gang weren't aware of what he had done. All that mattered now was getting out of here.

He moved the blade back and forth along the thick wire, knowing that he could cut it if he had the knife for long enough.

'Leave the clown where he is,' Johnny T grinned. 'Hey, Scotty. Go fetch me a beer, bitch.'

Scotty frowned.

Johnny T slapped his palm into the side of Scotty's face. The blow reverberated around the front room. Scotty looked up, tears in his eyes.

Luke moved the blade slowly back and forth, sticking at his grim task. His fingers were cramping a little from holding the knife in the strange position.

A trickle of what he thought was sweat made its way down his temple. When the descending droplet landed upon his lips he realised that it was blood.

Frozen into inaction, Scotty stared up at Johnny T. It looked like he was psyching himself up for having a go at the gang leader, but couldn't quite manage it. He turned away and slunk off to the kitchen.

'That's fucking right,' Johnny T crowed.

'Fetch me one too, faggot,' Otis laughed.

Luke watched the gang, his fingers all the while working at the wire with the blade. He heard glass bottles clanking together as Scotty raked around in the fridge.

Scotty reappeared, his arms braced to his chest to support the bottles he was carrying.

He offered one to Otis and Johnny T then put a couple more down on the floor. Dave and Billy each took a beer. As Scotty reached for one, Johnny T's foot pinned his hand to the floor.

'Who said you could have one?' the gang's leader said, a menacing glint in his eyes.

'They're my fucking beers,' Scotty complained.

Johnny T increased the pressure on Scotty's hand until it turned white. Scotty gasped with the pain.

One of the three strands of wire broke beneath Luke's efforts.

'Are you going to apologise for squaring up to me?' Johnny T wanted to know.

Scotty grimaced and tried to pull his hand out from under the leader's trainer. Johnny T increased the pressure, making Scotty cry out.

'I said are you gonna fucking apologise?' Johnny T said.

'I'm sorry,' Scotty said.

'That's better,' Johnny T smiled. 'Now, if you arrange for that pretty little blonde thing you're seeing to suck me off we'll be best mates again.'

Scotty frowned.

'I'm only joking,' Johnny T laughed.

Otis, Dave and Tommy joined in. Johnny T took his foot off Scotty's hand. Scotty pulled it to his chest and rubbed it hard.

'If you square up to me again I'll have to borrow her for an hour or two,' Johnny T grinned.

'I'll go twos up on her,' Otis leered.

'I'll have a piece of that action too,' Billy scoffed.

The three grinned at Scotty. He was ready to tear their heads off. Especially Billy. Billy was softer than he was. The other two would be a real handful, but he felt mad enough to take them.

'Hey, chill out,' Johnny T said. 'Have one of the fucking beers.' He nudged one of the bottles closer to Scotty with his foot. Scotty regarded it cautiously then opened it with his teeth.

He took a quick swig of it, eyeing the three suspiciously. *Who the fuck did they think they were?*

The more the gang bantered, the angrier Scotty got. He wanted to show them that he was in the gang for a reason, that he was just as tough as the others, not just Olly's kid brother. He drained his beer and shifted the bottle from hand to hand.

'Chill out,' Otis said. 'We were only joking, man.'

Johnny T grinned at Scotty. That was it; Scotty just snapped. Gripping the bottle hard in his right hand, he swung it at Johnny T's head.

The bottle smashed against Johnny T's temple, sending beer and broken glass cascading to the floor.

'Oh, you're going to fucking regret that,' the leader said.

Chapter 39

As Johnny T moved towards Scotty, Luke's blade cut through the last strand of wire. His hands came free.

While the gang's attention was diverted by the developing confrontation Luke launched himself up from the chair, the knife in his right hand.

Johnny T's fist collided with Scotty's jaw, dropping him to the floor. At the same time, Pete registered that Luke was not in his chair. He moved towards him to block his escape.

Luke punched the knife into his stomach at short range. The blow was satisfying for Luke, even more so when warm blood rushed out to meet his hand. He pulled the blade free and shoved the panic-stricken youth to the floor.

Johnny T was putting the boot to Scotty, still unaware of what was going on.

Pete writhed in pain on the floor, his hands clasped to his bleeding gut.

As Luke moved past him, Olly noticed his attempt to escape and cried out. Everything in the room cut off suddenly; Johnny T's kicking of the floored Scotty, the shouting of the gang to encourage the beating, and Scotty's pained cries. They all turned to look at Luke.

Billy was nearest and he moved towards Luke, who slashed the blade across at throat height as a warning.

Billy backed away, panic in his eyes.

Luke slashed the hand that Billy extended, then ran for the front door when he pulled back his injured limb.

He rattled the keys in the lock for a second before realising the door was unlocked and running out into the cold night.

'We've gotta fucking find him,' he heard Johnny T say.

Luke ran for all he was worth. He held the knife under his clothes. They were going to get every inch of it if they came for him again.

He was still unaware of what they had done with the tattoo gun but getting home safely took precedence over finding out.

He blundered into the back alleys, hearing the gang's footsteps behind him. His breathing laboured under the panic he felt. His face still burnt from the effects of the tattoo gun.

Through some miracle he managed to find his way home without seeing any of the gang. Norma and Bryony were in bed when he staggered through the door.

The knife still hidden under his clothes, he moved upstairs to the bathroom.

His heart beating fit to explode, he closed his eyes and stepped in front of the mirror.

When he summoned the courage to open his eyes, he saw the face that had haunted his nightmares for the past few years.

He saw the face of the man that had taken the lives of his father and his sister and almost killed him.

He saw the face of the clown.

Chapter 40

Luke stared at the black crosses that covered his eyes.

Stared at the dark circle the tattoo gun had scarred onto his nose.

Saw the permanent black grin that had been etched most of the way to his ears.

For a second, he just stared at how the gang had disfigured him in the worst possible way.

He stared, thinking of how every time he looked in the mirror he would be reminded of the two encounters he had had with the killer clown.

Then he started screaming at the top of his lungs.

He grabbed his face between his fingertips, pulling at it, trying to rip the tattoo out. He ran the taps as hot as they would go and started scrubbing his face.

The scalding water burnt his skin as he scrubbed his face until it was sore and bleeding. Still the clown's features were scarred onto him.

He screamed again, feeling so frightened his heart was going to stop. He pulled at his features, wishing he could tear them off his bones so he would no longer have to see the face of the man that had ruined his life.

Panic started to close a fist around his throat. It felt like he was going to die if he didn't get the black ink off his face.

He smiled as he remembered the knife under his clothes.

His right hand trembled as he raised the tip of the razor sharp knife to his forehead. He pressed the blade down to the top of the thick black cross. A ribbon of blood ran down his face. He applied more pressure and drew the blade round the cross.

The pain was intense and made him swoon, but he knew that it was nothing compared to the thought of seeing the clown's face every time he looked in the mirror. He pressed down harder still and drew the blade around to his temple.

Blood ran down his face like crimson tears.

The sudden intensity of the pain made him cry out.

He barely heard the knock on the bathroom door.

Barely heard Norma asking if he was ok.

Just continued to pull the blade around.

The blade carved into the tattooed skin on his cheekbone now. Finally he drew the blade up his cheek and over his nose, back up to the start of the wound on his forehead. There was now a thick red circle around the black cross that adorned his right eye.

He pushed the tip of the blade under the loose flap of skin and pulled. The pain made him curse.

Drops of blood spattered down into the sink. He bit down hard, grinding his teeth together. Worked the blade around inside the wound, loosening the skin.

Norma pressed her ear to the door and heard Luke making pained grunting noises. 'Luke, are you ok in there?' she asked, braying on the door with the flat of her hand. Luke grunted again in response.

Norma turned away from the door and went to get Bryony. Her daughter was fast asleep and it took some shaking to rouse her.

Luke grabbed the loose flap of skin and pulled. Part of the skin at the side of his eyebrow came away with a sickening tearing sound. Grimacing, he carried on pulling. The skin caught a few inches from his cheek bone.

He poked the tip of the knife into the bloody gash and pulled it down. The skin loosened enough for him to get his fingers in.

He gripped the end of his skin hard and pulled. Screaming, he tore the circle of skin away from his face.

Blood pissed out of the raw, bloody hole where the black cross had been.

Despite the agony he smiled at the knowledge that he was a little closer to removing the horrendous reminder of his childhood torment.

He put the blade to the other side of his forehead and cut a circle around the other cross. He moaned as the pain hit him anew but kept grimly on at his task. A piece of eyebrow came away as he slipped with the knife.

'Luke? What's going on in there?' Bryony shouted. She had heard Luke's screams and she knew that they couldn't be the result of anything good. She brayed on the door so hard it hurt her knuckles. 'Luke? Open up.'

Luke still didn't hear the knocking, so intent was he on removing every last trace of the gang's tattoo. The flap of skin hung from his eyebrow, pouring blood into the sink.

He took the blade to his right cheek, starting at the end of the enormous black smile that had haunted his nightmares for almost a decade.

He dug in hard, knowing that the deeper he cut now, the quicker he'd be rid of the heinous grin that mocked and tormented him. The tip of the blade poked through his cheek into his mouth.

He smiled. This part was going to be easier than he'd thought. Still smiling, he sunk the blade through the cut and pulled it hard. He screamed as the flesh tore and blood gushed from the wound.

Bryony gave up shouting for Luke and instead started trying to barge the door open. Her shoulder hit the door hard, making her bite down on her tongue. Cursing, she spat blood and hurled herself at the door again.

Luke had ripped the blade through his cheek and it was making its agonising journey towards his upper lip.

He hesitated for a second, the pain making his resolve weaken momentarily, but then he caught a glimpse of the remnants of the clown's grin on his face and he pulled the blade through slowly, severing his upper lip just below his nostrils. He smelt blood from the gaping wound. The sweet-smelling fluid ran into his mouth.

He pulled the knife down, cutting off the upper lip at the left side of his mouth. The loose skin dangled from his face.

He moved the blade back to the lower edge of the tattooed smile and dug it deep into his flesh. As it penetrated his cheek, he let out a pained cry and pulled hard, severing the skin and muscles that joined the hideous black ink to his face. Warm blood ran down his neck, plastering his clothes to his chest.

Bryony threw herself against the door again, screaming for Luke to stop whatever he was doing. The door remained solid, but her shoulder was becoming numb from the blows.

Luke ripped the blade up the left corner of his mouth, cutting loose the right hand side of the black grin. The dead skin fell into the sink like bloody strips of peeled-off wallpaper.

Luke smiled as he realised that he was more than halfway through his removal of the gang's sadistic handiwork.

He moved the blade back to his left eye, working the flesh loose. Blood gouted out onto the mirror.

The bathroom door buckled in as the lock gave way, dumping Bryony on the floor. Norma gasped then let out a scream.

It took Bryony a second to look up, but she already knew she didn't want to see the sight before her.

Chapter 41

Bryony raised her eyes and let out a bloodcurdling scream when she saw Luke sawing into his own face with a bloody kitchen knife.

'Luke, what the hell—'

He turned to face her and she saw the full extent of his handiwork. Saw the bloody hole running from his cheek to his chin. Through the gaping wound she saw his teeth swimming among the crimson that flooded his mouth.

His right eye was the only white in a vast raw bloody wound, gaping through the hole where he'd torn his eyelid loose.

She took in the blood that drenched his torso and ran down to pool at his feet.

Saw the bleeding strips of dead flesh in the sink.

'I'm getting rid of it,' Luke said, and he smiled. Actually smiled. Blood bubbled out of his mouth and ran down his jaw. His left eyebrow was hanging off, revealing gleaming bone beneath.

He moved the blade a little more, seemingly happy to carry on whatever the hell he was doing with or without their eyes on him.

'Luke?' Bryony said, but words failed her. She vomited on the floor. Tears streamed down her face.

'I'm nearly done,' Luke said. His smile returned. He looked monstrous. 'Nearly done.'

With that, he keeled over, hitting his head off the sink. The impact left a bloody imprint on the white porcelain. He landed in a heap on the floor, blood pouring out of his savage wounds.

Despite the revulsion she felt, Bryony ran to him. 'Don't just stand there!' she screamed at her mother who was still watching with a dumb look on her face.

Norma remained frozen, her eyes glued to the bloody remains of Luke's once-handsome face.

'Mam, fucking help us,' Bryony cried. In the end she had to throw the blood-drenched bar of soap at her to get her attention. 'Call the goddamn ambulance!'

Norma snapped out of her paralysis and ran downstairs to the phone.

Luke had still not come round by the time the paramedics appeared.

'Holy shit,' one of them said, unprepared for the horrific scene in the bathroom.

'Who did this?' the other paramedic said.

'He did it to himself,' Bryony said.

'What?' the first paramedic said.

'Why the—' the second began.

'I don't fucking know why. Just help him, for Christ's sake,' she snapped.

The paramedics moved in. The kid's chances didn't look good. He was pale as a corpse and, judging by the blood that coated a five-foot radius of the sink, he had hit a major artery during his crude attempts at facial reconstruction. They didn't voice their concerns to the two women; they looked terrified enough as it was.

They staunched the bleeding as best they could and took him to the hospital. Bryony and Norma followed in the car.

Luke woke, screaming and thrashing. It felt like burning ants were crawling over every inch of his face.

'Relax,' the doctor said.

Luke stared at him through a haze of pain. The vision in his right eye was distorted. Focussing with it was painful.

'What the hell were you doing?' the doctor said, his tone that of a man seeing something for the very first time.

'Is it off me?' Luke moaned.

'What?'

'Is the clown's face off me?'

'I'm not following you.'

Luke groaned. 'My face. They tattooed my face.'

The doctor nodded, seeming to understand. He said nothing else, just left Luke alone with his pain.

A few minutes later the doctor reappeared with Bryony, Norma and Sergeant Hirst.

'Some visitors,' he smiled.

Luke tried to smile but it felt like his face was wrapped in drying cement.

'Jesus, what happened?' Hirst asked, his face a mask of worry.

'They tattooed my face,' Luke said, then burst into tears.

'Was it?' Hirst asked. He needed to say no more, Luke knew what he meant.

'Yes, it was *his* face. The bastards tattooed his face-paint on me.'

'Who did this?' Norma asked.

Luke ignored her and continued. 'I had to get it off me. I'd rather die than see that every time I look in the mirror.'

Hirst nodded his understanding.

Bryony and Norma looked at each other, puzzled. It felt like they were being kept in the dark.

'Will someone please tell me what the hell is going on?' Bryony said.

Hirst turned to her, his face still shocked. 'They tattooed the clown's face-paint onto him.'

'Oh, fucking hell,' Bryony said. 'Who did this?'

'Gang,' Luke managed. He wanted to talk no more. The movement of his face was agonising.

'I think I know who did it,' Hirst said. 'I'll make some enquiries. I'll come and talk to you later, Luke.'

Luke nodded.

'Shit, are you ok?' Bryony said. 'They actually tattooed your face?'

'Yes.'

'They've got to fucking suffer for this.'

'Language, young lady,' Norma said.

Bryony's glare was enough to shut her mother up.

'I'm so sorry, Luke,' Bryony said, carefully hugging him.

Luke looked at her then burst into tears.

Chapter 42

When Luke's visitors had gone, the doctor came back in. 'We've got you booked in for a skin graft later today,' he said.

'Will you make sure it's all gone?' Luke said.

'Yes, of course. I realise now what happened. You're that boy aren't you? The one who saw his sister killed by the clown?'

Luke nodded.

'We'll get every trace of it off your face. We'll do such a good job of it that no one will ever know it was on there.'

Luke smiled.

'Now, there's some bad news. Because of the nature of the injuries, we need someone to come and assess you.'

'What do you mean?' Luke managed. It felt like his mouth was full of marbles.

'Well,' the doctor sighed. 'We need to assess if you're going to be a danger to yourself in future. If it seems that you are, we'll have to take steps to protect you.'

Luke groaned. This was the last thing he needed.

Later on, Hirst came back to see Luke. By his twitchy demeanour and the way he kept looking over his shoulder, it was obvious that there was something on the cop's mind.

He shut the door to Luke's room and pushed one of the chairs against the door.

'Hi, Luke. I wanted to express my regret for what happened to you.'

'Thanks.'

'But I have to admit, there is a more selfish motive for my visit. My son was the other lad who was attacked that night.'

'Tom?'

Hirst nodded.

'How is he?'

Hirst grimaced and stared down at the floor. A moment later he sniffed and looked up at Luke. Tears sparkled in his eyes.

'He's got severe brain damage and is paralysed from the waist down. Those cowards stopped him from ever walking again. It's breaking my heart seeing him like this.'

'I'm so sorry. It's all my fault. If he hadn't come to help me, this never would have happened.'

'I'm glad he helped you. You're a good lad.'

'So what do you need me to do?'

'I know the doctor already asked you if you wanted to press charges, but it might help our case a little if you identified the scum responsible for this attack. These cocksuckers have half of the court in their filthy pockets.'

'I'll help any way I can.'

Hirst looked Luke right in the eye. 'Thanks. I'll bring the photos in for you. You do realise that if you do this it will bring those fuckers down on you again, so think carefully.'

'I hope you nail the bastards. And I'll think about pressing charges, really I will.'

Hirst nodded again. 'I hope we do too, but in my heart I know I'm wasting my time.'

'Will you thank Tom for helping me?'

'I would if I thought there was the slightest chance of him understanding me. Thanks for your time, Luke. I wish you a speedy recovery.' Hirst gave him a very forced smile and left.

Chapter 43

The five unscathed members of the Marshton Eight were occupying one of the waiting areas on the ward next to Luke's.

Pete was being treated in intensive care as a result of the knife wound that Luke had given him.

Billy had needed stitches as a result of the vicious slash wound that Luke's blade had inflicted.

Johnny T was having his face stitched to repair the damage from Scotty's bottle strike.

Scotty himself was still shaking from the beating he'd sustained at the hands and feet of the gang's leader.

The five sat in the waiting room, smoking cigarettes despite the six-inch high sign that forbade this.

A doctor came in to tell them the news about their friends, but he paused, a puzzled expression on his face, when he saw the smoke billowing out of their mouths.

'You can't smoke in here,' he said.

'The fuck're you to tell us what to do?' Otis spat.

The doctor raised his hands in front of his face as a barrier. He spoke slowly, like he was talking to a child. 'This is a hospital, son. You can't smoke in here. Are you stupid or something?'

Otis got up from his seat, taking a good long while to do so. He swaggered over to the doctor, a placid look on his face. The rest of the gang looked on, giggling like stoners on their last joint of the night.

'Best put it out then,' Otis said as he reached the doctor.

'Yes, before I call security and have all of you forcibly ejected from the premises.'

Otis sucked in a last lungful of smoke, then nodded thoughtfully. Then, with sudden ferocity, he thrust his hand forward and crushed the cigarette into the doctor's forehead.

The doctor tried to shrink back, but Otis held him against the wall and shoved the blazing cigarette hard into his face.

'There ya go, Doc,' he laughed. The others joined him.

'Forcibly ejected!' Tommy scoffed. 'Who the fuck is this kid?'

Otis gave the doctor a slap for his cheek and slumped back into his chair.

'We do what the fuck we want, when we want to do it,' he explained calmly. 'Ain't much anyone can do about it. Now, tell me how my friend is doing.'

'He's stable, but we almost lost him,' the doctor blurted. 'Now, get out of here, because I'm going for security as soon as I get out of this room.'

'If you call security I'll cut off your shrivelled dick and make you eat it,' Dave said, flashing the handle of his knife to the terrified doctor. 'Now get the fuck out of here.'

The doctor's eyes widened when he saw the knife. He gulped and left the room without saying a word.

The gang collapsed in fits of laughter.

'Olly, go see if that little prick has called security,' Otis said.

Olly considered questioning, but Otis was the unofficial leader in Johnny T's absence. Otis was the cruellest motherfucker around, except for maybe Dave. The two of them usually agreed on everything, so it wasn't wise to front either of them.

With this in mind, he swallowed his pride and went out into the corridor.

Chapter 44

Olly was looking for the doctor when he saw Hirst making his way out of the next ward. He pressed himself against the wall as he saw the policeman approach.

It was obvious to him why Hirst was at the hospital. He carefully followed the cop out to the car park, hiding on the handful of occasions he turned to check behind him.

On the way to his car, Hirst stopped to talk to a girl. They talked for almost a minute, then he got into his car and pulled away.

Olly made a note of the number plate and wandered around the hospital, looking lost, until someone came and asked if he needed help. He gave them some bullshit, trying to blag his way onto Luke's ward, but the nurse called his bluff and turned him away.

'Hey,' Olly said. 'I think the freak's in the hospital somewhere. I've just seen that Hirst prick coming out of the next ward along. There was a girl too. He was talking to her.'

'Did you manage to get in?' Dave asked.

'No, the bitch of a nurse turned me away,' Olly said.

'We'll see if we can get to him,' Tommy said.

'Yeah, we'll have to finish him now the cops are involved,' Dave said. 'Ain't no way I'm going back inside.'

'Fuck that,' Otis spat.

They sunk into a sullen silence, then the door swung open. Johnny T and Billy swaggered in. Johnny T looked hard as fuck with his new facial stitches.

'What's up, pussies?' Johnny T beamed.

'Fuck you calling a pussy? Faggot ass bitch,' Otis snarled, getting out of his chair and squaring up to Johnny T. He held his stare for a few seconds then relaxed, smiled and slapped him on the shoulder. 'Good to have you back, man. Got some shit you need to hear.'

'It'll have to wait,' Billy said. 'There's a few big ass security guards on the way here. Did one of you pricks attack a doctor?'

Otis grinned. 'No match for me, I'm sure. I'll stab the son of a bitch so much he'll look like he's inside out.'

'No,' Dave said. 'We're gonna have to keep our noses clean so we can come back for the freak later. They'll be looking for us if we stab a security guard.'

'He's right,' Olly said. 'And I've been out there, there are cameras all over the fucking place.'

'Ah, shit, man, I ain't afraid of a few motherfucking cameras,' Otis said.

'Let's get outta here before we're all fuckin' lifted,' Dave said.

The rest of the gang looked at him for a moment then decided he was right. They ran out of the hospital into the night.

Chapter 45

A few hours later, after sharing a few beers and telling Johnny T and Billy that it seemed the freak they'd attacked was holed up in the hospital, the gang had gone their separate ways.

Olly was making a drug sale in the graveyard on the edge of town when he saw Hirst's car pass. Wanting to make sure he wasn't imagining it, he squinted at the rear license plate and confirmed it was the cop's car.

His buyer was fumbling in his pocket for money.

'This is a freebie,' Olly said. 'I gotta be somewhere else, man.'

The buyer grinned like he'd just found out he'd won the lottery. Olly turned and ran, trying to keep the car in sight as it turned into an urban area.

His legs and lungs already starting to burn (that's what smoking cheap dope does for aerobic fitness) he slowed to a walk.

He walked as fast as he could, hoping that he could follow the cop to his destination.

It was a disappointment when the car turned off and headed towards the hospital. He had hoped it was going to lead him to wherever the freak was living.

'I'm onto you, pig,' he muttered.

He moved to the hospital car park and hid behind a fence while the cop got out of the car.

Luke was just drifting off into a pained sleep when there was a knock at the door. Sergeant Hirst poked his head in. 'How ya doing?' he said, smiling.

'Been better,' Luke said, returning Hirst's awkward smile. He beckoned the policeman in and told him to sit down.

'Sorry to bother you when you're trying to recover,' Hirst began.

'Not at all,' Luke said.

'I'll get this over quickly,' Hirst said, 'and let you get back to your sleep.' He pulled a file out from under his long tan-coloured jacket. 'There are photos here of the Marshton Eight – the gang I'd bet attacked you and Tom. There are a few photos of known associates of the gang, and also a few dummy ones, so we can't be accused of putting ideas in your head.'

Luke nodded.

Hirst passed him the photos.

The first one showed the big youth who had broken Luke's nose.

'I recognise this dickhead,' Luke said straight away.

'I thought you might. That's Johnny T, the leader of the gang.'

'Yeah, he was the one who seemed to be in charge.'

Luke looked through the rest of the photos, nodding when he recognised one of the gang, shaking his head when he didn't.

Hirst put the photos in two piles, depending on whether they contained one of the gang.

In the end, eight photos were on one pile, ten on the other.

'Yep, it's the eight fuckbags I had thought,' Hirst said. 'Have you thought about pressing charges?'

'I've thought about it and decided not to. Sorry.'

'You've put your neck on the line enough as it is. I appreciate it.'

'It's the least I could do.'

'Well I'm grateful. As Tom would be if he knew what was going on.' He smiled, again the sad smile of a broken man. 'I'll not take up any more of your time. Thank you, Luke. I'm going to do my best to nail these fuckers.'

Luke nodded.

'Thanks for your time,' Hirst smiled, looking at Luke's raw, exposed face. 'And I'm sorry to interrupt your sleep.'

'It's worth it if it means you can catch those wankers,' Luke said.

'I couldn't agree more,' Hirst said, standing up and walking to the door. 'Take care, Luke. If you need any help give me a call. I hope you're feeling better soon.'

'Thanks,' Luke said.

Hirst drove away.

Chapter 46

Early the next afternoon the seven members of the Marshton Eight not in hospital got together and tried to decide who was the best man to go and finish the freak.

Billy drew the short straw, as he had been in the hospital already. The plan was for him to wander into the ward and, if challenged, say that he had left some of his belongings behind.

He snuck a small kitchen knife under his tracksuit top and made his way to the hospital, on the verge of panic for almost the whole journey.

He had never killed before, but had come close when a fire he'd started almost killed a father and his two young children. The thought of killing someone in cold blood terrified him but he knew he had to go through with it. The rest of the gang would look up to him if he did this to take care of their shit for them.

He shoved open the doors to the hospital, his heart slamming like the beat of his beloved house music. The knife felt cold as it touched against his back.

His eyes were on the floor six feet in front of him, not wanting to meet the gaze of anyone who worked at the hospital. He knew that guilt was written all over his face.

At the entrance to Luke's ward he straight-armed the door open. It smacked into the wall behind, making him jump a little.

Way to go, draw attention to yourself, he thought. *Like I don't look suspicious enough already.*

He ignored these niggling voices in the back of his mind and moved into the ward. A blonde nurse came to greet him. She gave him a kind smile and asked if he needed any assistance.

'Er, y-yes. I was in here yesterday,' he said, flashing his stitched hand to her as some kind of identification.

'Oh, yes. Did you leave something behind?'

'Erm, yeah. I did. I just got one of those new I-Phones. Left the fucking thing in the night stand.' He silently cursed himself for swearing. That would hardly help him remain inconspicuous.

'They're expensive,' the nurse smiled. 'You must have too much money if you're chucking one of those things away.'

He smiled but it felt forced. Awkward.

'Which room were you in?'

Inspiration hit him like a ton of bricks. 'I was in the bed next to the lad who had the black tattoo on his face.'

'Ah, yes. Well, he's not here anymore.'

'Shit. I borrowed a tenner off him,' Billy said, slapping his hand to his brow theatrically. He decided to push his luck. 'Do you know where he went?'

The nurse suddenly didn't seem so comfortable with him. 'No, I'm sorry, I don't.'

'Are you sure? I feel really bad about it. Poor sod had been through enough without me robbing his money too.' He laughed but it sounded painfully fake.

The nurse's face turned up like he'd unleashed a particularly potent fart. 'No, I'm sorry. I don't know where he went.' She paused, then added. 'And even if I did I wouldn't be allowed to tell you. Your phone should be somewhere in that room.' She pointed to a room down the corridor then hurried away.

Smooth, Billy thought. *Now I'm going to have to make believe while I search for my imaginary phone. Smart move, dickhead.*

Billy stepped into the empty ward, making a great show of looking under the beds and along the walls. If anyone was watching him he wanted to make it look real.

His instincts were telling him to run, this was way past the point of being a bad idea.

He paused, looking in the drawers of a nightstand.

As he stood up, he registered movement out of the corner of his eye. A split-second later, the fist struck him in the temple. The hard blow was even more destructive due to its unexpected nature.

The smell of bleach flooded into his nostrils as he fell. A strong hand gripped the back of his head and slammed it into the floor.

Facedown, he couldn't see his assailant. The strong hand smacked his head into the hard floor again.

While blood ran down the back of his throat, almost choking him, the hand snuck around his neck and, with practised ease, sunk into his trachea.

Billy's breathing laboured, panic and the strong fingers combining to make a dangerous team.

'Listen to me, you little prick,' the harsh voice breathed into his ear. 'I know what you and your shitty little gang did. You're going to pay for it. Mark my fucking words, sonny. You're going to pay for it. Pass this on to your bum-buddies.'

While Billy floundered, weakly trying to pull the vicelike grip from around his throat, the hand released. He wheezed, gulping in air.

The hand grabbed the back of his head again and lifted it high. Then it crashed down to the floor. Consciousness slipped away from Billy.

His unseen assailant gave his body a contemptuous kick then snuck out of the hospital.

Chapter 47

Johnny T wasn't happy when Billy told him that he'd been unable to find the kid they'd attacked.

'Fucking knew I should have sent someone else,' he said.

'He tried,' Olly said. 'Ain't his fault the fucker'd upped and gone.'

'No, I guess not,' Johnny T mused.

'There was someone there,' Billy said. For the first time, his mates noticed the blood around his nose and the way the appendage was swollen and twisted.

'Whoa, you look like you had the shit kicked out of you,' Otis laughed. 'What happened? Nurse throw you out?'

The others laughed until Johnny T quieted them. 'Who was it?'

'No fucking idea, I never saw them,' Billy said. 'But he said that we were going to pay for what we did.'

'Must be the kid,' Otis said. 'I'd want revenge if I was him.'

'Maybe it's the cop,' Olly said. 'I saw him at the hospital. The freak must have grassed on us.'

'You might be right,' Johnny T said. 'We'll give the freak's girl a message. No one fucks with us. We'll find out where she lives and scare the shit out of her.'

'I reckon we should put the cop out of commission before this goes any further,' Otis said.

'Na, I ain't killing a cop,' Johnny T said. 'We'd never get off with that. We just scare the girl. She'll not be able to prove it was us.'

Chapter 48

Luke woke in unfamiliar surroundings. Since the gang had tattooed him it seemed like he was constantly waking up in strange places.

This particular strange place was painted white, with a small barred window on the far wall. There were a few shelves on the wall to his right. The small bed he lay upon was soft and had a pile of his clothes neatly folded on the bottom of it.

He sat up, rubbed sleep out of his eyes. The pain in his face became more intense than ever, making him curse his decision to rub his eyes.

There was a stainless steel sink in the corner, over which was a small plastic mirror which reminded him of the events that had taken place the last time he'd seen his own reflection.

He recoiled in horror and let out a cry. The pain meant that all of it had been real. He'd really cut off most of his face to remove the tattoo of the clown's face-paint.

Standing, he approached the mirror, treating it as if it was a venomous snake.

He was torn. He didn't want to see what a mess he'd made of his face, but he needed to know whether he'd managed to remove all of the tattoo.

His heart sledging off his ribs, he paused by the sink. Then he looked.

The face that greeted him was not noticeably his own. The huge masses of scar tissue that surrounded his eyes and mouth were an abomination. His face, usually pale, was now sickly fish-belly white in colour. The stitches that lined the edges of scar tissue looked angry and inflamed.

He screamed, startled by the horrific sight that met his eyes. The black ink had gone, at least, but his right eyelid was just a fleshy nub. He had never been fond of his own appearance but now he hated what he saw. Screaming, he started to pull at the stitches.

As he did, a section of wall to his left retracted and two big men ran in. They were clad in white and had expressions of concern rather than anger.

'Please, Luke, don't do this,' the largest one said.

Luke ignored him and started pulling a loose piece of thread from above his eye. A drop of blood snaked down his face.

'We don't want to do this, but it's for your own good,' the second man said, grabbing Luke and twisting his arm up behind his back. Luke cried out in frustration as the two men dragged him to the bed.

'Fucking come on then!' he cried, trying to wrench his arm loose. His teeth snapped towards the first man's arm.

They put him facedown on the bed where he snarled and spat and snapped his teeth. The larger man sat atop his back, pinning him to the bed.

'Luke, you're here to get better,' he said. 'It's our job to help you.'

'You can help by getting the fuck off me.'

'Not until I'm sure you've calmed down,' the man said.

Luke thrashed for a good half an hour before his energy ran out. The man very cautiously lifted a little of his weight. Luke didn't react, other than to take a deep breath.

The man stood up from Luke's back. As he did so, Luke turned and threw a vicious punch, catching the man off guard and almost knocking him over.

The two men lunged at him, seeking to restrain rather than hurt. Luke grappled with them for a few minutes before a third man came in. The two men held him as best they could while the third man approached.

Luke's eyes widened when he saw the dripping hypodermic needle in the hand of the new arrival. His feet lashed out, bursting the lips of one of the men.

They doubled their efforts, pinning him to the bed facedown. There was little he could do. The third man snuck the needle into the side of Luke's neck and depressed the plunger.

Luke felt the anger and fear ebb away from him in a tide of pharmaceutical warmth. His body went limp. One of the two men rolled him to his back.

They smiled down upon him.

'Luke, you're here for your own good,' the first man said, a sad smile on his face. 'We're sorry if we hurt you but it's for your own safety.'

'The doctor is going to come and see you soon,' the second man said. 'She'll explain the situation to you.'

As if his words had been heard by some omnipotent deity, the door again retracted and a stern-faced woman came in. She wore a white lab coat and held a grey clipboard. Her dark hair was tied back in a severe ponytail that pulled her face taut.

Despite Luke's first impressions, she seemed kind when she smiled and spoke.

'Hi, Luke. I'm Doctor Mary Cullen. I'm going to be looking after you while you're in here.'

'Where am I?' Luke asked.

'You're in the Psychiatric Facility on the edge of your home town.'

Luke looked puzzled for a moment.

'You're here because of the injuries you inflicted on yourself recently. Your guardian and her daughter are concerned for your safety and your mental health.'

'Why?'

'Because they found you cutting off large sections of your own face, Luke. That's not the behaviour of someone who's in his right mind.'

'They put the clown's face on me,' Luke said, tears streaming down his face. The salt from the tears stung his wounds.

'I heard all about it,' Mary said. She smiled a very kind smile. 'We'll be discussing it in depth to help you come to terms with what has happened. From what I've been told about you, though, it sounds like you should have been brought here years ago after what happened at your home.'

Luke nodded, his eyes still bleeding tears.

'So, that's why you're here. We'll talk more later. You just try to relax. You're in good hands.'

Luke didn't reply, just watched her go. The three guards followed her out.

'You'll be fine, kid,' the one who had sat on his back smiled. 'I know it.'

Luke's head lolled forward onto his chest. His eyes rolled back into his head and he fell to sleep.

Chapter 49

Bryony's bedroom was cast in a dim glow as the light of dawn began to filter through her curtains.

She woke, drowsy and aching all over. Her stiffness and exhaustion was partly due to her exertions at the gym and partly from her excessive drinking the night before, both of which had been vain attempts to banish the feelings of anger and grief she felt for Luke.

She knew her mother was staying out at a friend's house, yet she was aware that she could hear the floorboards creaking on the landing.

She jerked awake, but still felt glued to the mattress. Her head was fuzzy, an inevitable side-effect of getting drunk after a ball-buster at the gym. The footsteps stopped outside the door.

Bryony tried to move, but found she couldn't. She didn't feel scared, more uneasy.

The door swung open, revealing a dark figure in the doorway. She pretended to be asleep.

As the figure crept closer, Bryony saw him pulling a knife from beneath his tracksuit top.

This jolted her into action. The figure seemed shocked, like he had assumed she was asleep. He stopped, seemingly not wanting to have to kill her.

'Tell your freak boyfriend to call off the cops or I'll kill you,' the figure said.

'What?' Bryony said.

'Make sure the cops aren't involved or I'll kill you.'

Bryony's next words were muffled as her bedroom window exploded, showering broken glass into the room.

While she looked at the brick that had landed on the floor, the figure beat a hasty retreat.

Another brick came through, shattering the other window.

'Don't threaten me, you fucking coward,' Bryony bellowed. 'Come back here. I'll slit your fucking throat.'

She staggered to her feet and shuffled out of her room. Her head swam like she was still drunk.

The landing window erupted in a hail of broken glass. The brick narrowly missed her as she turned away, covering her eyes from the flying shards of glass. She looked down to see a lad stood in her back garden.

'Fucking grass,' the lad shouted.

Rage overcame her. She ran to the window and hurled the brick with all of her might. The falling projectile slammed into the shoulder of the lad, causing him to cry out.

All around the house, Bryony heard the windows succumbing to the bricks being hurled by the gang. She looked out of the window and saw the lad prone on the lawn. Running footsteps came from seemingly every direction.

Bryony ran downstairs, pulling a knife out of the drawer in the kitchen. She heaved open the back door and ran out into the garden.

The youth was still there, trying to climb over the fence. His arm hung, limp, by his side.

Bryony ran at him, feeling utter rage. The lad looked round at her with wide eyes, then scrambled over the fence. Bryony followed him, but he had already gone.

She stood on top of the fence, holding the knife aloft like a triumphant gladiator.

'I'll kill the fucking lot of you,' she bellowed into the dusk sky as the gang disappeared into the night.

She slept badly that night, but it wasn't through fear.

She hoped they would return so she could grind their faces into the broken glass until they begged for mercy.

Chapter 50

The next morning, her neighbours awoke to see the house being tended to by both police and window fitters. They were shocked at the state of the place.

'Are you all right?' they asked her.

'Fine. Just really fucking angry.'

'Who did this?'

'The same assholes who attacked Luke. We need to get them locked up,' she growled.

The policeman at the scene frowned. 'We lock 'em up. They get released. We lock 'em up again. Just goes round in circles. Isn't really anything we can do. We just leave 'em to it now.'

'That's a fucking disgrace,' Bryony spat. 'These pricks want locking up.'

The cop shrugged. 'Are you going to press charges?'

'Trust me, they won't like that,' another cop said.

'No, I don't want to press charges,' Bryony said.

Her neighbours looked at her like she was insane.

'What's the fucking point?' Bryony said. 'If you cops can't do your fucking jobs and put these wankers away, there's no way I'm going to make the situation worse.'

The cop nodded.

'Ok, then,' Bryony said. 'If you aren't going to lock them up, get the fuck out of my house.'

The cop started to protest, but Bryony shoved him out of the front door and slammed it in his face.

'Fucking lazy bastards,' she spat.

Chapter 51

Early the next morning, Mary came in to see Luke. 'We need to do an assessment on your mental state,' she said. 'To see what we can do to help you.'

'I feel frightened,' Luke said. 'I feel like I'm going to hurt myself. Every time I look in the mirror I want to pull the stitches out and finish the job I started with the knife.'

Mary nodded, looking a little overwhelmed at first. She made a few notes on the clipboard. 'And how do you feel about the people who put the tattoo on your face?'

'I want them to suffer as much as I have,' Luke said, his voice devoid of all emotion.

Mary put on a brave face. She knew that she was going to have to keep Luke in the ward for a long time. He was a danger to himself and others.

She could not comprehend the extent of his hatred for the gang, but she knew that he was best kept under her supervision for the foreseeable future.

Something about the boy chilled her to the core.

Chapter 52

Time marched on. Not a great deal happened during the eighteen months following Luke's admission to the Psychiatric Facility.

The Marshton Eight kept their heads down, in relation to the charges pressed against them for the crippling of Tom Hirst. Though it appalled them to behave like normal human beings, they realised that if they were caught committing a misdemeanour it would reflect badly on their chances in the trial.

Hirst was doing things by the book too, also not wanting to cock up the forthcoming trial. He wanted to make sure the pricks all got what they deserved.

Luke spent most of his days in his small room in the mental ward. He found that he didn't mind life in the institution. He had his CDs and his books, and, for one hour a day, under supervision of course, he was allowed to play his guitar.

He also worked out hard, pummelling the plasterboard walls like his life depended on it. This was all he wanted out of life so he was quite content to stay inside.

The only thing that made him want to leave was the thought of Bryony, but their love for each other remained a secret so he had no urgent desire to escape life in the hospital.

Bryony and Norma visited him almost daily, their visits a highpoint in his days. His crush on Bryony had returned with a vengeance.

He was a model patient, mostly because he was content with his life, but also a small, sly part of him knew that if he ever wanted to get out he would have to play by the rules.

Chapter 53

The enforced period of good behaviour was worthwhile for the Marshton Eight, who were in high spirits as their trial for the crippling of Tom Hirst had been dismissed, despite Tom's father being a hall-of-famer in Marshton's police force.

Sergeant Hirst was furious about the gang being let off with the crime and went to the papers, announcing that a re-trial was necessary if they wanted to keep him on the police force.

From time to time, he toyed with the idea of visiting the Marshton Eight and riddling them with bullets, but he always managed to talk himself out of the idea.

Hirst's superiors took the threat of his resignation seriously, and a re-trial was arranged for the following month.

For now, the Marshton Eight were celebrating at Scotty's house. Otis had returned from the newsagents with an armful of papers, all of which showed the gang's mug shots on the front page, along with the headline, 'Marshton Eight escape justice again.' He threw each of his seven friends a copy.

The gang hooted, clapped and cheered when they saw themselves on the front page. They sprayed beer around the room and slapped each other on the back.

Laughing, they relived the night they had beaten up Luke and Tom. Each of the eight told their version of events, exaggerating their own role in the attack.

'No sign of the freak,' said Scotty.

'I almost forgot about him,' said Otis.

'For a while I didn't think we were going to put him away,' said Olly.

'I knew we would,' bragged Scotty.

'Shut the fuck up, Scotty, you can't punch for shit,' said Dave. 'We'd have still been struggling with him now if we'd left it up to you.'

'I wonder what happened to him,' Otis said.

'Ain't seen anything of him since we did his face,' Olly said.

'Learnt his lesson,' said Tommy. 'He won't fuck with us again in a hurry.'

They all laughed.

'Mouthy little fucker wasn't he?' Scotty said. 'But I shut his mouth for him.'

'Scotty, he could walk in here right now and kick your pansy ass,' laughed Otis.

The others joined in.

'Fuck you,' Scotty replied, flicking his cigarette butt at Otis.

'Who gives a fuck anyway?' Johnny T said. 'Fucker's dead for all I care.'

They all laughed and carried on the party, each of them looking with pride at their photo on the front page of the paper.

Chapter 54

The next night, Otis and Dave watched two young girls walking through the graveyard.

Otis smiled when he noticed that one of the girls was the freak's girlfriend, the one whose windows they had smashed. She had threatened them all. Now it was time to see if she could back it up.

When the girls were level with him, he broke his cover in the bushes and raced at them, his flick knife held above his head. Dave followed, bellowing a bloodcurdling war cry.

The girls screamed and took off. Otis and Dave cursed and set off after them.

Bryony and her friend, Clare, ran through the graveyard, not daring to look back. They could hear the two lads' heavy breathing and footsteps behind them. It sounded like they were getting closer.

Their limbs gradually tired. Every breath felt like acid in their throat and lungs. They both felt sick with panic and knew they couldn't keep this pace up much longer.

Clare chanced a look and saw that one of the grimacing youths was only a few feet behind them.

Her house was only a minute from here. If they could just outrun the lads, get home and lock the doors, then her dad would kick the shit out of the hapless bastards.

'Go… to… mine,' she breathed.

Bryony nodded but veered off to the left. Dave followed her.

Otis pursued Clare. She got to her house and started slamming her palms onto the door. Her eyes were bulging and seemed ultra-white.

Otis enjoyed the panic on her face.

She pulled the keys out and unlocked the door, then ran in and slammed it shut behind her. The lad disappeared from view.

She pulled breaths into her starving lungs and called out for her dad. He should be in. Her eyes landed on a note on the table, 'Gone out for a few jars. Be back around 10:30.'

Her watch showed 10:10. She'd be cold and bled dry by the time he got home. She needed to find a weapon.

Her heart punched against her ribs. She risked a glance out of the curtains and saw no sign that the lad was outside.

But she knew, deep down, that he was still there.

She hunted for a weapon, finding only an old length of wooden curtain pole. It felt hard enough but had a flex to it that made it highly suspect.

She ran to the kitchen and remembered with a groan that the knives were under lock and key thanks to a drunken argument between her parents which had got out of hand and led to her dad needing stitches.

'Thanks a lot, mam, you crazy bitch,' she said.

She scanned for another weapon. All she could see were rows of brown Bud bottles stacked in a neat formation by the back door.

A noise came from the back door to her left. She glanced down to see the lad's grinning face poking through the cat flap.

She screamed, drawing a laugh from him.

The handle to the back door wiggled back and forth. Luckily the door was locked. The lad said something which she couldn't understand. Then she made out Bryony's voice, shrill with panic.

She ran to the front door, and, despite all of her fears, hurled the door open and screamed for Bryony to come in.

Nothing happened for a long few seconds. Then Bryony echoed Clare's scream. Footsteps thudded up the path at the side of the house.

Bryony ran in. Clare slammed the door shut and peered through the spyhole.

Their pursuers were nowhere to be seen.

She waited a moment then turned to look at her friend.

'He got me in the back,' Bryony said, turning to show a ragged wound running diagonally between her shoulder blades. Blood welled up from the wound, soaking into her shirt.

'You'll survive,' Clare said.

'I know. Hurts like hell though. You gonna call your dad?'

'Yeah. Good idea. I hadn't thought of that.'

'No time to be sarcastic.'

'I wasn't. I'm not thinking straight.'

She picked out her phone and tried dad's mobile. The credit lady told her that she'd spent her allowance already. She cursed as she remembered the house phone was out of commission too.

'Best get some of those bottles,' she said. 'In case they get in.'

'I think it'll be fine. They won't have the balls to break in.'

'I hope not.'

They took deep breaths, trying to slow their frantic heartbeats. A few minutes passed.

'See, they've fucked off,' Bryony grinned.

As soon as she'd finished her sentence, there was a crash from upstairs.

Chapter 55

Bryony and Clare stared at each other for a frozen second. Time seemed to stretch out before either of them dared to move, but the second crash shocked them into action.

Clare remembered her habit of leaving her bedroom window open. Her dad had often told her about it and she had always ignored him. Now it looked as though her belligerence was going to cost her dear.

They ran to the front door but as they did so, fists beat against the wood, sending them scurrying back into the living room.

'What do we do now?' Bryony whispered.

'Get out of here. And quickly.'

'Your dad will be well pissed if this psycho gets his money out from under the bed.'

'He'll be even more pissed if he finds his only daughter chopped up into little pieces.'

'True, but—'

Bryony's next comment was blotted out by the sound of footsteps crashing down the stairs. Maniacal laughter accompanied the footsteps, sending shivers down both of their spines.

Otis poked his head around the doorframe, a hideous grin on his face. His hand curled up one finger at a time in a casual wave.

One of the Bud bottles burst on the wall next to his head. He didn't flinch. Fucker didn't even stop grinning.

Suddenly the bottles and the wooden rod felt totally inadequate. Clare hurled another bottle for good measure.

It bounced off the youth's shoulder as he came through the doorway.

Clare pressed a couple of bottles into Bryony's shaking hands then started rummaging through her pocket for the back door key so they could escape.

Bryony threw a bottle. It whizzed over Otis's head, missing him by a fraction. He let out a shrill laugh and ran at them.

Clare forgot her search for the key and instead swung a home run swing at Otis's head. The curtain rod smacked into his temple, confirming her doubts about the weapon when it snapped on impact.

The lad stumbled to the right but kept on charging.

Clare ran to the back door, hurling the remaining shard of wood like a spear. It bounced off the lad's belly, but did little else.

She fumbled the key, her sweating, trembling hands slipping from the polished brass.

Bryony raised the bottle to swing at the attacker but he slammed into her like a charging bull. The impact sent both of them off their feet. The world spun.

Clare pulled the key out and put it into the lock. She heaved the door open and ran to help Bryony, who was trying to pull herself out from beneath the lad's bulk.

The sound of sirens cut through the otherwise quiet night.

'Help,' she cried. Blood ran down her face and arm. She wheezed for air.

Clare tried to roll the semi-conscious lad off her friend.

'Come on,' Bryony whispered. 'Before he wakes up.'

Already Otis had started to stir. He grabbed Clare's leg, making her squeal.

Bryony managed to get out from under the intruder while he tried to keep his grip on Clare.

She kicked him in the bicep of the arm which held her friend. He let out a grunt and his hand let go of Clare's leg.

Clare pulled back and pushed Bryony towards the open door.

They ran blindly, not caring where they ended up as long as they outran the maniacs who seemed hell-bent on killing them.

Chapter 56

Wincing, Otis got to his feet. His head pounded. He reckoned he must have banged it when he and the girl landed on the floor. Still he smiled. The girls' terror was delicious. He was savouring every second of their fear.

This extended chase was like foreplay, only prolonging his fun. When he got his hands on them they were going to suffer for making him wait.

The girls found themselves on the edge of town. There seemed to be nothing for about a mile in every direction. Just lampposts and trees and bushes. Places to hide.

'I think we can stop now,' Bryony said, still winded from where Otis's head had met with her stomach.

'Think you might be right,' Clare said. She too was exhausted. Her mind was screaming thoughts at her.

'He cut my arm,' Bryony said. 'Only a little but it's bleeding badly.'

'It'll be fine. Try to keep quiet, just in case he's around.'

'I doubt he'll— Shit.'

'What?'

Bryony clamped her hand over her friend's mouth and pulled her behind a thick tree trunk. She pointed across the road.

Clare's breath caught in her throat as she saw the man in the shadows, carefully scouring the trees and bushes.

'I know you're here,' he said, loud enough that they could hear. 'When I find you, you're going to be sorry you made me wait so long.'

Clare and Bryony did their best not to gasp.

Clare felt paralysed with fear. Bryony grabbed her friend's arm and led her further into the trees and bushes. She looked over her shoulder every few seconds, making sure that their pursuer hadn't seen them.

The moonlight reflected off the knife in his hand. In the twilight he looked even more frightening than he had in the house.

They realised they were heading uphill. Bryony caught her foot before she stepped onto the gravel path which led up the driveway. The noise would have been certain to bring the lunatic straight to them.

Clare pulled to a stop.

'What are you doing?' Bryony whispered.

'That's the Murder House. We can't go in there.'

'Are you fucking kidding me? This nutcase is going to cut us up if he catches us.' She pointed down the hill for emphasis. The man was headed towards them, unwittingly for now.

'I'm shit-scared of this house too,' Bryony continued. 'But it's the lesser of two evils.'

Clare said nothing but let Bryony lead her again. They reached the top of the drive and headed for the gates which were slightly open.

'Besides,' Bryony said. 'No one's lived here for years.'

They both winced as their feet crunched on the gravel. The man glanced in their direction, making them both almost scream. He carried on following, but didn't seem to have seen them.

In the grounds of Peth Vale, the two girls felt a wave of unease. There was something plain wrong about the house and the land on which it stood. It was the epitome of bad vibes.

Just superstition, they both tried to console themselves. They hid in the corner of the grounds, behind the garage which was partly hidden by overgrown bushes.

They watched through a gap in the brickwork on the wall that marked the front boundary of the house.

The man was out of sight but they could hear his footsteps on the gravel. He was moving slowly, presumably in an attempt to stop them from hearing him, but he was undoubtedly on his way to the gates.

'He won't come in,' Bryony said.

He paused at the gate. They saw one gloved hand poke through the bars. It was like he was deciding whether to go in the grounds or not.

As Otis pushed the gate open a little more, making an unsettling squeal ring out, one of the upstairs windows of the house illuminated.

Chapter 57

Bryony and Clare stifled a gasp. They'd never have set foot in the grounds of this notorious house if they'd known it was occupied.

The silhouette of a man showed in the curtains, making the lad who'd chased them duck away from the gates. The girls heard his footsteps retreat down the driveway.

They breathed deeply for the first time since they'd set foot out of Clare's house.

Their breath soon froze again when they heard the door of the house open. Footsteps crunched across the gravel towards the gates.

The man came into view, his pale face hidden by a black hood. His right hand held a large cleaver.

'Who's there?' he said, his voice commanding and without even the merest hint of fear. 'You stay the fuck away from here or I'll cut you to ribbons.'

His eyes flicked across the garden and the girls were certain he had seen them. He didn't act as if he had, just continued to scan the darkness as he moved over to the gates. He wrapped a thick chain around the gates and secured it with a big padlock.

The girls were trapped in the grounds now. With an angry man who had threatened to cut up any intruders. Things were going from bad to worse.

Chapter 58

Bryony heard a noise in the bushes behind her. At first she thought it was a bird, but then something hairy and warm squirmed over her foot. She put a hand over her mouth, but not before the scream escaped.

The man looked over to their hiding place and started back across the gravel towards them.

'Who's there?' he shouted.

The girls remained silent, knowing they were discovered but too frightened to do anything about it.

'Come out now. Don't make me have to look for you,' the man barked. 'Put down your weapons and I'll let the cops deal with you, much as it pains me to do so.'

Clare and Bryony looked at each other.

Shrugged.

Raised their hands above their heads and left the cover of their hiding place.

Chapter 59

'Keep your hands where I can see 'em,' the man with the cleaver told them.

Clare and Bryony did so. They couldn't see the man's face so well in the dark.

'What are you doing here?' the man said.

'This fucking whacko was trying to kill us,' Clare blurted.

'One of that arsehole gang,' Bryony added.

'The one who crippled that lad?' the man said, his voice becoming much kinder.

Both girls nodded, eyes wide.

'Are you ok?' he asked, lowering the cleaver and tucking it into the back of his trousers.

'Shitting ourselves,' Clare said.

Bryony laughed nervously.

'I don't blame you. But you're safe here. Come inside for a drink, make sure he's gone.' He turned so he was facing Bryony. 'Looks like you're bleeding,' he said.

'Yeah, the crazy bastard got me with his knife,' Bryony said.

'I can treat the wounds for you if you like.'

Ignoring their misgivings, the girls took him up on his offer and went inside.

Chapter 60

The interior of the huge house was impressive, arguably even grander than the exterior, but looked like it hadn't been cleaned in a lifetime. Clare and Bryony were wowed by it, dust or no dust.

'Please, take a seat in the front room,' the man said.

The girls opened the door to see wall upon wall of heavily laden bookshelves. Pictures filled in the space between the books.

The girls found themselves unable to resist curiosity's pull and started to look at the pictures.

'Dr Arnold Kasabian,' Bryony said, reading aloud the certificate she saw framed on the wall. 'Sounds like one of the fucking X-men.'

Clare stifled a laugh. 'You're wicked. The man just saved our asses.'

'Yeah, you're right. He ain't exactly a shining beacon of humanity though, is he?'

Clare's reply never came because she heard a nervous laugh from the doorway.

She looked across to see the man standing outside the door with a tray of drinks. He looked very uncomfortable, like he had heard every word of their conversation.

'I've got beers, vodka, whiskey, mixers and ice,' he said. His face was still hidden in the shadows, giving the girls the impression that he wanted it to stay that way.

'Beer will be fine,' Bryony said. 'Thank you.'

The man nodded.

'Haven't you got any brandy?' Clare asked.

The man shifted uncomfortably for a second then Clare burst out laughing. 'Just messing with you,' she said. 'Beer's fine.'

The man laughed but it was forced. 'Do you mind telling me your names?'

'I'm Bryony.'

'Clare.'

'As you already know, I'm Dr Alfred Kasabian. I've just moved into this wonderful house. I'm pleased to meet you both and I'm glad your intrusion on my premises was justified.' He grinned at them. If it was meant to put them at ease it failed. Even without the cleaver he had an air of menace.

'Well, thanks for not cutting us up,' Clare said.

The man laughed. As he did so, his face moved into the light. His skin was pale and pock-marked, except for his fat cheeks which were red as though he was permanently blushing.

'We were just glad you weren't a psychopath,' Bryony laughed.

The man grinned.

For the first time he looked relaxed. 'Please, stay a while. Have a few drinks. I'm glad to share my home with you. When you're ready to go I'll call you a taxi. We'll split the fare.'

'That's very good of you, but—' Bryony started.

'I insist,' the man said, waving away her protests. 'I'm glad to be able to help. Let's just pray this clown gets what he deserves.'

'Fucking right,' Clare said, raising her glass.

'I'm sorry but can you please not shout,' the man said. 'I don't mind but my wife is asleep upstairs. If she were to wake and find me here with two such comely ladies,' he pulled a horrified expression.

'Keep it down, Clare,' Bryony said.

Clare scowled at each of her companions in turn.

'Where's the toilet, Doc?' Clare asked.

'There's one upstairs, but I'd rather you didn't use it. The one downstairs is straight along the corridor, second right then third door on the left.'

'Thanks.'

Bryony gave her a look that said, *you're not leaving me alone with this guy are you?*

Clare ignored her and said, 'Not be long.'

The man smiled at Bryony. It was the smile of someone who had no idea what to say next.

Chapter 61

Clare tried not to be nosey, but she couldn't help but take a look into the rooms she passed on the corridor.

Dead animal eyes stared at her from the walls. She flinched as if burnt and, cursing her curiosity, went to the door that the man had told her was the toilet.

After a second's thought, she locked the door. When she finished she left the toilet and walked back to the front room.

No detours this time. She didn't want to see the dead animals again.

It would be best if she and Bryony got out of here, as soon as they could. She had a very bad feeling about everything now.

Clare jolted when she reached the front room. Bryony was nowhere to be seen. The man was gone too.

Her mind started working overtime. Feeling a blast of cold air, she looked to the front door. It was open by a few inches and the smell of cigarette smoke drifted into the house.

She pulled it open to see Bryony and the man having a smoke.

The man noted her wild-eyed expression and said, 'Don't like to smoke in the house.'

'Of course,' Clare said. 'I just…' she didn't want him to know what she'd been thinking but he seemed to know anyway. 'So, we should be going.'

'Please, stay for one more drink. You've barely even relaxed yet,' the man said.

'He's right, Clare, you still look wound up.'

Clare didn't want to offend the man after everything he'd done for them, but she felt terrified. Something was wrong about this, but her mind was refusing to reveal it to her.

'One quick drink, Clare,' Bryony said. 'Half an hour at most. Then we'll go home.'

Bryony and the man stared at her, making her feel like a nerdy kid being cajoled into smoking a cigarette behind the sports hall at school.

'Ok. One more drink,' she relented.

'I need to pee,' Bryony said.

'You know where to go?' the man said.

'Yeah, thanks.'

The man nodded, stubbed out his cigarette. 'I'd best go sort out the drinks,' he said.

Clare nodded and took a draw of the cigarette. When the front door closed, she felt strangely alone and on show. Like unseen eyes were upon her.

She ignored the feeling (and her persistent thought that something was wrong) and instead looked at the grounds of the house, trying to see the beauty in it.

She failed.

Chapter 62

After her smoke, she went back to the front room. The house was strangely quiet.

The man came in with a second tray of drinks. 'Another beer?' he smiled. His grin made her sick to her stomach.

'Yes, please.'

He passed her a dew-covered can.

'Thank you.'

She popped the ring-pull and took a drink. Smiled at him. The atmosphere was still uncomfortable. The man was not one of the world's great conversationalists.

While she sat in silence, the answer to what was making her so uneasy leapt into her mind.

Arnold Kasabian. She knew she'd heard that name before. He had been a doctor at Marshton's hospital who'd gone missing a few years ago.

The weird guy who she was now sharing a room with was no doubt the killer, trying to pass himself off as the dead doctor. He'd even called himself Alfred instead of Arnold.

Her heart began to pound and a sickly feeling flooded over her.

As soon as Bryony came back they were going to get the hell out of here.

She sure was taking a long time considering she had just gone for a piss.

The man seemed to sense her unease and tried to console her. 'It's a big house. She probably just got lost.' His smile did little to lessen her thoughts of foul play.

A few minutes later, Clare was seriously worried. What was taking Bryony so long?

The man just kept smiling at her. The more he did it, the more creeped out she became.

'Mind if I check up on her?' Clare said.

Her strange companion shook his head and smiled.

Clare felt good not to have to look at him. The evening had taken a sinister turn.

She moved through the dark rooms, towards the bathroom she'd visited not long ago.

'Bryony?' she called, rapping lightly on the door. 'Anyone there?'

After waiting a tense minute or so, she knocked again. The silence of the house was almost deafening.

She tried the handle.

Pulled it open.

Saw Bryony slumped over the toilet bowl, limp and pale.

Turned to see the man stood with a length of rope in his hands.

'Shh,' he said, lunging at her.

Clare fought as best she could but he was just too strong. The rope drew taut around her throat and crushed the air out of her.

She felt like she was drowning, like her eyes were bulging out of her head. Her hands clawed at the rope. Panic welled up inside her then she felt nothing at all.

Chapter 63

Alfred had been wrong about the first girl. She hadn't died just yet. That was good, he could have some fun with her before he put her out of her misery.

While she was still out cold he ran his knife up her top, slicing it in two. The removal of the torn garment revealed two perfect breasts.

His mouth watered. His groin pulsed and tingled and stiffened. She was beautiful but he would let her wake before he touched her.

Bryony stared up at the clown. Just her luck to end up in his clutches after escaping the first nut with a knife. She fought back the panic which threatened to consume her and tried to think.

With her hands bound behind her like this, the clown could do anything he wanted without too much of a struggle. She needed to be smart.

Though it sickened her to do so, she winked at the clown and turned her back to him. She reached back with her hands, trying to reach his groin.

She tried to speak, but the gag muffled her words.

Her hope was that he would be stupid enough to remove the gag. He didn't take the hint, so she knelt in front of him and mimed giving him head.

He smiled but shook his head.

Moving too fast for her to react, he grabbed her legs and pushed them apart. His flabby bulk pinned her to the damp cellar floor.

The smell and feel of him made her retch.

Chapter 64

A few days later, an ashen-faced Norma came to see Luke with the newspaper article declaring the Marshton Eight's escape from punishment. Upon seeing it, he punched the wall and bellowed his rage.

The two guards eyed him nervously. Since Luke had been admitted to the asylum he had put on a stone and a half of muscle. His lean frame belied his strength and power.

He had always possessed a steely determination – they knew that from the first time he'd kicked off with them – but now his temper was volcanic. The last thing they needed was for him to go ballistic.

'Fucking bullshit,' he screamed, grabbing his hair and bending double, doing his best to process the information, then stood and slammed his fist into the wall again. Another chunk of plasterboard fell away.

'Luke, are you ok?' Norma said. She was worried about him, and she may have been one of the only people not to be terrified by his temper.

He lapsed into an uneasy silence and put his arms around her, resting his head on her shoulder.

'It's ok to be pissed off,' she said.

He nodded. 'I just can't believe they got away with it. They crippled him and did this to me.'

'I know. I know.' She looked him in the eye. There seemed to be nothing she could say to comfort him, so she planted a kiss on his cheek.

'Luke, there's something else you should know,' she said, her voice faltering and cracking.

He looked up at her with his big blue eyes and she was startled how childlike he appeared.

'What?' he said, his heart already sinking.

She sighed and looked down at the floor. 'It's Bryony. I haven't seen her in three days. She and Clare were supposed to be spending the weekend at a friend's house, so I assumed she would just turn up tonight. When I called her friend, it turned out she and Clare never got there.'

'Fuck's sake,' Luke bellowed. His fist smashed another section of plaster loose. It crumbled to dust beneath his foot.

'I'm shitting myself, Luke,' Norma said.

He shared her fear; Marshton was a breeding ground for psychopaths.

Chapter 65

'I just wish I could help you to look for her,' Luke said. 'But I'm no good to anyone stuck in here.'

She leaned in close, whispered, 'Then don't be stuck in here.' As she pulled back he saw a glint in her eye.

He looked puzzled for a moment.

'Why don't you escape?' she said.

For a second he thought she was joking, but, after studying her face, he saw that she was entirely serious.

'And how the fuck would I do that?' he whispered.

'I overheard the guards saying that they're having a party tonight, so the reserves will be down to skeleton staff. That'd be your best chance.'

Luke looked at her.

'I'd wait for you in the woods across the road,' she said. 'I'll give you a lift out of here, because they're bound to come looking for you.'

Luke thought about it for a second.

'One more thing, Luke, I think you have a right to know this. The last time I saw her, Bryony told me she was in love with you.'

Luke put his head in his hands. Any sliver of doubt he had held evaporated. He looked up at Norma and nodded.

Norma snuck her hand under his top and pushed something into his waistband. He wasn't sure what it was but it felt a little cold against his skin. She kissed him on the forehead and pulled away.

'Act normal,' she whispered in his ear.

He sat on the end of the bed, taking care not to stab himself in the gut with the hidden object. She took his hand and smiled at him.

'How's life then?' she asked.

'It's not bad, actually, I don't mind it.'

'It's for your own good, I suppose.'

'Yeah, it's the best place for me.' From the way he played with his hands, it was obvious that something was on his mind.

'What is it?'

'Just the thought of Bryony out there on her own. She could be anywhere.'

Norma opened her mouth to say something but the door came open.

Hirst stood in the doorway, his face grim. He stepped in, his eyes scanning the ceiling and walls for the camera he knew was concealed somewhere. After finding it, he flicked the off switch.

He shifted from foot to foot, then cleared his throat and nodded a greeting to Luke and Norma.

'Norma, is it ok to catch up with you later?' Luke said, sensing that Hirst had something he wanted to say to him in private.

'Yes, of course.' Norma hugged Luke, whispered, 'See you tonight,' and left.

'Sorry to interrupt you,' Hirst said, loud enough for Norma to hear. 'I won't keep you long, if Norma wants to stay.'

'It's ok,' Luke said. 'Stay as long as you want.'

Hirst stared at the floor, his face slack. 'So, I'm sure you've already heard that those dickless wonders have got off with it.'

'I know. Don't worry, they'll get what they deserve.' Luke said.

'I will help you kill them,' Hirst said. He stared Luke in the eye, and Luke saw that he meant it. 'Anything you want to do will be legal. I'll make sure the heat stays off you.'

Luke couldn't help but smile at the idea. 'No. I won't be doing that. And even if I was going to, I couldn't ask you to risk your career like that.'

Hirst said nothing, just stared at Luke. 'I understand. And you're a good lad for being able to let what happened to you go. I just hope I can be as forgiving.' He leant in close. Luke smelt stale cigarettes and alcohol on his breath. 'I lie awake at night dreaming of shoving a twelve gauge into each of their mouths and blowing their worthless brains into the sky.'

'I can imagine,' Luke said. He wasn't sure whether he could trust Hirst or not, so he decided to play it safe. 'Being in here is starting to mellow me. I was angry, but now I am starting to let it go.'

'Well, you're a better man than me. Take care, Luke. I'll come and see you again soon. Thanks for listening to my bullshit.'

'You look after yourself, Sergeant.'

Hirst smiled. The gesture was forlorn, hopeless. Luke felt for him. The sad smile made him even more furious about what had happened.

'Nearly forgot,' Hirst said, flicking on the camera again. 'See you soon, Luke. You're a good lad.'

Luke settled back on his bed and waited for the party to start. Under his duvet, he pulled the object that Norma had given him from his trousers.

It was a metal ballpoint pen. He tested it against his hand. It wasn't the best weapon in the world, but it would be enough.

After hiding it under his pillow, he laid back and stared at the ceiling.

Chapter 66

Luke opened his eyes to see that a few hours had lapsed. The party would be in full swing. He rubbed the pen, relishing the chance to use it.

His wish was granted ten minutes later when Swick, one of the few guards that Luke didn't like, strutted into the room, holding a syringe and a plastic tub full of tablets.

Swick was a bully to most of the patients and had stolen from a number of them too. The prick was long overdue retribution.

Luke smiled when he saw him.

'Evening, cumstain,' Swick smiled. 'Got your crazy pills.'

'Just stick 'em on the side, I'll take 'em later,' Luke said, knowing full well that Swick would feel the need to force-feed them to him.

'Come on, Miller, I've got strict orders to make sure you're taking these tablets. Wouldn't want you trying to peel your face off again now, would we?' The corners of his mouth twisted up in a malicious grin.

Luke laughed. He was going to be wearing his grin on the other side of his face in a moment.

'I don't think you're tough enough to make me,' Luke smiled.

'Oh, yeah?' Swick pulled his cosh.

'Yeah.'

Swick took a step forward.

Luke held the pen tight in his left hand, keeping it hidden beneath the bed clothes until Swick got close enough.

'Last chance, Miller. Don't make me kick your crazy ass.'

Luke stared defiantly at him.

Swick rushed in. Luke leapt to his feet and brought the pen down in a stabbing motion.

The hard metal tip sunk into Swick's eye, pushing blood out onto Luke's hand. Luke kept driving the pen in until it disappeared into Swick's eye socket.

Swick stood for a moment then fell, a sea of gore rushing out of the wound. Luke watched the blood flow for a second, feeling alive for the first time in a long while. He pulled Swick's key-card from his lapel and ran out into the corridor.

Chapter 67

Knowing he didn't have long before the sirens started, he tried to think. Even on skeleton staff, there would be between five and seven guards lurking around.

Being caught was not an option, or else he'd never be allowed out of here. Adrenaline coursed through him, making his whole body shake.

The thrill of being out of his cell turned to terror when the sirens started to blare.

The noise stabbed into his mind, threatening to blot out all semblance of rational thought. He forced panic back and tried to come up with a plan.

He swiped the key-card on the magnetic strip by the door of the nearest cell. The door clicked open.

Luke opened the next few doors using the magnetic key-card. Soon, a dozen patients were running down the corridors, screaming their joy at finally being free.

Luke saw a white-clad figure at the far end of the corridor and ducked into the shadows.

His breath came fast and hard as the figure approached. It was one of the guards he knew and liked. It was a shame to have to hurt him, but he couldn't be allowed to fuck up Luke's escape plan. Luckily the guard ran past.

Luke made his way along to the stairs, opening every door he passed. The patients flooded out onto the corridors.

At least he'd given himself a valuable distraction. He may even help some of his friends to escape.

A pair of guards came upon the scene and stood, mouths open, looking at the large group of patients loose on the corridor.

Luke watched them wade into the mass with their coshes flailing. He saw one of his friends fall beneath a heavy cosh strike then moved away from the scene.

He ducked into a shadowy corner as two more guards ran into the melee. They were under no restrictions, laying into the mob with extreme prejudice.

Luke was too busy watching them to notice one of the guards creeping up behind him.

The first thing he knew was the cosh hitting him in the side of the head. The blow was unexpected but he took it well. His head moved to the side, pulling his neck a little, but he was otherwise unharmed.

Turning fast, he grabbed the guard's head and jammed it into the wall. The guard slid to his knees, clutching his pounding skull.

Luke ran for the stairs and shoved the handle on the door that led to the fire escape.

Cool air from the rear staircase caressed his face, a small taste of freedom that further strengthened his resolve to escape.

A glance down the spiral staircase revealed distant shapes running up the stairs towards him.

Moving into the shadows at the top of the stairs, he let the first guard run past. He was certain they'd seen him, but they passed without reacting to his presence.

He cursed as the second guard stopped halfway up the stairs.

He was going to have to risk being discovered if he wanted to escape.

Chapter 68

His body shaking like a leaf in a tornado, he stepped towards the top of the stairs. Fear tried its utmost to weld his feet to the floor.

His eyes glued to the guard standing sentry two levels below him, he dropped to his butt and slid down the stairs, keeping out of sight behind the waist-high rail. Every step he took seemed to make his heart beat a little faster.

He was still a good distance away from the guard, who was built like a brick shithouse. Looking down at the immense guard, his mouth suddenly felt like it was lined with cotton wool.

He slid down each step, making sure not to make a noise. As he neared the guard, he started to feel sure he couldn't pass without being discovered.

Looking down, he found a loose rock on the floor. He shuffled on his knees towards the rail, then flung the rock at the wall to his left. When the guard went to investigate the noise, Luke ran.

He found a nice shadowy corner in which to hide while he waited for the guard to come back. His back pressed against something cold as he moved back. He turned to see a fire extinguisher mounted on the wall behind him.

Grinning, he lifted it free of its bracket and waited, allowing his heart rate to settle. When the sickly feeling disappeared, he stepped out of the shadows.

The guard turned as Luke was close enough to touch him. His cosh flew through the air, just missing Luke's head and bouncing off his shoulder.

Luke grunted in anger and thrust the fire extinguisher at the guard's face. The guard staggered away then fell on his back.

Luke slammed another few blows in, grinning at the sickly crack and the ribbon of blood that snaked out of the guard's ear. Though he desperately wanted to bray the guard's head into mush, longed to bathe in the thick, warm blood, he knew he had to escape. There'd be plenty of time to indulge his bloodlust later.

Luke left the twitching guard in the growing pool of blood and raced down the stairs.

Chapter 69

The commotion from upstairs came through on the monitors in the security room where a guard sat behind a desk watching the screens. A pizza the size of a bin lid rested on his lap.

Luke dropped to his knees and crawled towards the desk. The guard laughed as he watched his colleagues hitting the crazies with their coshes. Some of the crazies were pulling pained expressions which made him snort laughter again.

Luke shuffled forward, taking a quick breather when he reached the desk. His heart once again began to thrash. He took a deep breath and carried on.

The security guard was too busy watching his screens to notice Luke gradually appearing from behind the wooden desk.

When Luke had passed the desk he crawled until he was hidden by the wall and stood up. His breath stinging his throat and lungs, he shuffled along the wall until he was sure he had passed the guard station.

Then he ran full pelt for the main entrance to the asylum.

He scanned his key-card against the swipe reader by the entrance. The doors clicked open, allowing him to run out into the cold night.

The air was cool and refreshing on his face as he ran towards the woods where he'd arranged to meet Norma. For a few frantic seconds, he didn't think she was there, but then he saw her leaning against a tree.

'Hey,' he whispered.

'Hey. You made good time.'

'Yeah. Let's get out of here.'

'My car's on the other side of the hill. Let's go.'

They ran over the hill, towards the dark shape of Norma's car, which was hidden under a sprawling oak tree. Then they made their escape.

Chapter 70

Norma wanted to find Bryony and get out of Marshton, but Luke refused to leave until the Marshton Eight had suffered for destroying what remained of his sanity.

They went to Bryony's sister's house, right on the edge of Marshton. She was on holiday so Norma said they could stay there for a few days.

The house was cramped, but it was going to be worth a few days of discomfort to get his hands on the gang who had attacked him. He just hoped he could find Bryony.

He and Norma ate while she told him of all the places that had been searched previously then they put their heads together and tried to come up with a plan to find her.

Luke said he'd cover Marshton, while Norma decided to check if Bryony had turned up at her dad's house in Scotland.

Luke was startled out of his thoughts by someone knocking at the door and hid behind the settee.

He was dismayed to see Hirst stroll into the front room.

'You can come out from behind the settee, Luke,' he said.

Luke stood up, feeling awkward.

'Don't worry I haven't come to send you back.'

Luke relaxed a little.

'I just wanted to see how you were, in light of what has happened.'

'Erm, I've been trying not to think about it.'

'I don't blame you. Are you worried about her?'

Luke nodded his head slowly.

'I thought as much. I'm going to keep a close eye on you here.'

Luke shook his head. He didn't want police surveillance when he was carrying out his vengeance. 'I just want to have a normal life,' he muttered. After a moment's thought, he added, 'Or as normal as possible.'

Hirst seemed to understand. 'Tell you what I'll do. I'll say you were killed in the riot at the asylum. It'll take them at least a few days to figure out that this wasn't the case. By then you can make your escape or whatever it is you want to do.'

'Thank you,' Luke smiled.

'It's ok. You're a good kid. I don't want you to be locked up in there like a fucking criminal. You look after yourself, Luke.'

Luke nodded. Hirst left, looking around himself to make sure he hadn't been seen going into the house. Then he called the press and told them that Luke had been killed in the asylum riot.

Chapter 71

Alfred saw the breaking news about the breakout at the mental hospital. Four dead, according to the report. *No skin off my nose*, he thought with a smile. *Four less nutters to waste taxes on*.

The news report said that two of the bodies had been battered beyond recognition. *Nice work*, he thought. *We all have a little bloodlust in us, when it comes down to it*.

One of the dead was identified as Luke Miller. The name was familiar to him, but he didn't immediately know why.

When a photo of Luke as a child popped up on screen, he remembered. The kid he'd almost killed, then orphaned, had been committed. The little fucker had died in the asylum which he'd been sent to as a result of Alfred's own crimes.

He felt a sense of pride at this, although he was a little pissed he hadn't gotten to finish the kid himself. Still, if he was out of the picture, there were no living witnesses to his crimes.

He was finally free of the worry of having someone identify him. Now the fun could begin in earnest.

Alfred felt a surge of blood to his groin upon imagining the acts he'd carried out on the family of Luke Miller and decided to vent his frustrations on the pretty little thing in the basement.

He whistled a happy tune as he descended the stairs. The tune was still on his lips when the girl lunged at him, swinging a piece of wood.

The sheer shock of seeing her out of her shackles caught him off guard and the blow hit him hard in the face. Surprise doubled the impact of the blow.

His head went sideways, hitting the doorframe. Transparent sparks flew across his vision. Cursing, he threw an instinctive punch that burst the girl's nose.

It didn't deter her. The wood hit his head again, sending more sparks flying across his vision.

Bryony saw the clown's arms grabbing for her, but was too slow to avoid it. His arms pulled her in, crushing into her ribs.

His breath was foul, even worse than it had been the last time he had been upon her. He smelt of blood and death. His arms squeezed harder, forcing the air from her lungs.

He's going to crush me to death, she thought.

Acting on instinct, she pulled her head back and whiplashed it forwards, smashing her forehead into the clown's chin.

The impact hurt.

But it hurt him too.

His grip slackened and he grunted in pain.

While she had him hurt, she slammed her knee into his groin. An old playground move that dropped him like a sack of shit.

She ran but one of his hands grabbed her ankle. She let out a cry of frustration and stomped out at him with her free leg.

Her first stomp caught him in the face. The noise it made was horrible, like a hammer hitting a side of beef. She kicked out again, catching his forearm. His fingers kept hold of her leg, squeezing so hard her foot started to go numb.

She twisted and pulled, wrenching her leg from his grip and giving her calf the mother of all Chinese burns, but she was free. His hand came towards her again.

She stomped out at his face a second time, making him groan. His fingers pulled away a little, but he was still too close. She stomped his head again. This time there was a sickening crunch.

The hand dropped to the damp floor.

Without looking back, she ran for the stairs.

Chapter 72

The house was a dark maze, seemingly designed to bemuse and disorient her until the clown could catch her.

Her feet pounded the bare floorboards, sending each step through her like a shotgun blast. His footsteps were mere seconds behind her.

She did her best to stay hidden, stay safe, but she knew he would find her eventually. She had to get out, fuck staying silent.

Her aching legs propelled her towards what she hoped was safety. The back door was locked (things were never *that* easy).

Again the debate between staying quiet and getting away raged. Once more safety reigned supreme.

She found a metal lawn chair tucked in the corner and swung it at the window.

Cracks shivered down the glass, but it stayed in the frame, mocking her.

The clown's loathsome breathing filled the darkness behind her.

She thrust the chair at the window again, making a fist-sized hole in the glass. Ignoring the pain and damage it would cause her, she shoved her hands into the hole and started trying to enlarge the gap.

Blood ran down her forearms as she struggled to break the glass.

The clown appeared out of the shadows like a foul, bloated nightmare. She pulled a shard of glass from the frame and slashed it at his face.

He ducked back, as the glass carved a bloody trail across his brow. He cried out and lunged at her, knocking her off her feet.

Her head connected hard with the door, and the scene distorted like it was made out of melted wax. The clown was on her, his fists plunging into her face and gut, winding and stunning her.

A part of her knew it was useless, but still she fought. Her thumb caught the clown's eye, making him cry out in pain, but it seemed to only incense him further. He smashed the back of her head against the floor and this time she blacked out.

Chapter 73

A few hours in, Bryony was torn and bleeding.

Numb with terror and humiliation, she stared at the ceiling, wondering how much more of this she could take.

Her mind seesawed between wishing he would just kill her and holding on for an opportunity to escape.

Finally, the clown left her alone with her pain.

She'd refrained from crying in front of her captor, not wanting him to know he'd broken her. Now that she was alone she let her tears fall.

Chapter 74

The images from Luke's childhood nightmares returned with a vengeance, making him beat his fists against his head in an attempt to dislodge the macabre images. But it was no good; they remained no matter what he did.

He knew he was supposed to go to Peth Vale, the huge, abandoned house on the hill, and confront his fear that Bryony was in the place which terrified him most.

When darkness started to fall, he decided to chance it and set out for the house from his nightmares.

The dying light cast the town in a strange glow. It was like the underbelly was emerging now that the sun had sunk behind the horizon.

Luke checked around himself as he moved out of town towards the house. Many people were beaten just for setting foot in this part of town, so he knew he had to have his wits about him.

He saw no one that bothered him, just a couple of ten year olds sharing a stolen cigarette. Ignoring them, he moved further out of town. He had not set foot out here since the clown had kidnapped him all those years ago.

The place awoke terrifying feelings in him. He cursed his decision to explore the place in darkness, but he knew that in daylight he stood more risk of being spotted sneaking into the grounds of the house.

At least no one dared to hang around the house at night, in respect of its reputation.

No one sane, anyway.

Chapter 75

The house was very secluded; built on top of the hill, with no houses for a quarter of a mile in any direction. The large detached house stood on its own land, surrounded by ten foot high mesh fences.

It was rarely visited by the people of Marshton, due to its bad reputation, which made it ideal for sneaking into.

In the darkness, Luke found it easy not to draw attention to himself as he walked around the perimeter of Peth Vale.

He managed to find a small hole in the bottom of the fence at the side of the house.

After making sure no-one was looking, he squeezed through the hole and carefully manoeuvred himself through the thick hedge on the other side of the fence.

Treading carefully on the gravel drive, he moved around to the front of the house and peered in through the filthy window.

A dim light penetrated the murk, allowing him to see a fat man squashed into an armchair. There was no mistaking the face of the clown who had murdered his family.

Upon seeing him, Luke felt suddenly exposed, as though he was a helpless child all over again.

His legs felt like he'd sunk a litre of vodka, his head like he'd done twelve rounds with Tyson.

He gripped the wall to keep from falling and gulped in as much air as he could, eventually steadying his body and his nerves.

Now that he knew the clown was back, he could keep an eye on him. He smiled, despite the unease that the sight of the man from his nightmares had stirred up in him.

He was going to regret ever laying eyes upon Luke.

Chapter 76

With the knowledge that his last surviving victim was laid on a slab in the morgue, Alfred felt a celebration was in order. He'd refrained from killing in Marshton, just taking out his impulses on girls from the neighbouring towns, and, recently, the pretty little thing in the basement.

He wanted to kill something and didn't want to sacrifice his plaything, so he decided to go out and find a fresh victim.

Shrugging on a coat, he doused himself in cheap aftershave then left, not noticing the pale, scarred face that watched him from the bushes at the side of the house.

Luke watched the clown go, for a moment unsure of how to react. He wanted to rush him, but he had seen the blade inside the clown's coat. As he hadn't expected to find his enemy at home he hadn't brought a weapon.

It wasn't wise to take on such a dangerous foe unarmed so he decided to wait, despite the rage that formed a white hot ball in his stomach.

The clown left the grounds of the house through the gates and vanished from Luke's line of sight.

Luke waited a few minutes then left the cover of the bushes. He listened, in case there was anyone around, or, worse, the clown returned.

The front door was solid and he knew he'd make a real mess busting it open. He needed to find another way inside.

Luke made his way across the darkened back garden, which looked expansive, even in the dim light provided by the streetlights around the house's perimeter.

He moved through waist-high overgrown grasses towards the back of the house. Small animals made noisy movements in the bushes along the left-hand side of the house. Rats, Luke guessed.

He fought his way through the grass and up a small flight of wooden steps, which led to a long stretch of decking.

He crossed the decking with trepidation, noticing that a few of the panels were cracked and hanging down into the grass.

After what seemed like an age, he reached the old wooden back door, which had a large, boarded up window.

The door looked sturdy, although the handle looked like it was made entirely of rust.

Satisfied that he couldn't be seen from outside Peth Vale's grounds, he tried the handle and found the door was locked.

After patiently working on the board for a time, the top corners came loose, allowing him to bend the rotten wood until the gap was large enough to climb through.

A fetid smell greeted his nostrils as he climbed in and looked around.

The house would undoubtedly have been impressive once upon a time, with its varnished wood floors and ornate wall decorations, but had now fallen into disrepair.

The room in which he stood was dimly lit through the hole he had left in the boarded window. A dusty, discarded toolbox occupied one corner of the room.

He shone the torch into the room to his left. The dim light revealed a spade in the corner, next to a pile of rusted pots and pans. On a grimy workbench, Luke found a large box of cooking matches which he pocketed.

Dust seemed to cling to every surface in the house. Spider webs decorated most corners. Glassy, dead eyes stared out at him from the walls, the mounted animal heads watching his every move. He felt privileged to be the object of their attentions.

After running his hands over the pretty dead things for a time, Luke remembered the reason he was here and went into the master bedroom. The bare floorboards creaked as he walked in.

There was what looked like a trail of blood across the floor, leading to a broken double bed. The wall next to the bed was dented, looking as though something (a human head, Luke's mind told him) had slammed into it.

He explored the house, avoiding the room where he'd been imprisoned as a child.

Finding nothing of any real interest, he went outside to the garage. In here, among piles of rusted car parts, he found a long line of jerry cans. Petrol fumes greeted his nostrils as he loosened one of the caps. The garage also contained a pair of garden shears, a full roll of silver duct tape and a few lengths of rope.

He went back into the house and found a key ring in one of the kitchen drawers. One key was clearly marked for the back door. He tried it, satisfied when he heard the lock click open.

Something about the wood panelling running along the staircase drew his eye. When he looked closer, he saw a faded, dust-covered handprint on the panel. The handprint abruptly cut off halfway up the fingers, leading Luke to believe that it was a door.

Even with the flashlight trained on the door, it was hard to see the line where it opened. Luke had to run his hand along the panel to find the keyhole. He tried a few keys from the key ring, finally getting one to snack the lock open.

Chapter 77

Gripping the key, he levered the door open. The cupboard beneath the stairs was dark and dusty and he could hear something scuttling in the gloom, beyond the reach of the flashlight's beam.

There was only an old, dust-ruined chest of drawers in the cupboard. He played the flashlight over the wood, peering into the drawers.

Inside were torn, bloody pieces of clothing. Most were women's – panties, bras, a shredded skirt – but there was also a man's shirt, mud-smeared and tattered.

Wanting no part in whatever had happened to the owners of the clothes, Luke didn't touch them. Whatever had happened, it couldn't be good.

He slammed the drawers shut, knocking the flashlight out of his hand. It hit the floor and rolled against the leg of the chest of drawers. Luke expected the impact to smash the bulb, but it didn't.

As he bent to pick up the torch, he noticed a line in the floor. Like the edge of the cupboard door, there was a partial handprint. This one was the strange rust-coloured shade produced by dried blood.

He ran his hand along the edge of the trapdoor. Ten inches of it were visible, then it disappeared beneath the chest of drawers.

That's to weight it down, so it remains shut, Luke's mind tormented him. *To keep the beast in the basement.*

He silenced these thoughts and concentrated on moving the chest of drawers. It was like trying to push a tree down.

Sweating and panting and itching from the dust, he finally managed to get the drawers off the trapdoor. Another line on the floor marked the edge of the hatch.

He crouched down, flinching at the popping sound his knees made, and ran his hands along the dusty hatch.

The key for the cupboard door also worked on the trapdoor. He hesitated for a moment then pulled the trapdoor up.

As the hatch creaked open, the smell of damp drifted up to him, along with a rotting smell.

Cursing his curiosity, he shone the torch into the hole. Damp, concrete stairs led down into the dank basement.

The smells intensified as he moved down the stairs. The flashlight helped his vision, but he wasn't sure if he really wanted to see what was down here.

The faint glow provided by the torch gave the basement the feel of a nightmare or a cheap horror film.

The basement was stone walled, rather than the brick walls which made up the house. A drop of water landed on his head, making him jolt. He looked up to see drops of condensation hanging from the low ceiling.

He moved into the dark, wishing he'd found a more powerful torch. Or not come here at all. Yes, that'd be much better.

At the far end of the basement, he found the cause of the rotting smell.

Chapter 78

Alfred went into one of the many pubs in Marshton's town centre. The square was shoe-horned full of pubs and bars, testament to the fact that there wasn't much to do in Marshton except drink.

He swaggered up to the bar and ordered a coke, not wanting to dull his senses with alcohol.

Scanning the crowd for a likely victim, he saw plenty of girls to choose from, but most of them were day-glow slappers with their tits and arses hanging out. Still, they'd do for a few hours of fun, he supposed.

One particularly loud girl was propping up the bar, already pissed. Her voice grated on him. *See if she can still talk with my cock shoved down her throat*, he thought with a grin.

'The fuck you smiling at?' she shouted, looking him up and down.

'I was just thinking how good you'd look naked,' Alfred confided with a wink.

'Eugh, as if,' she pouted.

Her friends all laughed. The sound was excruciating, but Alfred laughed along.

'Reckon you should get out of here, pervert,' the girl said.

'Just leave him, Kelly, the bouncers'll get him out,' said a girl wearing even more fake tan than Kelly.

'Oh, cheers, now he knows my name, you tit,' Kelly said.

'Seriously, Kelly, you and me,' Alfred said. 'I've got plenty of money. I could be the dream date for you.'

'I really don't think so, weirdo. Now get out of here before I set my boyfriend on ya.'

'I'm doing nothing wrong, just having a quiet drink and enjoying the scenery.'

'Right, that's it,' Kelly said, swanning off out of the front door.

Alfred admired her arse as she walked.

'You'd best get out, yeah?' one of the other girls said.

'Yeah, her boyfriend works on the door,' another girl said. 'He'll kick your fucking head in.'

The girls laughed at this.

Alfred shrugged. Stood his ground.

Kelly came back in with a brick shithouse of a bouncer. He had no neck and his arms were as thick as tree trunks.

Alfred tried not to look scared, even though he was shitting himself.

'You 'arrassin' my girl?' the bouncer grunted.

'No. Just having a drink and taking a look at the talent.'

'He was eyeing me up,' Kelly said. 'Couldn't take his eyes off my tits.'

'Come on,' Alfred said. 'She's a good-looking girl. I couldn't help but look.'

'Right, get your fat arse out of my pub now,' the bouncer said. 'Or you and me are gonna be fightin'.'

Shit, Alfred thought.

Loathe to draw more attention to himself, he decided to leave. The fact that he'd avoid a kicking was a good incentive too. As he walked out, the bouncer gave him a dig in the belly for his cheek.

'Nice one, Deano,' the super-fake-tanned girl laughed.

'I see you in here again, I'll cripple you,' Dean said.

Kelly kissed Dean then turned and spat at Alfred. 'You hear that, you freak?' she scowled.

Alfred laughed despite the pain in his belly.

Dean, Kelly and friends were a little freaked out. No one laughed off one of Dean's punches.

They went back inside, leaving Alfred in the gutter, eager to continue the night's revelries.

'That's the last we'll see of him,' Kelly laughed.

But it wouldn't be.

Chapter 79

Luke counted four decaying rodent corpses before he looked away in disgust. The small bodies were laid in an arc on the floor. Some of the bodies had bite marks in their flesh. Others had been mashed to a pulp, presumably by the blood-covered half of a brick that lay a few feet in from the array of dead vermin.

Luke suspected what he was going to see when he moved the torch further up the basement, but it still didn't lessen the shock when his suspicions were confirmed as reality.

The corpse was sat hugging its knees, its hands were chained to a large metal ring on the wall. He gasped when he saw it, scaring a rat away from the ear on which it was feasting.

Time had not been kind to the chained body. Its flesh was discoloured and sagging away from the bones like wet wallpaper.

Feeling the contents of his stomach starting to rise, he closed his eyes. Swallowed hard.

When he opened his eyes, he forced himself to look at the body. It did little to reassure him when he saw that it was that of a girl with long blonde hair.

He looked at the tattered clothes and realised that it was the same outfit Norma had said that

Bryony had been wearing the last time she'd been seen.

Tears started to drown his vision. He wiped them away with the back of his hand. Forced himself to concentrate on the body.

He knelt next to it, in his panic not caring that his knee crunched into the mangled remains of one of the rats.

He shone the flashlight on the face, hoping and praying that it wasn't Bryony. The features were unidentifiable, thanks to putrefaction and the feasting rodents.

The flashlight hit something shiny, causing the light to wink at him. He moved closer, squidging his knee further into the rat's corpse.

He recognised the heart-shaped necklace that hung from the neck of the dead girl. Luke had bought it for Bryony as a present last Christmas, but had never plucked up the nerve to give it to her. His heart slamming, he reached for the necklace. The silver locket felt cold to the touch.

Tears again filled his eyes. He blinked them back. Pulled the necklace open. There, inside, was the message that Luke had paid to have inscribed: 'My heart belongs to you, my love. Forever. Luke XXX'

Chapter 80

There was a sliver of doubt in his mind that the body was Bryony but still he let out a scream that echoed around the dark basement. Tears flooded down his face, making tiny sounds as they hit the floor.

The love of his life was dead. Only God knew what horrendous acts she'd endured.

Then it sunk in why the dead rats were there; she'd been eating them to stay alive. Showing such courage in the face of utter hopelessness.

Somehow that was worse than the fact of her death. *She must have been waiting for me to save her,* he thought.

He fell to the floor, sobbing uncontrollably, cradling her corpse. Her flesh was cold and hard and pocked with tiny teeth marks from where the rats had been at her.

No way was he going to let her be eaten by vermin!

He kissed her lifeless face.

As he sobbed, he heard a shuffling sound behind him.

He spun, startled by the sudden noise. A heavy piece of wood smashed into the side of his head. Stars flew across his vision and his legs wobbled.

The wood hit him again, accompanied by an animalistic, but unmistakably female, cry of rage.

The wood slammed his head a third time. The haze of tears still blurred his vision, but he could see a pale, dirt-smeared face framed with lank blonde hair.

The wood swung for his head again. He was still too stunned to react but this time the wood stopped an inch from his jaw.

'Holy shit, Luke, what are you doing here?'

Luke stood, dumb-founded.

'Luke, it's me, Bryony. How did you get out of the hospital?'

Luke's mouth moved but the words wouldn't come. He couldn't believe she was still alive. He sobbed, tears of relief.

'I'm here,' she said. 'Thank God you came. He's had me here for a few days now.' She burst into tears, the salty fluid cutting paths in the dirt on her face. He held her and they both sobbed for a moment, until Bryony came to her senses and said, 'We'd best get out of here, before he comes back.'

They snuck out of the house the way that Luke had come in, taking the time to replace the drawers over the trapdoor so that the clown wasn't immediately alerted to her escape.

They paused by the side of the house, hearing footsteps on the gravel outside the gates. The sound soon passed.

They both let out a sigh of relief as they fled the house, heading home as fast as their aching limbs would carry them.

Part Two – Hunter

Becoming: to suit or give a pleasing effect or attractive appearance, as to a person or thing

Chapter 81

Once home, Bryony collapsed as the events of the last few days hit her like a speeding juggernaut. Luke cradled her, stroking her hair.

'I kept praying that someone would come,' she sobbed.

'And someone did,' he said, kissing her forehead.

'It had to be you too. It's fate.'

'Your mam told me you'd gone missing. She helped me to break out.'

Bryony nodded.

'What did he do to you?'

The question made her break down again. Incapable of speaking, she let him hold her as she cried.

When Bryony finally stopped crying, Luke stared at her bruised, dirty face.

'What are we going to do about this? Luke asked. 'Do you want me to call the police?'

'No. They're fucking useless. Look how they've let the Marshton Eight off time and time again.'

Luke said nothing. He knew what he wanted Bryony to say next, but he didn't want to be the first to bring it up.

'You are gonna kill him, right?' she asked.

'I only wish I could kill him twice.'

'You've got to make him suffer.'

'Oh, I fucking will.'

'And those pricks who attacked you too. It was one of them who chased us to the Murder House.'

Luke snorted at the thought of the gang. 'Every last one of them,' he said. 'I promise they're all going to fucking suffer.'

She nodded, a final tear cutting a path through the grime and dried blood on her face. 'You'd best get on with it,' she said. 'Before they realise you've gotten out.'

'I don't want to leave you on your own after what's happened.'

'Please, I need to be alone for a while. I need to try and come to terms with all of this.'

'I really don't think—'

'—LUKE!'

'Are you absolutely sure?'

'Yes, I am. I love you for wanting to stay with me and I'm grateful for you rescuing me, but I need to get my head straight. And I need a fucking drink.'

Luke nodded. He pulled her into him and kissed her forehead.

'Now get out there and kill someone already,' she laughed.

He took in her face a final time. His mournful expression made it look as though his heart was broken. He sniffed and wiped his eyes then left the room. 'I'll see you later,' he called over his shoulder.

'I love you, Luke. Thank you so much.'

'I love you too,' he shouted.

Now that Bryony was alone in the house, she went downstairs and poured herself a wine glass full of vodka.

She slung it back without pausing, grimacing only slightly at the fire that grew in her belly and made its way up her throat. Gasping in appreciation, she poured another glass. She slung back a mouthful of this one too. Paused. Gulped the rest down.

She found two more bottles in the cupboard underneath the sink. *Plenty to be getting on with,* she thought with a sad smile.

She wanted to drink until she couldn't feel.

Chapter 82

With most of his face hidden beneath his hood, Luke took to the streets. He wasn't sure if the news of his escape would have been released yet, so he wanted to be careful.

Sneaking through the back alleys, his anger rose as he passed the place where the gang had beaten him and Tom.

He pushed the feeling down for now, knowing that he needed to think clearly. The time to use his growing anger and hatred for the gang would come.

Until then he needed to stay focussed and avoid anyone who might be trying to catch him.

He tried to remember everything about that night from eighteen months ago.

The feeling of being helpless flooded into his head.

The darkness inside the bag as he was bundled into the car.

His sense of terror as they had tied him to the chair.

Wait! There was something in between, a dim recollection that struggled to make itself known.

That was it! The smell of curry on the way into the house. He couldn't remember fleeing;

that was all a blur, but he remembered that the house was on the same street as the only curry house in Marshton.

His grin widened. The scarred skin by the sides of his mouth ached with the grin, but he kept smiling.

He made his way to the curry house, knowing that he was drawing closer to his prey with every step.

Chapter 83

Bryony swayed as she slung back the dregs of the first vodka bottle. The liquid burnt its way down to her stomach, filling her with warmth from belly to throat.

Drops of the cold liquid ran down her chin, soaking into her top. It didn't matter. The blood, dirt and semen that already stained the garment were enough to ruin it.

She swallowed the last of the vodka and hurled the empty bottle against the wall. It showered her with broken glass. She cared not. Her body was already broken, abused. A few small cuts weren't going to make any difference to her.

She uncapped another bottle of vodka and took a long pull.

The alcohol was kicking in nicely now, her head was warm and fuzzy, her vision beginning to blur. Encouraged by the feeling, she slung back another mouthful.

The curry house was a blackened husk. Marshton didn't take kindly to foreigners, or anyone who was slightly outside the boundaries of normality.

Luke tried to remember out of which house he'd ran. He knew it wasn't the one next to the curry house. But it could have been the one next to it, or possibly the one next to that.

He did a quick check around him, then strolled up the path of the first house and pressed his hands to the glass. The front room was in darkness but he made out nice furniture and toys strewn about the floor.

This wasn't the place.

He hopped the fence, ducking out of sight as a car's headlights illuminated the stretch of darkness by the road.

He paused for a minute, making sure the car wasn't looking for him, then stood up. The need to get this done quickly had been reinforced by the car's passing.

Peering through the window, he saw bare floorboards and multi-coloured walls.

This was undoubtedly the place.

He smiled.

Tried the door.

Cursed when he discovered it was locked. Best go round the back, he was way too exposed out here.

He snuck round into the back alley and pushed the gate open, wincing when the hinges squealed. He ducked down behind a wheely bin when lights came on in the upstairs window.

Luke saw the silhouettes of at least three lads. Somehow he knew that they were members of the gang who had attacked him and threatened Bryony.

He glanced up as Johnny T came to the window, a double-barrelled shotgun broken over his arm.

'Fuck,' Luke hissed.

His heart was pounding fit to burst. He felt every beat in his head as the blood rushed through.

Maybe this was a bad idea. *There must be a better way*, he thought.

An idea formed in his mind. In the few minutes it took for the light to extinguish he had explored the possibilities and decided that it was the best course of action.

He waited behind the bin for another minute in case the gang had switched it off to trick him out of hiding. Then he snuck out of the yard and made his way down the alley into town.

Chapter 84

Alfred checked his watch. Half past one. The King's, the pub where Dean worked the door, was open till two.

After that, he knew that the doormen from the King's worked the doors of the Lounge until closing at half three. At least that's what used to happen. He'd been out of town for a long time but he hoped the times hadn't changed.

Not much changed in Marshton, so he was relatively confident that this wouldn't have either.

He figured Kelly would go home with Dean at the end of his shift and decided to just wait in the alley until the Lounge kicked out. Better that than get another punch from Dean when he caught him in the Lounge.

Then fortune smiled upon him.

Dean and Kelly were leaving the King's, heading for the car park across the road from him.

Kelly was paralytic, Dean realised with a smile. Even by her standards she was drunk.

Dean liked to make sure she got home safely. If working the doors in Marshton had taught him anything, it was that there were weirdos everywhere. He didn't want to run the risk of anything happening to her when she was in such a vulnerable state.

Dean tried to lead Kelly along towards the car but her legs were shot. He realised it would be quicker if he carried her and pulled her into a crossing-the-threshold-style carry.

Though Dean was fit and strong, he moved slowly. Kelly was practically unconscious and was a dead weight. It had been a long night, too, so he wasn't feeling particularly energetic.

Dean was so focussed on getting Kelly to the car that he didn't hear the footsteps behind him.

Chapter 85

Upon reaching the car, Dean swung Kelly high onto his chest while he scrabbled in his pocket for the car keys.

Kelly stirred.

'Hey, babe, just getting you home,' he said.

She nodded and slumped back over his shoulder.

He found the keys and got the door open. Put Kelly on the back seat. As he did so she leaned out of the car and opened her mouth.

A stinking flood of wine, vodka and red bull gushed out onto his trousers and shoes.

'Jesus Christ, Kelly,' he said.

She looked up and let out a cry.

'Just sit up and try not to be sick,' he said, ignoring her protests as he slammed the car door shut on her.

She hit the window, but he didn't acknowledge her. He was too pissed off about his clothes. His legs were too big for regular trousers, so he'd spent a week's wages having these specially made. Now they were ruined.

He pulled the boot open and found the bag of clothes he'd stored for later.

Kelly screamed.

While he struggled into his clean pair of trousers, he heard a voice behind him.

'Remember me, fucko?'

He turned to see the man he'd punched earlier. Something sharp was clutched in the fat man's hand. Before Dean could do anything, the man had punched the blade into his belly.

The pain was like nothing Dean had ever felt.

While he looked on in disbelief, the man stabbed him twice more and shoved him into the boot. His head thudded into the wall of the boot then the lid slammed down, leaving him in darkness.

Alfred got into the driver's seat and pulled away. The girl was in the back, too drunk to do anything.

'Told you we belonged together,' he smiled.

He drove to a quiet road and turned and looked at the girl. She looked terrified and he knew she was too drunk to defend herself.

He devoured her with his eyes, and, unable to wait for some time alone with her, climbed into the back of the car and took what he wanted.

Chapter 86

Bryony was officially fucked-up.

The last mouthful of vodka she'd guzzled seemed to have been the one that tipped her over the edge.

But instead of the oblivion she craved, the memories of the torments she'd been forced to endure in the grimy basement re-surfaced.

Without anyone to comfort her, she felt unable to cope with the feelings. She sobbed uncontrollably, her tears mingling with the mass of stains on her shirt.

She moved over to the neck of the broken vodka bottle that lay in the corner. The weight of it felt comforting in her hands.

'Let's not do anything stupid,' she muttered, setting it down on the bench.

She decided to take a bath, wash all the filth off her. She ran the water as hot as it would go and stripped.

While the tub filled, she stared at her bruised, pale skin in the mirror.

The bruises don't tell the full story, she thought. *The real damage is in my head. Those are the scars that will last the longest.*

She went downstairs to get the full vodka bottle.

Steam curled out to greet her as she stepped through the door.

Despite her alcohol-numbed skin, the bath water drew a gasp from her as it scalded her foot. She ignored the sensation and put her other foot in too. It felt like a thousand blazing needles were being jabbed into her feet and ankles.

She took another slug of vodka while she waited to get used to the burning temperature of the water. Her unsteady legs wobbled beneath her, making her sway like a trainee tight rope walker.

Lowering herself carefully, she again gasped as the scalding water consumed her pale frame.

She breathed in, savouring the pain that brought her back to her senses. Every detail of the incidents in the basement was scarred into her mind.

Suddenly, she doubled up as if she'd been punched in the belly. Burning bile shot up her throat and out of her mouth, floating on top of the water in a stinking yellow cloud.

Tears flooded her vision. She took another deep swig of the vodka, put the bottle on the side of the bath and started scrubbing her skin with the loofah. No matter how much she scrubbed she knew she'd never feel clean. She'd always feel used, dirty.

Her skin was red now, burnt from the extreme heat of the water. But the water could never be hot enough to cleanse her. She had that insight now.

Luke, the man she knew was the love of her life, would no longer want her, not after this. She was impure, filthy. He'd not want anything to do with her. She'd seen the carefully-concealed disgust on his face as he'd scrutinised her. No, he wanted no part in it. She could tell.

The thought of living seemed pointless. There was nothing to live for now. The clown's repeated assaults had taken away her soul, left her an empty shell, with no chance of ever being filled. She knew that now.

There was no way things would ever improve.

No way she could live her life.

No way the man she wanted could ever feel the same way.

And there was no way she could go on living.

She knew that now too.

Chapter 87

After finishing with Kelly, Alfred throttled her and dumped her body in the boot of the car with Dean.

Then he drove to the edge of the council estate and, leaving the keys in the ignition, abandoned the car there, knowing that some chav would have it stolen within minutes.

He walked home and went straight to bed, his hands shaking with the rush of what he'd just done. Though he'd calmed down a little, he stared at the ceiling, unable to sleep.

Luke had been walking back towards home when the car went past him. He shrank back into the trees by the side of the road as he recognised the pale, flabby face of the clown at the wheel.

The clown didn't seem to see him, but still he waited until the car pulled into the layby on the far edge of the council estate.

The clown got out, leaving the engine running, and walked right past Luke, close enough for him to smell the fresh blood on his clothes. The sight of the clown so close to him chilled his blood, but also made him furious.

He almost ran at the clown and started swinging his arms like a threshing machine but he remembered the knife that the clown held and knew he'd be better off biding his time.

When the clown had passed, he approached the car, eyeing it like it was a hostile animal. The car was still turning over. There was no one inside, but there were a few bloody smears on the back seat.

Without hesitating, he climbed into the driver's seat and drove away.

Chapter 88

Bryony's eyes rolled back in her head as she finished the last of the vodka. Her arms felt limp, like they were made of rope rather than bone.

The drunkenness served only to deepen her depression. She knew she had nothing to live for and was preparing herself for the end.

She ran the bath even hotter. Now she was so drunk that she couldn't feel the millions of needles pricking at her skin. She hurled the vodka bottle at the tiles, raising an arm in weak defence as the shards of glass flew at her face.

She picked up the neck of the bottle. The jagged edge of the glass looked perfect for what she had in mind.

Tears streamed down her face as her shaking hand moved the glass to her wrist.

Just do it, don't hesitate, she implored herself. *No going back.*

She drew the glass across her wrist. A few drops of blood bubbled out of the wound.

Don't be a pussy, do it lengthways. Going across means you want to be saved. It's too late for that.

Do it lengthways.

Do it do it do it.

She pressed the glass to the crook of her elbow and dug it deep. The pain made her gasp, despite her drunken state.

She pressed harder. Blood ran out around the tip of the glass which was now embedded a few inches into her forearm.

Do it!

Do it! Now!

She pressed harder still and drew the glass down her forearm. Her hand went numb as the wound opened to reveal bone and glistening, ropelike tendons.

Blood jetted out, spraying the tiles in front of her.

This is it. No more sadness. No more pain. No more shame. No more.

The bloodied piece of glass slid from her grasp and disappeared beneath the crimson water.

She slumped back, no longer feeling capable of sitting up. Her eyelids felt like they had ton weights attached to them.

She felt herself weaken, felt darkness creeping into her as the blood left. Her eyes rolled back into her head.

Dimly visible was the note she'd left on the toilet lid for Luke. A tear rolled down her cheek, then she sunk into the merciful darkness.

Chapter 89

Luke pulled the car into a deserted stretch of road at the edge of town. He climbed out and opened the boot.

Two pairs of glassy, dead eyes stared up at him. Unable to help himself, he stared at them, ran his hands over the dead girl's body, savouring the clammy, waxy feel of her dead flesh. It awoke feelings in him that had laid dormant for too long.

He enjoyed the sight of the two bodies for a time then parked the car behind the graveyard where his father and sister had been buried. He knew that the bodies were the clown's victims and figured he may be able to use them to get back at him.

He walked back into town, stopping to pick up a box of cigarettes at the all night garage.

As he queued up behind an old man who seemed to be paying his bill with pennies, he turned and scanned the magazine racks. His gaze was drawn to a familiar face that stared out from the front cover of one of the lads' magazines.

It took him a few moments to place the girl, but then he saw that it was Kate, the bitch who had set him up to get attacked by the Marshton Eight.

An idea hit him like a thunderbolt and he bought the magazine. He flicked through it, eager to find the section featuring his nemesis. She was a glamour model now, according to the blurb on the article. The photos of her brought back the memories of how she'd led him on.

He was going to make her suffer too.

And he knew exactly how to do it.

Chapter 90

When, an hour later, sleep still eluded Alfred, he went downstairs. A small white envelope lay on the floor behind the front door.

At first he took it to be a scam and was about to tear it into pieces, but curiosity made him open it.

He was pleased when he did, as a glossy photo of one of the hottest girls he'd ever seen greeted his eyes. She was blonde and slim, with tits that most porn stars would kill for. The glint in her eye made him hard just looking at it.

Beneath the picture was a message reading, 'I'm a huge fan of your work. Meet me tomorrow night, eight o' clock, outside the Black Cat x.'

He had an urgent need to ejaculate – which was so strong it stopped him worrying about how someone knew his secret – and he was regretful that he'd finished with the mouthy slag from the pub so soon or he could have taken his frustrations out on her.

Still, he had the girl in the basement to satisfy his desires, but decided he couldn't be arsed to struggle with her tonight.

He took care of the problem using his imagination to dictate what would happen when he got his hands on the pretty blonde girl.

As he drifted off to sleep he couldn't get her pouting lips and come to bed eyes out of his head.

Luke smiled as he made his way home. The picture of Kate had surely done the job. The clown's lust would be his undoing.

Luke was going to put him through hell and then put him in a shallow grave.

Chapter 91

As the front door swung open, Luke was instantly aware that something was wrong. He had no idea what it was, but he had a cold squirming feeling in his bowels.

He called out to Bryony, then stopped himself. It was after two. Chances were she was asleep and he had no intention of waking her. It was better for her to sleep as much as possible. That way she wouldn't be thinking of her ordeal at the hands of the loathsome clown.

He moved into the hallway, noting the bathroom light was still on. Still he couldn't shake the sense that something was wrong. *So she's forgot to switch the light off,* he thought. *It's understandable she'd forget that after what she's been through.*

He moved up the stairs. The bathroom light blazed a hole in the darkness.

There was a dripping sound coming from the bathroom. *Nothing to be scared of,* he thought. *A dripping tap that's all.*

When he saw the large pool of bloody water on the bathroom floor he instantly knew what had happened.

Screaming, he ran into the bathroom, skidding on the water and nearly pitching headfirst into the bath.

Bryony was laid back in the blood-filled tub. Some of the thick gore had spilled over the side, forming the pool that lay on the tiles.

Her left arm was laid open from elbow to wrist, showing off gleaming bone and shredded arteries. The immense wound was clotted with blood.

Her eyes stared up at him as if accusing him of abandoning her when she needed him most. The image of her blurred as his sorrow streamed down his face.

He dived forwards, his arms encircling her. The coldness of her body startled him. Usually he loved the feel of dead flesh, but this was different. He hated the cold feel of her skin, knowing that it was his lover, his best friend, who was the owner of the bulging, glassy eyes that seemed to bore into him.

He cried, his tears falling into the bathwater to mingle with his lover's blood.

When he'd finished, he cradled her carefully and lifted her out of the water. Blood red water dripped off her still form, leaving a trail behind them as he carried her to her bed.

He laid her down, closed her staring eyes and looked down at her body.

He was still staring at her when she sat up and let out an ear-piercing scream. Luke jolted, certain that she had been dead already.

Her voice was weak when she spoke. 'It hurts so bad, Luke.' Tears rolled out of her glassy eyes.

Luke joined her in her sorrow.

'I can't bear this, Luke. I don't want to live.'

He stared her in the eye. 'Is this really what you want?'

She nodded, a further stream of tears pouring from her eyes.

His eyes streaming, he picked up the pillow and pushed it over her face. He expected some sort of a struggle, weak though it would be, but she welcomed the cessation of her oxygen supply. She thrashed a little but made no conscious effort to save herself.

'No one will ever hurt you again,' Luke whispered. He held her convulsing form, his body racked with sobs. He kissed her, held her, stroked her hair. Whispered to her.

Chapter 92

When he came out of his daze, he brought a kitchen knife upstairs and cut the skin at the back of her neck. Blood slowly dripped out from her dead flesh. He put his hands on the nape of her neck. The drops of blood that fell onto his palms were still a little warm and felt sticky.

He held his hands in front of his face, then licked the blood from his fingers. The taste was like no other. He put his hands on the back of her neck again, until they were covered in blood, then pressed them into his face, feeling, seeing, smelling her on him. He felt so good, so warm, so alive. He had never loved her more than now.

He reached behind her head again, feeling her blood on his hands. The colour was so bright, so beautiful. He sucked all the blood from his fingers for a second time. The taste was even stronger.

Every one of Luke's senses was heightened. He could even hear her blood dripping onto the bed.

He was euphoric. This was the best he ever felt.

He kissed her cold, dead lips as he rubbed his hands into her blood again.

He stripped himself and held her, like he had longed to for such a long time. She felt even better than he had imagined.

He enjoyed her still-warm embrace, while stroking her hair, kissing her face and telling her that he loved her.

After a time, he realised what he had done. Letting go of Bryony as if she was red hot, he let out a stunned cry and scrambled off the bed.

Covered in her blood, he rocked backwards and forwards, staring at the pool of crimson on the bed. He had never seen so much blood.

He muttered to himself, trying to justify what he had done.

Realising he had zoned out, he picked up his knife again and sat next to Bryony, staring at her, stroking her beautiful soft face. He kissed her again.

Placing the knife against the back of her neck, he applied a great deal of pressure and dragged the blade up into her hairline. The knife continued its path down her back, further opening the wound on the nape of her neck. The cut was extremely deep. But that was good.

He made a deep slash around her neck, going around her shoulders, and began to peel the skin back.

After a lot of care and effort, he managed to loosen the skin. He cut carefully around her eyes, unable to bring himself to damage something so beautiful.

Eventually, he pulled the skin from her head and neck. It was so beautiful. He held it in front of his face, kissing the soft, perfect skin and laughing to himself.

Chapter 93

Luke wanted to see what it was like to be beautiful, so he tried to put Bryony's skin over his head as a mask.

He knew that once the news broke that he had not been killed in the asylum riot, people would be looking for him. This would hide his identity for long enough to take out his enemies. He laughed at the thought of the terror his new face would inspire in his victims.

It went on easily, like it was made to fit him. The still-warm blood and the feel of her dead skin pressing onto his face felt divine.

It was a struggle, but he managed to stitch the back of the neck together. A couple of times, the needle punctured his own skin. When it did, he continued, sewing the mask to the back of his own neck in places. The thread bound them together for eternity now.

Admiring his new features in the mirror, he found that he looked beautiful, like he knew he would.

He went back to Bryony and attempted to take off the rest of her skin. The arm that she had slashed was easy, he just pushed his fingers into the wound and worked the skin until it was loose enough to get a blade in to cut loose the connective tissue.

Bryony's right arm was more of a problem – the skin was seemingly clamped tight to the muscle and bone beneath.

Luke wandered around the kitchen, looking for inspiration. He raided the drawer and found a pair of kitchen scissors. The next drawer down yielded an assortment of tools, including a hacksaw. Grinning, he took his two new tools upstairs.

He set the hacksaw to Bryony's right wrist and started sawing into the bone. The sound was the older, uglier brother of nails being dragged down a blackboard.

Blood seeped from the cut, clogging up the blade. He stopped every dozen strokes and wiped the sticky paste of blood and bone dust onto the bedclothes.

Finally, one of the bones in Bryony's forearm snapped. The hacksaw blade sunk through the gap in the bone and jammed against the other bone at an angle. Cursing, Luke tried to pull the blade out but it was wedged in awkwardly.

He gripped her wrist with one hand and bent it slightly, trying to make enough room to pull the blade out. The sensation of the shorn bone moving beneath the skin was nauseating but he continued with his task.

He managed to work the blade free and started again, sending sprays of congealing blood flying everywhere. His mask was spattered with it and the sticky flux of blood and bone felt warm on his face where it had gone through the eyeholes.

Finally the second bone gave way and the wrist went slack. Just a few tendons and layers of skin held the hand on. He sawed into these, which were a piece of cake compared to the bones, until the hand came free with a liquid splat.

When he had the hand loose, he ran the scissors up the skin on the inside of the arm all the way to her armpit. The scissors chewed through the dead flesh, the nauseating sound of the blades grinding against each other not registering in Luke's mind.

Using the kitchen knife and his fingers, he carefully managed to work the skin loose.

After this, he took the saw to her ankles and repeated the process. The ankle bones were much thicker and harder to cut. He found himself wishing he'd done them first. The wrist would have been a breeze in comparison.

Itching from the mixture of blood, sweat and fragments of bone that coated his skin, he panted for breath. The mask did not inhibit his breathing in any way. It was like it was made for him.

It took all of his care and patience, but after a time he managed to remove all of her soft, beautiful skin. He had the arms, up to the wrists, the legs up to the ankles, the chest and belly and back. He left the genitals in place – he knew he'd need to piss – and also he had something else in mind for these beautiful, secret parts of her.

The hardest part had been getting the skin off her ribs. The limbs – once he'd got the skin loose – were relatively easy, just a pulling and weird wet sensation that Luke assumed felt very much like taking off a wetsuit.

There were gaps from where he had needed to cut the skin off – which he kept to the inner edges of the limbs and the outer edge of the chest and stomach – so he stitched the skin together as best he could and dressed himself in it, stitching the front together once he was inside.

As with the sewing together of the mask, the needle punctured Luke's skin, sewing Bryony's dead skin to his.

He went back to the mirror, running his hands over his new skin. The task was complete.

He was finally beautiful. Behind her lifeless features, tears of joy rolled down his cheeks.

He stared at her skinless body, which lay in a vast pool of blood on the bed, for a few hours then slept beside her.

Chapter 94

When he awoke, Luke touched his face to see if it had been a dream. It was a relief to discover it was real.

His eyes refused to leave the skinless body of his love on the bed. He felt a little sick, but this was dwarfed by the euphoria he still felt. She was his forever now. This thought made him laugh.

He spent the next few hours holding Bryony's body and running his hands over his new skin.

Alfred dressed himself nicely for his date with the pretty girl. He knew he wasn't the greatest looking guy in the world so he had to make the most of what he had. Luckily the girl was a fan of his work, so he already had her on his side.

He whistled a happy tune as he walked to the Black Cat. He stood outside the back of the pub for a while, checking his watch.

The night felt colder than it looked, but he would have stood naked in a snow blizzard to get his hands on that blonde girl.

The idea that he'd been stood up came to him a good hour after he'd arranged to meet the girl.

Cursing, he left the pub and went home. When he got in he found another envelope on the floor beneath the letterbox.

'Just making sure you were serious about me,' the message read. 'See you at ten xx'

'Fucker,' he muttered. The last thing he needed was a cock tease, even when it was for such an angelic being.

'You gonna show up this time?' he muttered.

His breath plumed around his face as he set off to the pub for the second time that night. He was so eager to meet the pretty blonde girl that he was out of breath.

As he reached the corner before the pub he slowed. He didn't want her to see him as some fat, out of shape loser.

When his breathing returned to normal he carried on and saw a dark figure by the rear of the pub. Its face was hidden by a hood.

He hoped it was her, but he didn't think it was. The figure gave him the creeps.

By the time Alfred reached the figure, he knew that it wasn't the girl from the picture.

Disappointment made him want to hurl the imposter to the floor and stomp a hole in them.

'Good to meet you,' the figure said.

He couldn't see the face, concealed as it was beneath the hood. The voice sent a chill through him.

'Sorry to mislead you with the girl, but I needed to get your attention. You and I are kindred spirits, Alfred,' the figure's creepy voice said.

'The fuck are you?' Alfred said, trying to get a better look inside the hood.

'Doesn't matter right now. But you and I can have a lot of fun together. The girl you killed earlier this week. She is just the start.'

'And why the fuck should I believe that? You already lied to me about the blonde bitch.'

'I know where she lives and I'll be only too happy to show you when you've allowed me to be a part of one of your crimes.'

Alfred salivated at the thought of finding the girl's house, but he tried to play it down, not wanting to look too desperate. 'What do you want me to do?'

'Just let me play too,' the figure said. 'And once we're done I'll show you where she lives. Deal?'

Alfred thought about it for a second. 'Deal.'

'I'll be in touch.'

The figure disappeared into the shadows.

Chapter 95

A few hours later, the Marshton Eight's party had died down.

Billy and Scotty made their excuses and set off home. They lived in the same part of town, so it made sense for them to accompany each other.

A street away from their homes, they heard a noise behind them. Billy turned to see a black hooded figure following. He looked like Death itself.

Billy did a double take and turned to see the figure again. It stood a few feet away, staring at them. 'Well look at this, Scotty,' he said, feigning fearlessness. 'Some fucker dressed up like it's fucking Halloween or some shit.'

Scotty snorted laughter.

'The fuck you want, freak?' Billy challenged.

The figure laughed, sending icicles racing through their veins.

'I said what the fuck do you want, freak?' Billy shouted.

'Your hearts on a fucking plate,' the figure snapped.

The pair looked to each other for a second. The challenge terrified both of them but they wanted to look tough. They leered at the figure and began to advance on him.

Scotty edged closer. His nerve broke and he charged at the figure, swinging a looping punch.

The figure's arm intercepted the blow then his other arm shot out, punching Scotty in the chin. Billy aimed a punch at him, but Luke kicked him savagely in the ribs, driving him backwards.

Luke grabbed Scotty by the collar of his tracksuit, punched him in the face and swung him into the wall. He brought his right knee up into Scotty's midsection. Scotty doubled over and took two hard punches to the face.

Billy punched Luke in the back of the head. Luke saw stars for a second, but turned and threw a vicious left hook that landed perfectly. There was an audible crack as Billy's jaw shattered.

Billy fell to the floor, his unconscious head slamming off the cobbles. In a frenzy, Luke kicked his fallen enemy.

Four kicks later, Luke registered a blow to his back. As he turned, Scotty punched him on the jaw. Luke laughed as the blow had no effect on him whatsoever.

He grabbed Scotty by the throat and drove him back into the wall. They struggled for a few seconds, moving further away from Billy.

Luke drove his fist into Scotty's ribs. He cried out, but Luke's fingers crushed into his throat, cutting off the cry.

Luke brought his fist up again, thrusting it hard into Scotty's chin. Scotty fell to his knees, his mouth open, about to scream.

Luke moved behind him and put the bony part of his right wrist across Scotty's windpipe. He clasped his hands together and pulled his forearm towards himself, into Scotty's throat. The scream cut off. Instead, Scotty gagged as Luke's wrist cut off his air supply.

Scotty's eyes bulged, his throat struggling for air. Luke pulled harder, maintaining his chokehold until Scotty started to convulse. There was a crack and Scotty stopped fighting for air. Luke held his grip for a minute longer, then he let go of Scotty's throat.

Scotty slid, lifeless, to the alley floor. Luke spat on him, then started dragging him up the alley to the car.

Chapter 96

Billy had regained consciousness shortly after Luke started to attack Scotty.

His head pounded and he knew he was better off hiding, so he watched from the yard opposite Scotty's body. He had seen the lad choke the last breath out of Scotty, had watched his friend's life ebb away.

Had seen the utter lack of remorse from the killer.

Adrenaline made his body tremble. The thick, coppery smell of his own blood filled his nostrils. He hoped the guy who'd taken Scotty out couldn't smell it too.

Billy wasn't a praying man, but he uttered a few frantic words now, hoping for divine intervention to prevent the killer finding him.

Fuck knows what he'll do if he catches me, he thought. He wondered if he should call Johnny T and let him know the score.

It took less than a second to decide that he should do just that.

Patting down his pockets, he cursed as he realised he had left his phone at home.

Hope lit up his mind. Scotty always had his phone with him, was always fidgeting with it. If he could get to Scotty, he could use his phone to call for help.

He put his eye to a crack in the gate. Saw the killer dragging Scotty up the alley.

Opening the gate, he took a quick glance around and saw the dark rectangular object on the floor.

Scotty's phone.

He grinned, unable to believe his luck.

When the figure had disappeared round the corner, Billy sprinted to the phone and picked it up, flicking his thumb across the screen to switch it on.

After repeating the gesture a few times, he came to the reluctant conclusion that the battery had died.

'Bastard,' he muttered.

Footsteps approached, sending him scurrying deeper into the alleys. Otis lived nearest, so he'd give him a knock.

Smiling at Scotty's dead-eyed stare, Luke dumped the body in the boot of the bouncer's car.

He returned to finish off the lad he'd knocked unconscious, but he had gone. Luke shrugged.

He'd get him eventually.

He'd get all of them.

Chapter 97

Billy brayed on Otis's door, unable to believe that his friend was out. The day was quickly turning into a nightmare. He ran from Otis's, desperate to get home to his phone.

Luke caught up with Billy a few streets from where he'd killed Scotty.

The stricken youth was running away from a row of terraced houses. He didn't see which house he'd been at, just saw him beating a hasty retreat up the back alley. He followed him, keeping his distance to maintain the element of surprise.

The fool led Luke directly to his door. Luke watched him enter the house and casually strolled away, a smile on his lips.

Johnny T's phone was switched off, so Billy left a number of messages on his answerphone. The rest of the lads weren't answering either, and he knew that Olly hated mobiles. He cursed and slammed his phone down on the floor.

He decided his best move was to get cleaned up – he was still covered in dried blood – and get to the police station.

The dried blood stunk and was starting to itch. His head was swollen and bruised. The guy had one hell of a punch, no taking that away from him.

His jaw ached. Eating was going to be a chore for the next few weeks.

He ran the bath nice and hot and put some dance tunes on, to try and take his mind off the image of Scotty's bulging eyes and purple face.

Hopefully he could forget the way his body had twitched as he suffocated.

He was in the bath only a few minutes when his eyes became heavy. Before he had chance to fight it, he had drifted off to sleep.

Chapter 98

The bathroom light dazzled Billy's eyes when he woke up. The music still played.

He didn't feel like getting out for a while yet, so he ran a little more hot water in and settled back into the warmth.

The light flickered, then the house was plunged into darkness. At the same time as the bathroom light went out, the CD player shut off. The sudden silence was startling after the blaring racket of his music.

Shivering, despite the heat of the water, he muttered curses under his breath. The fuse must have blown again. Why was it always when he was in the bath?

He hastily dried himself then dressed. Feeling uneasy, he stepped out from the bathroom.

Just the after-effects of seeing Scotty die, he thought.

But he couldn't help feel it was more than that.

As he set foot on the top step, he heard movement behind him and turned to see a dark shape rushing at him.

Before he could react, he was flying down the stairs. His shoulder hit first, flipping him so that his legs sailed over his head. He cried out in pain and dismay as his back twisted.

He bounced all the way to the bottom, his head landing hard on the floor at the foot of the stairs.

The dark shape followed him.

He knew it was Scotty's killer and knew why he was here.

There was little Billy could do to stop him. Something had torn in his back as he fell, sending shooting pains racing down his legs. He felt unable to move.

The figure said nothing, just grabbed his ankles and started dragging him out of the house.

He was too weak to put up a fight.

Chapter 99

Luke shoved Billy into the boot of the car and drove to Peth Vale. As he opened the boot, Billy struggled weakly, traumatised by his time in the darkness with his friend's corpse.

Luke carried him a short distance, then dropped him on the grass, knocking out what little fight remained in him.

He dragged the weakly struggling youth to the front door and brayed hard on the black-glossed wood.

Angry muttering came from behind the windows, then footsteps approached the door.

'This better be good,' the clown growled.

The door opened upon Alfred. He was half-asleep, his hair mussed and his eyes puffy with sleep.

'What in hell are you doing?' he asked the hooded figure that greeted him.

'Brought you a present,' Luke smiled, indicating Billy who lay, stunned, on the gravel drive.

Alfred nodded and smiled a wolfish smile as he ran his eyes over Billy's body. Then he and the figure grabbed Billy's arms and legs and carried him into the house.

Alfred directed them to the cupboard beneath the stairs. He lifted the trapdoor and they dragged Billy down into the dank cellar.

'Shit, where's the girl?' Alfred exclaimed, puzzled by Bryony's absence.

Luke smiled beneath his mask.

'For fuck's sake,' Alfred bellowed, charging at Billy like a raging bull, slamming fists and feet into his startled opponent until his limbs were exhausted and his chest heaved with the effort.

'You want in?' he asked the hooded figure.

'Not yet. You enjoy yourself.'

Alfred continued to kick the youth, hitting him so hard that it hurt his foot. Blood poured from Billy's busted nose. His eyes bulged, staring up at his assailant.

Alfred grinned as he took in the shivering youth. 'Say,' he said, rubbing his groin. 'I got something in mind for you.'

Billy winced at the realisation of what the fat man had in mind. Luke felt a little sickened too.

'What are you, queer or something?' Luke said.

'A hole's a hole, whether blood or spit or shit comes out of it,' Alfred leered.

'I love the dead no matter what their gender,' Luke said. 'But I can only stomach relations with the females.'

Alfred shrugged. Like fucking dead girls was something to be proud of.

'You joining in?' he asked.

Luke shook his head, feeling sickened by the idea.

'Then leave us in peace,' Alfred said.

'Don't kill him.'

'I won't.'

Luke made his way up the stairs, and waited in the garden.

Trying his best not to imagine what the clown was doing to Billy, he covered his ears to blot out the occasional muffled grunt and cry of pain that came from inside the house.

He was pleased that Billy was in pain, but the thought of what the clown was actually doing reminded him of the attack he had carried out on Jane when Luke was a kid. The memories made him angrier and angrier.

Deciding he was going to finish the vile clown there and then, he pulled his knife and headed into the house. His plan was disrupted when he saw a bloodied and bruised Billy

running up the corridor towards him. All
thoughts of attacking the clown were gone.

Luke instinctively sent his right hand sailing
out towards the fleeing youth. It met his chin and
buckled his legs. For the second time that day
Billy was out cold.

Luke dragged him out onto the paved side
yard and started slapping him across the face to
wake him up.

Chapter 100

Billy woke, cold and wet. There was a smell that he couldn't place at first.

He took in the roiling dark clouds in the grey sky above him and wondered what was going on.

The feel of blood on the backs of his legs made him remember where he was and what had happened. He retched, sending pain spiralling through his body. His eyes struggled to focus on the dark figure standing over him.

'I believe this is what you would call a special occasion,' the figure said. By the sound of his voice it seemed he was grinning.

Then Billy recognised the smell. While his mind struggled to process the situation, the figure scraped a match across the cobbled floor. He held it up for a second, his sickening features illuminated in the flickering flame of the match.

'No, please, no,' Billy pleaded.

His begging fell on deaf ears. Luke threw the match at his feet. There was a loud *wumph* as the petrol ignited.

Luke watched the flames climb Billy's back, inhaling the sickly smell of burning flesh. With a hearty, yet depraved, laugh, he took a deep breath in. This made him retch, but he overcame it as he watched Billy twitch in agony.

The clown came out, his flabby chest heaving up and down with the effort of running. 'You…got…him?' he panted.

Luke pointed to the flaming pyre that marked Billy's remains.

'Nice. I like that,' he smiled.

Luke wanted to rip his own eyes out of his head to avoid seeing the smile as it brought back the events of his family's deaths anew. He wanted to take the blade beneath his coat and ram every inch of it into the clown's gut.

But he knew that the clown was the only person bad enough to help him take out the infamous Marshton Eight.

He resisted his impulse, though it physically sickened him to leave the clown alive for a second longer.

And in spite of his hatred and disgust at the clown he was thrilled at the possibilities his loathsome accomplice provided.

'Beer?' the clown asked, raising his eyebrows suggestively.

Luke shook his head. 'Another time,' he said.

'Hey, I was impressed there. Setting fire to him like that was fucking genius. This is going to be fun.'

You have no idea, Luke thought, his smile hidden by the dead skin that covered his true features.

He put a cigarette into his mouth, lighting it with the flames on the burning body. He walked back to the car, enjoying the nicotine rush – which further enhanced the much stronger rush of his triumph over two of his attackers. His blood lust was satisfied for the time being.

He took Scotty's corpse out of the boot, enjoying the way the dead eyes stared into the night sky, and left the body on the gravel drive.

At the front of the house, he had a quick look to make sure that nothing looked out of place in the garden.

He could not risk being caught until he and the clown had killed all of the gang. The thought of leaving any of them unharmed made his blood boil.

They were all going to fucking suffer.

Chapter 101

An involuntary shudder went through Alfred as he watched his strange associate walk away. Something about the kid freaked him right the fuck out.

Alfred wrapped the body in one of the tarpaulins from the garage, placing some bricks inside. He tied the tarpaulin up with a length of rope and dumped it in the pool. The black cylindrical form disappeared beneath the murky water.

He turned back to Billy, who had stopped moving. The flames dwindled.

Alfred got some water from the pool and poured it over the smouldering corpse. There was a loud hiss as the water put out the dying flames.

He wrapped Billy in a tarpaulin in the same way as he had Scotty, dragged him to the pool and watched another corpse sink to its watery grave.

He made sure that the bodies were submerged – just in case anyone happened to look in the pool. The thick layer of scum atop the water made it difficult to see the bottom.

He covered the pool with the tarpaulin and went back into the house.

A few hours later, a noise in the dark awoke Alfred.

His head pounding, he opened his eyes and glanced towards the source of the noise.

Nearly jumped out of his skin when he saw the masked man's dead face hovering in the dark above his bed.

'Shh,' the masked man said, clasping a cold, coppery-smelling hand over Alfred's mouth.

Alfred's eyes bulged as he saw the mask properly for the first time. It looked like the kid had skinned someone and was wearing their face. Seriously fucked up.

'Jesus, what the hell have you got on your face?' Alfred shouted when the figure's hand had retracted from his mouth.

The masked figure laughed, a low ominous sound that scraped across Alfred's ears.

'Brought you a present,' he said. With that he switched on Alfred's bedside lamp. The light, dim as it was, hurt Alfred's eyes after the darkness of his bedroom.

He found himself staring at the bound, gagged form of a pretty brunette girl. She struggled against her binds, trying to scream for help.

Alfred's eyes bulged as he took in the naked, shivering girl. She was wide-eyed and whimpering. Just how he liked them.

'I haven't touched her,' the masked stranger said. 'Feel free to have some fun with her. Think of it as a thank you for your help with the lad I set fire to.'

Feeling like the offer was too good to be true, Alfred looked from the girl to the man and back again.

'Or there's a dead one, if that's more to your liking?' Luke asked.

Alfred shook his head and looked back to the girl, salivating at the thought of getting his hands on her.

'I'll leave you to it,' Luke said, shutting the door as he left.

Chapter 102

Luke gave it half an hour before he ventured back to the bedroom. He had no desire to catch the clown in the act, risking the return of the nightmares from the night his family had been murdered.

As he reached the top of the stairs, he heard a grunt of satisfaction which sickened him.

Again he felt the urge to run in and gut the clown like a fish, but he knew that his plan would be worth it in the long run.

He pulled the door open to see the clown lying next to the whimpering girl.

'My turn,' he said, trying to make it sound as though he was smiling. Taking the girl by the arm, he dragged her out of the bedroom.

Alfred was basking in the glow of his recent orgasm and felt no need to intrude on the masked stranger's fun. He'd been good enough to bring him a naked stunner, that meant he deserved some alone time with the girl. His eyes closed and he settled back into sleep.

Luke dragged the traumatised girl to the car and took her to his home. He led her up to the bedroom, where he chained her to the radiator before leaving her in darkness.

He drove back to Peth Vale and let himself in using the key he had taken for the back door.

'This is a reality check,' Luke told the drowsy clown. 'So you don't get any ideas of turning me in. You do and I'll drive the lady you've just raped right to the cop shop where, I'm sure, Marshton's finest will hang on every word of the story of what you've done to her. If that's not enough, I also have the bodies of the slut and the bouncer that you killed. If you agree to play, I'll not only let you have them to dispose of as you wish, but I'll keep my promise and take you to the house of a truly tasty piece of ass.'

With that, he flashed a photo of Kate from her glamour site. Alfred couldn't stop the strand of drool which ran down his chin. He'd loved the previous photo, but this one was even better. She was wearing the tiniest panties and nothing else.

'Yes, if you play along with my game, I'll lead you right to her door. What you do then, of course, is up to you. I'm sure you can think of something fun to do with her. So, do I have your attention?'

Alfred nodded.

'Good. Because we can have such fun together, Alfred.'

Chapter 103

'In choosing victims, there's more thrill where there's more danger,' Luke said.

Alfred thought about it and decided that the masked lunatic had a point. 'Who do you think we should go for?'

'I think these fuckers would be a good test of our skills,' Luke said, pulling out a newspaper clipping he had of the Marshton Eight. 'Besides, we've already killed two of them, the others will be looking for us.'

'Fuck it. Why not?' Alfred said.

'I'm glad you said that. These twats will be fun to kill. And we'd be doing the town a favour.'

Alfred nodded. 'So what do we do?'

'Why don't we head out now? I know where one of them lives.'

'How do I know that this isn't a trap?' Alfred said.

Luke chuckled ominously. 'You don't, I guess. But as a show of trust, I'll let you have the bouncer's body. The slut's you can have after we've had our fun with these wasters.'

Alfred looked him up and down and decided he wasn't bluffing.

'And the blonde girl's address too?'

'I'll even drive you there,' Luke beamed.

'Yeah, alright then.'

'Well, let's go,' Luke said.

Chapter 104

They left Peth Vale and parked up at the end of the back alley where the Marshton Eight had beaten Luke.

Alfred waited in the shadows while Luke walked down the alley. A wolf-whistle made him turn to see Olly standing behind him.

Olly was accompanied by another youth, who Luke did not recognise, probably one of the hangers-on, the hapless wannabes who followed the Marshton Eight around, dreaming of one day being as feared and respected as the gang-members.

Luke waved to them and then began walking away. They followed him, as he knew they would.

He turned and looked at them again. They continued to follow. He turned a corner and waited for them.

When they got closer, they noticed the stitches around the neck of Luke's new skin.

'What the fuck?' Olly said, a look of terror spreading across his face.

'Let's get the fuck out of here,' the hanger-on said.

They both ran, but Alfred burst from behind a bin and stabbed the hanger-on in the throat. The lad went down, choking on his own blood, his hands scrabbling uselessly at the spurting wound.

Alfred watched him die, then hid the body in a wheelie bin. He carved a cross into the side of the bin so he knew where to find the body later.

Luke pursued Olly, who ran into a house a few streets away. Olly came back out with Pete, a fellow member of the Marshton Eight. They were both armed with baseball bats.

'I think he went this way,' Olly said, pointing to the alley where the attack had taken place.

Luke hid under a car and watched as two pairs of feet ran past him. He waited a few minutes, then climbed out and searched until he found them in the back alley behind Pete's house.

'Who we looking for here?' Pete asked.

'I don't know. It looked like some young girl, but dead.'

'Dead? What the fuck are you talking about?'

'I mean she looked dead. Like I fucking said.'

'So she died and suddenly decided to walk the streets for something to do? Lay off the fucking crack pipe, Olly. I'm going back inside.'

Luke crept up behind them. Olly was nearest to Luke, with his back to him, imploring Pete to stay outside. He was wasting his breath; Pete had already returned to the house.

Olly turned and ran over to Luke, thrusting the bat into his ribs.

Luke doubled over, laughing. 'You think you can fucking hurt me?' he said, his disturbing laugh echoing round the alley.

Olly lost his nerve and ran, dropping the baseball bat. Luke scooped it up as he passed. Olly slipped on his friend's blood and bumped into the wall. This slowed him enough for Luke to catch up to him and smash the bat hard across his legs.

He fell to the floor, screaming for mercy. Luke put his lights out with a solid blow to the temple.

He dragged his unconscious enemy to the car, the lateness of the hour making for a distinct lack of witnesses. The locals knew better than to visit the alleys after nightfall.

At the car, he bundled Olly into the boot then followed Alfred to the body of the hanger-on. They lifted the body into the boot and Luke drove them back to Peth Vale.

In Peth Vale's yard, Luke and Alfred removed the corpse from the boot, wrapped it in a tarpaulin and dumped it in the pool.

Luke dragged Olly, the corpse-to-be, out of the boot and dropped him on the floor.

Olly awoke screaming as he saw the grinning, bat-wielding clown standing over him.

Alfred laughed and brought the bat down hard, just as Olly thrust his arm up to protect his head. There was a snapping sound and the forearm hung at a strange angle, the white bone sticking through the skin on the side of Olly's arm.

'Nice,' Luke remarked, watching proceedings with a sickly grin.

Olly screamed for the clown to stop. The bat sunk into his abdomen with a nauseating crack. Alfred brought the bat down hard on his head a few times. Olly twitched, his head hanging limp on his neck.

Alfred gave him one more smash then leant down and took his pulse.

He was already dead.

'That's how it's fucking done,' Alfred shouted, adrenaline coursing through his veins.

Smiling beneath his dead skin mask, Luke shook his head and snatched the bat from Alfred's grasp.

Luke laughed as he brought the bat down repeatedly on Olly's head, refusing to stop until it was a bloody pulp.

His face, hands and clothes coated in a thick layer of dripping gore, he stared at the body.

'That was fucking incredible,' Alfred hooted, high-fiving Luke. Drops of blood flew from his hand as the palms connected. 'True fucking brutality,' Alfred raved. 'Fucking A!'

Luke felt a euphoric rush at having battered Olly's head to mush.

'We doing any more tonight?' Alfred said.

'Na, I'm beat.'

'We have been busy,' Alfred said. His black painted grin seemed to stretch all the way to his ears. Luke looked away, feeling ill from staring at the face.

'I'll be in touch,' Luke said. 'And we'll kill the rest of the bastards.'

'Fucking right we will,' Alfred smiled. He turned and went back into the house. Luke washed himself in the pool, then drove away from the house.

He headed towards home, but then changed his mind and went back to the alley where he'd been earlier.

Chapter 105

After dismissing Olly's ramblings, Pete had gone inside, neglecting to shut the kitchen blinds. He also left the back door unlocked, reasoning that Olly would eventually give up his search for the drug-induced hallucination and come in to steal a beer or two.

He woke an hour later, on the settee, his glass of Jack and coke perched next to him.

His sleep had been disturbed by a persistent banging sound. At first, he had thought that the young couple next door were playing one of their kinky sex games.

The noise came again. He rubbed his eyes and got off the settee, setting his glass down on the dusty coffee table.

In the corridor he heard another bout of banging. It sounded like the back door hitting off its frame.

Someone was in the house with him, he could sense it.

'Olly?' he called out.

Silence.

He moved into the kitchen and pushed the door open.

His eyes scanned the darkened room, looking for the knife block, which usually held a single big, sharp kitchen knife that he kept, in case anyone ever broke in.

The knife was not there.

He switched on the kitchen light. It flickered on for a second and he saw his own reflection in the window.

The light flickered off for a second, before coming on properly.

He jumped.

The reflection in the window now showed a figure standing behind him. The intruder's face was grotesque, its eyes full of malignant energy.

Pete turned to see that the figure held the missing kitchen knife.

As he stared in disbelief at the intruder's dead face, his eyes registered a number of flashes across his vision.

Too late, he realised that the figure was slashing the knife at him.

There was a searing pain and then he felt blood running down his cheek. His throat let out an involuntary cry of pain. It was a pathetic sound, and it made the figure laugh at him, before the knife again carved a path towards his face.

The blade cut into Pete's face again and again, sending sprays of blood up the walls.

As Pete doubled over, clutching his bleeding face, Luke grabbed him and stabbed him through the stomach.

Pete's eyes widened. He looked as if he didn't think that this was really happening to him.

Before Pete could even raise his hands to protect himself, Luke had already stabbed him frenziedly, creating a dozen eye-shaped wounds.

The blood streamed out of Pete and he fell to the floor, struggling to breathe. Blood bubbled from his chest.

Luke watched Pete die, wrapped him in a bed sheet and put him in the boot of the car. He drove to Peth Vale, where Pete joined his friends in the pool.

Luke washed the blood off himself and went home. He put a couple of petrol cans in the car boot, washed himself, and sat in the grounds of the house, thinking about what he had just done.

Chapter 106

The next day, he crossed Scotty, Billy, Pete and Olly off the newspaper photo, taking this with him when he went out in the car that night to look for the remaining gang members.

He remembered he'd seen Billy running from a house earlier, and guessed that it was the home of one of the gang.

Leaving the car at the end of the street, he approached the houses. He pressed his face against the window of each house in turn, spotting Otis slurping a bowlful of chilli on the settee in the fourth house.

When Otis left the house, Luke went round to the back door and booted it off its hinges.

He went through the house, destroying everything he saw, then got one of the jerry cans from the car and began throwing the petrol around. He lit a cigarette, then dropped the smouldering match into the petrol-soaked carpet.

When the entire downstairs caught ablaze, he laughed then walked out into the street and watched the scene from his hiding place.

Five minutes later, Otis returned. Luke stifled a laugh as he saw Otis looking upset and confused about the situation.

Otis stayed for a while, trying to put out the fire with buckets of water from his outside tap.

After a while, he sensed he was getting nowhere and left.

Luke followed him and listened in as he called the fire brigade, who recognised his voice from tapes of his infamous prank calls and laughed at his plight.

Otis slammed the phone down and went to one of his friend's houses. The friend was not one of the Marshton Eight.

Luke found a brick on the floor near his hiding place. He picked it up, taped the amended newspaper page to it then approached the house occupied by Otis and his friend.

After he had checked no-one was watching him, he threw the brick at the window.

The glass shattered, breaking the silence of the sleeping street. Luke ran away. When he reached home, he laughed till he threw up. This was more fun than he could ever have imagined.

That night he dreamed a great deal about Bryony. She appeared to him, but she was out of focus. Her voice seemed distant, unobtainable.

He woke up, sweating and panicked, and looked over to see her lying on the bed. His panic subsided after he cut off her head and put it on his bedside table. He smiled. It looked good there, watching over him while he slept.

He stared at her head, at her beautiful eyes, which lifelessly stared back at him, then moved her body across the bed and got in next to her.

Chapter 107

A few hours after the brick had come through the window, Otis told his three friends the story of his house burning down.

His face was pale and his hands and voice shook as he spoke. 'Then whoever it was followed me to Paulo's and put a brick through the window. This was taped to the brick,' he finished.

He showed them the newspaper article, which showed the four dead gang members, crossed out with a thick black marker pen.

'It's the cop, the guy's dad,' said Tommy.

'Yeah, I think so too,' said Dave. 'He's got the most reason to want us dead.'

'I don't know, man,' Otis said. 'I only caught a glimpse of the guy but he looked like a fucking zombie. I saw him throw the brick, then he was gone.'

'Like a zombie?' Dave scoffed. 'I'm telling you, it's the cop.'

'It did look like a zombie,' Otis insisted. 'Or some fucking weird mask. Sure as hell weren't no cop.'

'Never mind that,' said Tommy. 'What are we going to do about it?'

'We take the cop out,' said Johnny T. 'This will all stop.'

'Are you fucking stupid?' said Tommy. 'Kill a cop? You have any idea how long we'd get for doing that?'

'*We* wouldn't get any time for it,' said Johnny T, 'Cos *we* wouldn't be the ones who killed him.'

'Louie,' said Dave.

'Exactly,' said Johnny T. 'He's always wanted to be in our gang. This is his opportunity to show us that he's serious. If he takes the cop out, he's in. If he gets caught, so fuck, at least it ain't one of us.'

'Think he'd do it?' asked Otis.

'Yeah, he really wants in. And plus, he grew up with Olly, knew him pretty well. I think he'd appreciate the chance to avenge his death,' Dave said.

'Louie it is then,' said Tommy, smiling.

Johnny T called Louie and told him about what had happened, neglecting to tell him that the intended target was a cop.

Chapter 108

An hour after Johnny T had called him, Louie had his shit together. This was his big break, the opportunity of a lifetime. If he pulled this off, he was a big deal, an official badass, one of the infamous Marshton Eight.

'I'm in, baby,' he said, a shit-eating grin plastered across his face.

His car was flying along the bypass on the outskirts of Marshton, headed towards the address he had written down on a grubby piece of paper.

The handgun his late father had left him sat on the seat next to him. His eyes darted to it now and then.

Louie had been in the year above Olly at school and had helped him out when the school bully was shaking him down for lunch money. Since then the two of them had become firm friends and had watched each other's backs.

Now Olly was dead, and Louie felt honoured to be the one who was to avenge him. It did not occur to him that he was being used.

Louie congratulated himself; the phone call from Johnny T had been a pleasant surprise. He had left his mistress and had been going straight for the last few weeks, trying to re-build the bond between him and his wife and kid.

But this was, as they said in the movies, 'an offer he couldn't refuse.' This thought made him smile.

Turning left off the bypass, he pulled into a quiet alley a few streets from his intended destination.

Smoking a cigarette to calm his nerves, he killed the engine. His foot tapped nervously on the floor. Staring into the rear view mirror, he took a deep breath in and shoved the gun into his jacket pocket.

'This is it, Louie,' he said. 'What you've been waiting for.'

He got out of the car and walked along the street, the grubby piece of paper in his hand.

After checking the address for the last time, he dropped the paper between the bars of a drain and walked into the next street, looking around to make sure he wasn't being observed.

He whistled to himself, trying to take his mind off the panic he was starting to feel. The nerves disappeared when he told himself that he was doing this for Olly.

He reached the correct street and followed the house numbers which led him into a small cul-de-sac, finally reaching number 63, a detached house in the corner.

Taking a deep breath in, he looked around and walked up the drive. He climbed the fence into the back garden and saw that one of the rear windows had been left open.

The open window was a few feet above a flat roof. If he could get onto the roof, he could get in through the window. He dragged a plastic wheelie bin over to the wall. The bin gave him the extra height he needed to climb up onto the flat roof.

He crossed the roof to the open window and climbed in, finding himself on the upstairs landing.

The house was in darkness, but he could see pretty well. Crossing the landing, he noted a photo of Sergeant Hirst, in full uniform, on the wall.

'Shit, he's a fucking cop,' Louie hissed under his breath.

He froze for a minute, weighing up the odds.

Killing a cop was serious shit. But if he did it, everyone would look up to him. He may even go straight into the gang at the top, right under Johnny T.

The idea made him grin and he knew he had to go through with it.

He walked past the photo and towards the bedrooms.

Two of the doors were ajar, faint snoring coming from behind one of them. His target was unconscious on the bed. Louie's heart began to race as he moved towards the sleeping cop.

He was roughly halfway across the room when Hirst sat up and pulled a gun from beneath his pillow.

'Stop right there,' Hirst said, pointing the gun at Louie.

Louie's hand had been halfway to the gun in his pocket, but now he raised it above his head.

'Johnny T sent you, didn't he?' Hirst said.

Louie nodded, feeling panic twist knots in his stomach.

'On the floor, face down,' said Hirst.

Louie obeyed.

Hirst flicked on a lamp and got out of the bed. He gave Louie a stiff kick before frisking him. When he found the gun, he pulled it out and put it down on the bed.

'Mmm, breaking and entering, an unlicensed firearm, conspiracy to kill,' Hirst said. 'You'll not see the light of day for a long time, son.'

Louie grunted, disappointed with himself; if he had just fired the fucking gun that would have been it.

'Unless, that is, you tell me exactly what Johnny T told you.'

Louie was torn between saving his own skin and saving his reputation. In the end, he went for the first option. 'What will you do if I tell you?' he asked Hirst.

'I'll frame some other poor bastard for it.'

'Ok. Johnny T told me you were responsible for the murders of four of the Marshton Eight.'

'Really? I didn't even know they were dead. Which ones?'

'Scotty, Billy, Olly and Pete,' Louie told him.

'That *is* an interesting development,' Hirst said, smiling. 'I'll tell you what we'll do, Louie. You call Johnny T now, tell him I'm dead.'

'Why?'

'Because if he thinks I'm dead, he can relax, let his guard down. So can the rest of your friends.'

'But then the real killer will find it easier to get to them,' said Louie.

'Precisely, Louie, precisely.'

'Some cop you are. You're supposed to serve justice.'

Hirst's face went a beetroot colour. Grabbing Louie by the lapels, he pushed his own head forward so they were eye to eye. 'Because of those pricks my only child is forced to live the rest of his life in a wheelchair. He doesn't dare leave the house. When he does sleep he has nightmares. My happy, sociable son is gone. He can't even feed himself. So don't you fucking speak to me about justice. They deserve everything they get.'

He shoved Louie's head away and threw a mobile phone at him. 'Make the fucking call,' he said. 'Or God help you I'll kill you myself.'

Louie hurriedly typed the numbers into the phone. Johnny T answered.

'He's dead,' Louie said. 'I'm just leaving the house now.'

'Did he say anything?'

'Yeah, he confessed to the killings, then begged for his life.'

Johnny T laughed. 'Thanks, Louie, you did us a big favour. You're in the gang.'

'Thanks,' Louie said.

'We're gonna have a party at mine to celebrate, if you fancy it?'

'I think I'd better lay low until this all blows over,' Louie said.

Hirst nodded his approval.

'Good idea,' Johnny T said. 'I'll see you when the shit storm's all over.'

'Yeah. Bye, Johnny.' Louie hung up and passed the phone back to Hirst.

'Good, Louie, you're a first rate bull-shitter,' said Hirst.

'You'll not get away with this.'

'I'm not the one killing them.'

'But you're helping.'

'No, I'm just choosing not to waste police resources by investigating. Trust me; the world will be a much better place without them.'

'You'll be found out. I'll tell everyone what you've done.'

'Tell away, there is no blood on my hands. True, I have a good motive, but you have an even better one. Picture this, the wannabe gangster who killed the gang that had rejected him time after time. I can almost see the headlines.'

'No-one will ever believe that.'

'It happens all the time, rival gangs, and takeovers from the inside. All we have to do is wait. I have to say, I'm looking forward to seeing what he does to the rest of your friends.'

Louie opened his mouth to protest, but, before he could say anything, Hirst clubbed him over the head with the gun, knocking him to the floor.

Hirst cuffed his arms and legs and dragged him to the garage where he gagged and tied him, before dumping him in the boot of his car.

He pierced a few small holes in the liner of the boot, then slammed the hatch shut and went back upstairs to bed.

Chapter 109

Hirst's attempts to get to sleep were disturbed by the sound of screaming from down the corridor.

At first he thought it was Louie calling out from the boot of the car, but he knew he'd done a good job of gagging and binding him.

Besides, Louie was downstairs, locked away in the garage. The screaming was coming from upstairs.

Tom, having another nightmare, no doubt. The dreams were merciless and, in his decreased mental capacity, Tom couldn't tell that they were just dreams.

Hirst's face contorted as he sobbed, remembering all the good times he and his son had shared.

The shell of a man he had become was a mockery of those happy times.

He wanted his son to suffer no longer.

Taking Louie's gun, he crept into Tom's room. Tom was asleep again, his face stained with tears and snot.

Tears rolled down Hirst's face as he stood in the doorway and watched his sleeping son. After loading the gun, he moved across the room, wincing at the creaking floorboards. His son slept on.

Hirst held his son's hand for a few seconds, trying to decide whether he should do what he had in mind. One look at his son's vacant expression convinced him he was doing the humane thing.

He kissed his son's forehead and pushed a pillow over his face. His body shook with sobs as he lifted the gun to the pillow and pressed it into his son's temple.

'Please forgive me, son. I just can't bear to see you like this,' he said.

He stiffened and pulled the trigger. The gunshot was not silent, but the pillow did a decent job of muffling the report.

Blood covered the pillow and started soaking through the bed.

'I'm sorry,' he said, wiping his eyes. He left the room, closing the door behind him, and cried himself to sleep.

Chapter 110

Despite the insistences of his three friends and fellow gang members, Otis wasn't convinced that Sergeant Hirst was responsible for the deaths of his four friends.

He knew that what he had seen sounded impossible, crazy even, but the thing that had put the brick through his window was not a cop. Of that he was certain.

He suspected it was the weird kid they had beaten up and tattooed. The guy whose house they had trashed. He had as much motive as the cop.

Apparently he'd been killed in the riot at the asylum, but mistakes could be made in such chaotic circumstances. Otis reckoned the fucker was still alive and causing trouble.

He took Paulo, one of his buddies, with him. Paulo was a real scrapper, but Otis intended him as cannon fodder more than anything.

If this guy had already killed four of their gang (all tough lads) he didn't want to risk tackling him alone. He didn't care if it was yellow, it was common sense. Safety in numbers, or something like that.

Or a human shield, if he was honest about it.

He and Paulo kerb-crawled to the street behind Luke's.

'It's somewhere round here,' Otis said, scanning the houses. He chewed his lip as he tried to think.

'Maybe we should call Johnny T, see if he remembers.'

'Na, he'll just get pissed that I went behind his back. I want to get this guy myself, wipe the smug looks off their faces. No-one fucking laughs at me.'

'Any idea which house then, brainbox?'

'Fuck you. Let's get out and walk. More time to look, that way.'

Paulo groaned. He had no desire to be out in the cold, rainy darkness any longer than necessary. Hell, he was only here because he'd been caught boning Otis's sister. She'd been a crap shag too, which was salt in the wound.

'Yo, lardass,' Otis said, smacking Paulo across the head. 'Outta the fucking car.'

'Hit me one more time and I swear I'll—'

'What? You swear what? I'll pull your eyes out and fuck the empty sockets, Dolmio boy.' Otis stared at him, holding the gaze long enough to make Paulo back down, then burst into laughter. 'Man, are you soft as shite!'

Paulo said nothing, just got out of the car.

'Let's go,' Otis said. 'Quicker we nail this freak, quicker you can go back to wanking over Johnny T.'

'Your sister, more like.' Paulo knew he was pushing his luck, but he was too pissed off to care.

'That is not cool. I've told you what I'm gonna do to you if you keep running that mouth of yours. Don't make me stare your ass down again.'

Paulo again backed down.

They reached Luke's street, their faces hidden beneath their hoods.

'Ah, there's the fucker,' Otis said, his tone triumphant. 'See, new windows. Cos we smashed the fuckers to bits.'

Paulo nodded, grinning. He was feeling up for a ruck now. 'Yeah, let's show this kid who's boss.'

'Now you're talking my language, man.'

They laughed for a second then crept up to Luke's home. Paulo watched while Otis jimmied open one of the downstairs windows.

They froze as next door's kitchen light came on. The light remained on for an impossibly long time, before finally flicking off.

'Wait,' Otis said. 'Dozy bat'll probably come back for her glasses or something.'

The light remained off.

'Maybe this ain't such a good idea,' Paulo said.

'Ah, don't go all Boy George on me, man. The cops are scared of us. They won't even come out. Trust me.'

Paulo took a look at the utter confidence on Otis's face, and nodded.

'Now, let's go,' Otis said, climbing in through the open kitchen window.

Chapter 111

Otis stood in the kitchen, his heart already starting to race. It was always this way when he was in someone else's house. All part of the thrill, he had come to learn.

His eyes adjusted to the gloom now, he pulled open the drawer next to the sink and searched for a suitable knife. Always best to use their own knives on them, he found.

While he searched, Paulo climbed in. He wobbled on the worktop for a few seconds, his arms wheeling like those of a cartoon character on the edge of a cliff. He caught his balance and crouched to step down to the floor.

The sound of breaking glass shattered the silence in the house. Otis cursed under his breath and glared at Paulo.

Paulo froze atop the workbench, feeling Otis's eyes bore into him. He whispered an apology.

They waited for a tense few minutes, certain that the masked psychopath who had taken out four of Otis's best friends was going to make his appearance.

But nothing happened.

Otis finally decided that the moment had passed and beckoned Paulo down from the bench. He found a suitable knife for each of them, keeping the better of the two for himself.

'For that, you can kill him,' Otis whispered.

'I think we should go. It's not our night.'

'I'm fucked if I'm not going through with this after this shit. Now get your fat arse up them stairs before I make good on my earlier threat.'

Paulo shrugged and climbed down from the bench. He had the feeling that they were in for a bad night.

Otis went up the stairs first, cursing every creak of the shifting boards. At the top, he took in a lungful of air. Christ, the air up here was rank. It smelt like something had died.

'Something's *about* to die up here,' he muttered to himself, grinning.

'What?'

'Shh. Get in there and stab that murdering son of a bitch before he wakes up.'

'I really think you should—'

'For fuck's sake, Paulo. This guy's dangerous. We need to take him out before he wakes up. This is serious shit. You get in trouble, I'll be in straight away.'

He clapped a comforting hand on Paulo's shoulder.

'Ok,' Paulo said, moving towards the door before he had time to change his mind.

Otis's eyes scanned the darkened landing, searching for the hidden killer. He was nowhere to be seen.

Paulo moved to the door, his heart already slamming.

The bedroom door was open a few inches. A sickening smell drifted out through the gap. He blotted it out and pushed the door open, wincing as the hinges squealed.

A few feet behind him, Otis moved forwards. Paulo looked over his shoulder.

Otis nodded firmly.

Paulo took a deep breath and moved into the room. His hand faltered on the light switch. *No, leave it off,* his mind screamed at him. *Are you trying to wake him up?*

He jumped slightly as the door bumped against the wall.

There was a shape huddled beneath the covers on the bed.

He's still asleep, his mind screamed in triumph. *He won't even know what's happened until it's too late.*

His eyes glued to the sleeping figure on the bed, he crept closer.

Otis stopped at the threshold to the room.

Paulo reached the bed and paused for a second, the knife trembling in his hand.

He then slammed the knife down hard into the body, aiming for the chest area. The blade sunk into the flesh, surprising him with how good it felt.

'Take that, you freak,' Paulo cried, feeling sheer relief at making it this far.

Behind him, he heard a deep, mocking laugh. *No time for Otis to be playing tricks,* he thought. Before the thought had time to sink in, the door to the room slammed shut, hitting Otis in the face.

Light stung Paulo's eyes.

In the light, he found himself staring at a dead body on the bed.

A skinless, headless, bloody mass of dead flesh.

He let out a scream and turned to see a sight even worse than the corpse.

Like Otis had said, the figure did look like a zombie. It was charging straight for him.

Chapter 112

Paulo was too terrified to even lift his knife hand. The figure ploughed into him at chest level, taking him off his feet.

The door slammed behind them as Otis tried to open it, but the bookcase that Luke had tipped over was barring it shut.

The noises were far away to Paulo. Otis may as well have been in another town, for all the good it would do.

The horrid masked face of the man he thought he'd killed stared down at him. He retched, and vomit crept up his throat.

Luke twisted the knife out of Paulo's hand and slammed the blade into his belly.

He got up – he wanted Otis, not this fat bastard – and ran to the door. Pulled the bookcase aside and heaved open the door.

He expected Otis to rush him, fists flailing, but he didn't.

'You do right to fear me, Otis.'

He turned to see the fat man fumbling in his pocket, probably for a mobile phone. He pulled the hand out and dug around in the pocket. After stomping the phone, he turned back to the doorway.

Still no sign of Otis.

'You disappoint me, Otis. I thought you had balls. But bringing a friend, and now hiding, that's bad form.'

Otis, hidden behind the curtains in Norma's room, tried to stifle his breathing.

He was beginning to regret his rash actions tonight, but he knew that if he kept it together, he could get out of this alive.

Paulo's moans and cries came from the next room, and Otis's sensible side said he should forget him, let him get sacrificed. But it was his fault Paulo was here and his conscience (such as it was) wouldn't let him do that.

He just had to hope that the psycho didn't realise this.

Paulo cupped a hand to his bleeding gut. There was a shitload of blood and he was starting to feel lightheaded, but he figured the wound wasn't fatal.

He crawled along the floor, trying to make his escape. Luckily, the nutcase was busy trying to find Otis, and seemed to have forgotten about him.

He reached the landing and heard nothing. The house was eerily quiet.

'Silent as the grave,' Luke said from behind him, making him jump.

Otis heard the voice and his pulse began to race. He had an image in his head of the gruesome mask, and he had no desire to see it again.

'Otis, your fat friend here is going to suffer a painful death if you don't come out of your hidey hole.'

Otis heard the words, but didn't want to believe them. He wondered if he should give himself up – knowing, deep down, that a violent death awaited him if he did surrender.

His mind was made up for him when Paulo screamed.

'Well, I'm impressed,' Luke said, upon seeing Otis emerge from hiding. 'I didn't think you had a decent bone in your body. Guess I was wrong.'

Otis stared at the knife stuck a few inches into Paulo's stomach then glanced at his agonised expression.

Mercifully, the shadows hid most of Luke's macabre mask from his sight.

Luke watched Otis get into range, then he stomped the knife's handle, driving it deep into Paulo's bulging gut. Paulo screamed again.

Otis charged, flailing the knife towards Luke's face.

Luke dodged and slammed a fist into Otis's ribs. His breath exploded out of him. His chest laboured, trying to pull air into his starving lungs. The knife flew from his hand, disappearing into the darkness.

Luke bent down and pulled the knife out of Paulo's stomach. Otis still struggled for breath.

Paulo's arms wrapped around Luke and pulled him down.

'Run, Otis,' he yelled. 'I'll hold him while you get away.'

'Got a better idea,' Otis wheezed. He pulled an acrid breath into his lungs and aimed a kick at Luke's face. He let out a cry of disbelief as his shin hit Luke's raised elbow and made his foot go numb.

Seemed he was fucked whatever he did.

'Come get me, you twisted fuck,' he said, shuffling off down the stairs.

Luke grew sick of trying to get his arms free and instead raised his weight off Paulo. He dropped fast, slamming the crown of his head into the fat man's nose.

'Ah, shit,' Paulo cried out, and, like magic, his arms released Luke.

Luke dropped another heavy headbutt onto Paulo's shattered nose, then set off after Otis.

Chapter 113

Pain had been consumed by fear, allowing Otis to move fast, despite the pins and needles feeling in his leg.

He rolled out of the open kitchen window, wincing as his sore leg hit the floor, and made his way across to the bushes near the back fence.

A stone from the rockery was the best weapon he could find. It was no match for a knife, but it would have to do.

The sound of approaching footsteps jolted him out of his thoughts. Through the gap in the bushes, he saw a dark form. He knew it was the killer as it was too small to be Paulo. Shadows still hid the mask from him.

'Know you're still here, Otis,' Luke whispered. 'I know you didn't want to leave your buddy. Come out and play. I'll make it quick for you, then I'll go in and finish the fat man.'

Otis remained silent, straining to keep his breathing inaudible.

The figure approached him, like he knew exactly where he was hiding and was just toying with him.

Just as Luke neared the hiding place, Otis heard a thud as Paulo fell from the kitchen window. Blood poured from the wounds in his middle.

Luke turned.

Otis took his chance, charging Luke and slamming the stone into the back of his head.

Luke jerked forward, cursing his lack of awareness. He saw stars for a second, then the two attackers separated and started to scale the fence.

Luke spun and saw that Otis was already on the other side. He ran at the fat man and jammed the knife hard into his back.

Paulo clung to the fence for a second, his whole frame twitching. The fence shook in its foundations. Blood pouring from his mouth, he fell heavily to the floor.

Luke heard Otis gasp from the other side of the fence. He started over the fence, but Otis had disappeared by the time he reached the top.

Not to worry, Luke knew exactly where to find him.

Chapter 114

The next day, Luke woke late. He waited until nightfall, smiling as he relived the killings he had carried out.

When it was dark, he picked up the car and loaded Paulo's corpse into the boot. On the way to Peth Vale, he stopped to pick up the bouncer's body.

Alfred was puzzled when he opened the door upon Luke. He saw the two bodies slumped on the gravel drive and grimaced. The frown turned upside down when he realised that one of them was the bouncer he'd killed.

'I haven't had the police braying down my door just yet,' Luke smiled. 'So I reckon it's time we teach the other fuckers a lesson.'

Alfred smiled.

'Gotta confess I've had a bit of fun without you last night. Hence the fat boy's body.'

'It's fine.'

'I'm a man of my word so I brought you the bouncer's body. Like I promised I'll give you the slut's when we're through.'

Alfred nodded.

'So, hide the bouncer's body and let's get moving. And you may as well put the fat man in a safe place too while you're on.'

Alfred muttered under his breath. He had no liking for being bossed around by his strange associate, but he did as he was told.

They got into the car and Luke drove them to Paulo's, the house where he had broken the window a few days earlier.

He parked up and took a petrol can out of the boot.

Otis and Dave were sitting in the front room. The broken window had been replaced. *What was the point in that?* he thought and almost laughed. He scolded himself: this was serious.

'I'll smoke them out,' he told the clown. 'You wait by the front door.'

Luke walked to the back alley and began to scale the wall to get onto the roof. When he got there, he stood swaying, feeling drunk on both the height and his anticipation of what was to come.

He poured the fuel can down the chimney and heard a scream as the petrol ignited on the coal fire burning in the front room. He climbed down into the back yard and watched while they ran to the back door.

They tried in vain to escape – Luke held the handle tight, making it hard to turn. Their screams grew in volume as they saw the terrifying death mask that covered his true face.

He watched through the window as they made their way through the inferno in the living room towards the front door.

He got there mere seconds before they did, but the clown was there to back him up.

Alfred stabbed Dave in the knee cap as he ran, panicking, into the street. Dave fell, screaming.

Otis hurdled over his writhing friend and ran down the middle of the road at a hell of a pace.

'I'll get the runner,' Luke said.

Alfred nodded, booted Dave hard in the face and dragged him into the burning house.

Otis swerved into the alley behind the house. Doubting he could run that fast, Luke got into the car and sped after him.

Otis heard the approaching car enter the alley and turned, his face contorted by terror. Luke accelerated and the car hit the runaway with a sickening crunch. Luke drove over Otis again then got out. Otis cradled his shattered limbs on the alley floor.

Laughing, he put him in the boot and drove back to the flaming house, where the clown told him that he would meet him back at Peth Vale after he'd had some fun with the unconscious Dave.

Luke remembered what that had meant for Billy and wanted no part in it. He sped away to Peth Vale.

Chapter 115

Otis was still – barely – alive in the boot of the car. Luke picked him up by his shattered limbs and dropped him hard on the grass.

When Otis saw Luke's mask he shuddered with revulsion and pleaded for his life.

'I've heard it all before,' Luke told him. 'You're wasting your time. As good as dead. You may as well pray I let you die quickly.'

Otis's eyes grew wide and he trembled with fear. Luke reached into Otis's pocket and pulled out his mobile phone. The screen was cracked down its middle, some of the plasma leaking out.

'Who's left from your little gang?' Luke asked.

'I don't know what you mean.'

'Don't fuck me around,' Luke hissed, using his foot to put a little pressure on one of Otis's shattered legs. Otis stiffened, his terror visible in his eyes.

'Tell me now,' Luke said.

'I told you, I don't know what you mean.'

Luke put all of his weight onto Otis's leg, making him scream in agony.

'Otis,' he said, 'Why make it hard on yourself? As I said, you're already dead. So why suffer more than necessary?'

Otis whimpered a little.

A mammoth burst of adrenaline coursed through Luke's body.

He put all of his weight on Otis's leg again. Otis went pale and looked as if he was going to pass out.

'OK, OK, there's Dave, Tommy and Johnny T.'

He could probably cross Dave off once the clown had finished with him.

That just left Johnny T, the fuck who had instigated the attack, and Tommy.

'Do you have Johnny T's number?'

'No,' Otis said. Luke put all his weight on the leg again. 'Yes, yes OK, fuck man.'

'Call him now.'

'OK, just get off my leg. Please,' Otis begged, the pain hewn into his face.

Otis dialled and Johnny T answered.

'Talk to him,' Luke said.

'Hey, Johnny, the freak wants to talk to you. He says we fucked up his life.'

'Give me that,' Luke snapped, snatching the phone out of Otis's hand. 'I'm coming for you, Johnny T, you piece of shit.'

He held the phone close to Otis's mouth and stamped hard onto his shattered left tibia. Otis screamed into the phone.

'This is what's coming to you,' Luke told Johnny T.

Otis's blank eyes stared into the pale grey sky and he silently prayed that he would die soon.

'You still there?' Luke asked.

Johnny T answered, sounding terrified.

'If you're a man, Johnny,' Luke spat, 'you'll meet me at Scotty's place, alone, in five minutes. If you do that, your boy Otis here'll die real quick. If not, you'll hear every last tortured scream.'

Johnny T hung up.

Luke rang him back, but Johnny T had switched off his mobile.

He coerced the phone number for Johnny T's house out of Otis and dialled.

Johnny T let the call go to the answer phone.

Luke rang again, once more reaching the voicemail. He waited for the beep then stamped on Otis's leg.

The scream from the answer phone echoed around Johnny T's front room.

'We're just getting started here, Johnny,' Luke said, bringing out a pair of small, sharp garden shears from the garage. He parted the blades and put them around Otis's little finger.

'Please don't do this,' Otis pleaded. 'Please.'

Luke squeezed the handles together. There was a crunching sound, a spray of warm blood and Otis's little finger fell to the floor.

Otis's pained scream sounded ungodly through the speaker on Johnny T's answer phone.

Luke put the shears around Otis's thumb and squeezed the handles. Otis screamed as his thumb fell to the floor and floated in a pool of blood.

Luke cut off each of Otis's fingers with the shears, waiting a while between each one, so Otis received the maximum amount of pain possible.

Luke watched Otis for a while, then went to the garage.

He returned holding a propane blowtorch which he used to cauterise the stumps where Otis's digits had previously been.

He didn't want Otis bleeding to death just yet: the party was just getting started.

Chapter 116

Otis screamed – partly at his burning, fingerless hands and partly because he saw that the grinning Luke held a large, lethally-sharp kitchen knife.

Luke heard movement behind him and, lost in his sadistic euphoria, readied the knife to attack his unseen company.

'Jesus, what the hell are you doing to him?' the clown said. 'You're a fucking psycho, man. I love it.'

'Please just kill me. I can't take no more. Please,' Otis broke down.

Luke laughed, shaking his head. What little mercy he had held for the gang and their kind had died with Bryony.

Otis tried to drag himself away on his shattered legs. Luke stood heavily on one of the legs, again making Otis scream.

He pinned Otis's face to the floor, with his right arm out to the side. Knelt on the arm and began sawing into his wrist with the knife.

The sound of blade on bone was nauseating, even making the clown wince.

Otis screamed in agony, puking into the grass. Luke cut ten brutal strokes into the wrist, then paused.

Chapter 117

Johnny T cowered in the corner of his living room, wondering what they had done when they had attacked the freaky kid. It must have been him, the cop was dead. They had thought he had been responsible, but it seemed they had been wrong.

He stopped the answer phone. Seconds later, the phone rang and went to the answer phone again.

'Come on, Johnny,' the voice implored him. 'Poor Otis here just wants to die. Don't you, Otis?'

'Please, Johnny, this guy's fucked up.'

There was a pause for thirty seconds. Then Luke said, 'Ok, Johnny. Have it your way.'

The answer phone speaker echoed wildly as Luke resumed sawing into Otis's wrist. The room was full of Otis's panting, pained breathing and his screams.

Johnny T heard another horrendous, blood-curdling scream, then menacing laughter came down the phone.

Deep in shock, he vomited on the floor of his living room.

Another scream from Otis echoed around the room, making him jump.

Unable to listen to any more, he pulled the phone cable out of the wall-socket and sat in the corner, crying and trembling, fearing for his life.

Chapter 118

'The bastard's hung up on us,' Luke said, disappointed. He was surprised that Otis wasn't dead judging by the amount of blood that was pouring out of him.

He re-dialled Johnny T and again the answer phone came on. Luke continued sawing until he had cut through Otis's wrist.

Otis was now in such agony that he couldn't keep quiet, but for the entranced Luke it was like the scene had been muted.

Luke lit the blow torch and held it above Otis's severed wrist, enjoying the pained look on his face.

Luke made sure that the answer phone was still taping his 'message', then turned the lit blowtorch to Otis's wrist. Beads of sweat stood out on Otis's forehead as the blowtorch drew closer. He tried to hide his stump from the searing flame.

Luke laughed at how pathetic he looked. Otis screamed when the blowtorch began to sear his flesh. The skin turned red and started to blister, making a horrible crackling sound as it burnt. The thick smell of Otis's burning flesh filled his nostrils.

Luke laughed as he played the blowtorch over Otis's screaming face.

He turned the blowtorch off and let Otis's pained utterings settle for a while, then called Johnny T's answerphone again.

'You want to play?' Luke asked the clown.

'No, man. You're an artist. It's a privilege to watch you at work.'

Luke snorted laughter and picked up his kitchen knife. Otis stared up at him with eyes as white and prominent as golf balls.

'Y'know, Otis,' Luke said, his tone of voice making it obvious that he was smiling. 'I'm reminded of an incident about eighteen months ago. Let's see if I can refresh your memory.' He paused dramatically, like an actor trying to think of his next line. 'Ah, yes. A friend of yours said, "What about cutting off his lips and making him eat them?" But you had a better idea, didn't you?'

The clown looked at Luke, unsure of where this was going. He enjoyed the pain hewn into the youth's features. The masked man was clearly disturbed, and was getting something off his chest here.

Somehow, Otis's face dropped further. This confirmed the identity of the killer beyond doubt.

'Do you remember what you did to me, Otis?' Luke asked, his tone now deadly serious.

Otis gulped and nodded. His eyes were glued to Luke.

'Now, I'm not sure if you know what I did when I got home, but I'll enlighten you.'

Otis's whole body trembled.

'After you tattooed my face, I went home and stared in the mirror. Then, using a knife very similar to the one in my hand, I cut off most of my face to get rid of the tattoo that you had put on me.'

Otis let out a shrill cry when he realised Luke's intent. The clown whooped and clapped his hands together. Neither Luke nor Otis paid him any attention.

'Do you see where I'm going with this, Otis?' Luke said, the smile back on his face.

Chapter 119

Otis nodded, making little whimpering noises in his throat.

Laughing, Luke moved in. Otis tried to crawl away, but his shattered legs were useless.

The raw stump on his arm blazed with agony when he used it to try to drag himself away. He let out a forlorn cry as Luke sat on his chest.

Luke savoured the panicked look on Otis's face as he brought the knife closer with agonising slowness.

Alfred watched with an immense grin. It felt like all of his birthdays had come at once.

Luke took another few seconds to enjoy his enemy's anguish, then he brought the knife down to Otis's right temple.

'I started up here,' Luke said, pressing the blade hard against Otis's face so that a bead of blood snuck out of the wound.

Otis let out a cry. Then Luke traced a path round Otis's eye in the same way he had his own.

Otis screamed, his stump flapping towards his face in an attempt to hold the wound.

Luke moved the knife slowly, wanting Otis to feel every millimetre of the blade's progress.

After what seemed like an eternity to Otis, Luke had taken the blade in a full circle of Otis's right eye. 'Then I grabbed the skin and tore it off,' Luke said, his hands taking hold of the loose, blood-slicked skin at Otis's temple.

He paused for a second, to let Otis aware of what was going to happen, then he tore it loose. Part of it got stuck, so he stabbed the knife in and worked the skin free.

Otis screamed and writhed beneath Luke. Blood coursed down his face.

The clown watched, open-mouthed.

Luke held him down for a minute, letting the pain fully sink in.

'Please, just fucking kill me!' Otis screamed.

Luke laughed. The death mask around his real mouth moved out of sync with the noise of the laughter, creating a deeply disturbing sight for Otis. Luke's eyes looked dead. The blood-spattered mask was a vision of hell.

'This is the last face you will ever see,' Luke told him, again the mouths of mask and face not quite in unison, further adding to the nightmarish scene in which Otis found himself.

Luke looked blankly into Otis's eyes, feeling no remorse, no pity, only hate.

Without warning, he thrust the blade through Otis's left cheek. A jet of blood sprayed into Luke's face.

He laughed insanely as Otis convulsed in agony, his screams echoing around the grounds of the house.

'I then sawed through my cheek and cut off the smile that you had put on me,' Luke said.

Otis screamed as the knife continued its path down towards his mouth.

Each inch of its progress sent more blood spewing from the wound. The thick gore flooded into Otis's mouth and nose, choking him with his own life fluid. He tried to scream but it came out in a liquid gurgle.

'Are we having fun yet, Otis?' Luke laughed.

Otis tried to beg for his life but the blood filling his mouth and throat strangled his cry.

Otis faded in and out of consciousness for the next few minutes, screaming and flailing when he was awake. Blood pumped from the wounds in his face.

He came round for the last time, his bulging, terrified eyes staring up at Luke who had just finished tearing away the left side of his cheek and his upper lip. The pain barely registered now.

'It's looking good, Otis,' he said, then started laughing again.

Otis let out a weak cry that sent more blood bubbling out of his mouth and nose.

The maniacal laughter echoed around Otis's head. Though his eyes were now too weak to stay open, in his mind's eye he could still 'see' the mask moving out of time with Luke's mouth. It was his final, terrified thought.

'I said it's looking good, Otis,' Luke said.

Otis did not reply this time: the last of his blood had drained onto the paving stones.

Luke neither noticed, nor cared.

He laughed and gripped Otis's head with his free hand. With his other hand, he continued his reconstruction of Otis's face.

When he'd recreated his own facial wounds on Otis, he stared, entranced, at the body.

When he came out of his trance he noticed that the clown had gone back into the house. He sawed Otis's head off his neck, wrapped the body and dumped it in the pool.

Johnny T's answer phone tape was full of Otis's misery and terror.

Luke was going to make sure that the gang leader heard every second of it.

Chapter 120

Luke woke to find it was four am and still dark.

He went up to Peth Vale, leaving the bag containing Otis's head in his car, and knocked on the clown's door.

Alfred took an eternity to answer and seemed less than impressed at being woken.

'I'll do this one,' he muttered. 'But after that I gotta get some fucking sleep.'

They drove around until they located the houses of Johnny T and Tommy, the two remaining members of the Marshton Eight.

Choosing to visit Johnny T first, Luke looked the house up and down, then unzipped the sports bag and looked at Otis's severed head. He had been an ugly motherfucker – lucky that Luke had killed him, to be honest.

'What's the plan here?' Alfred asked.

Luke pointed to the open skylight on Johnny T's roof. 'I'll climb up on the flat roof near the bathroom and get up to the skylight and open the door for you.'

'Thank fuck for that. The flat roof'd be a piece of piss but I'd never have got up on that roof.'

'Just keep an eye out in case there are more of them.'

Leaving the sports bag hidden in the back yard, Luke carefully climbed up the wall and onto the flat roof, which he used to climb up the cast iron drain-work to get onto the roof.

He inched his way across the wet tiles, trying to be as quiet but as fast as he could – he was easy to spot up here. He tugged at the skylight, smiling to himself as it lifted, then carefully climbed in.

Chapter 121

He looked around Johnny T's house, allowing his eyes time to adjust to the darkness.

There were three doors on the upstairs landing. One was clearly the bathroom as it had a lock on it. One door was open. Luke crept to it and peered inside. It looked like some kind of office; there were files on the shelves and many metal filing cabinets.

Luke silently slid open one of the drawers. Inside were hundreds of small bags containing fragrant green herbs.

So, it seemed Johnny T was dealing drugs.

Luke smiled, reckoning he could use this to his advantage. He looked through all of the drawers, finding a set of electronic scales and a wide range of drugs, all packaged up and ready to sell.

One drawer in particular caught his eye. There were a few small vials – they looked like the tubes that the doctor used for urine samples – which were labelled 'Special K' and contained a clear liquid.

Luke knew that this was ketamine and reckoned this could be of use to him.

A small key hung on a nail above the cabinet. This unlocked the next row of cabinets. In the second drawer down he found some hypodermic needles. He unwrapped one and filled it up with the drug.

He crept along the passageway to the third door and slowly turned the handle. The door creaked as he opened it.

Luke silently cursed and ducked back behind the wall. He waited, his heart almost pumping out of his chest, then looked through the doorway.

Johnny T slept on while Luke made his way across the darkened room. He was halfway across the room when a floorboard creaked.

Johnny T stirred and turned towards the doorway.

With a feeling of dread coming over him, Luke realised that he had been spotted.

Johnny T sat up in bed, grabbing a flick knife off his bed-side table. While he fumbled the knife open, Luke dived at him and punched him in the face.

Before Johnny T could react, Luke twisted the knife out of his hand and stabbed the needle into his neck. His thumb pushed the plunger down.

Johnny T struggled wildly, hitting Luke in the face and driving him back. The blow made Luke angry and he slugged Johnny who threw up his hands in defence, then suddenly stopped.

The drug had taken effect quicker than Luke had expected. Luke refilled the syringe and injected Johnny T with another two doses – he was a big man and Luke wanted to make sure he had drugged him sufficiently.

The effect of the Ketamine left Johnny T frozen on the bed.

Luke searched downstairs and found the answer phone, still unplugged. He brought it upstairs and plugged it in. The device beeped and declared that there were fifteen new messages.

Luke turned the volume on the machine to full and pressed 'Play.'

Otis's final moments of misery echoed around the room.

Johnny T lay, conscious but paralysed, forced to endure every scream, every tear, every ragged, agonised breath of his friend's torment. The colour drained out of his face.

Luke went downstairs, leaving Johnny T to his recorded symphony of screams. He found a key to the front door, unlocked it and beckoned Alfred in.

He took Otis's head out of the bag and brought it inside as a surprise for Johnny T.

They both laughed at the thought of the gang leader finding the mutilated head – especially after he had endured the tape containing his friend's torture.

They waited in the front room until Johnny T could move again.

Chapter 122

When the paralysing effects of the Ketamine wore off, Johnny T, traumatised by the tape of Otis's suffering, dragged himself off the bed. His eyes were wide and staring, his legs tingling as the feeling flooded back into them.

Now that the answer phone tape had finished, he could hear the TV downstairs.

Instinct told him that he needed to get the shotgun from behind the settee in the front room and get the fuck out of the house, in case the guy with the dead face came back.

His skin crawling, he moved downstairs. The TV gradually grew in volume as he neared the front room.

Fear raked icy fingers down his spine when he saw Luke sat on the settee, swigging a beer and watching TV.

'Come in, sit down, let's discuss the tape,' he said, without looking round. It sounded to Johnny T like he was smiling.

As Johnny T moved into the doorway to the front room, he saw Otis's mutilated head sat next to Luke on the settee. He recoiled in horror at the gruesome sight.

'You should see your face,' Luke laughed.

Johnny T's eyes darted to the gun. Luke leapt to his feet and saw the shotgun leaning against the wall behind the settee.

As Johnny T lunged for the gun, Luke kicked him savagely, his shin connecting with the gang leader's face in a typical Thai boxing roundhouse kick.

The impact knocked Johnny T off his feet, but he got up almost as fast as he had fallen and punched Luke hard in the face, sending him reeling back.

Johnny T grabbed the shotgun and ran to the front door. Heaved it open.

In front of him was a big, blood-spattered clown smoking a cigarette. A huge black grin was painted on his face. He gurgled laughter like a broken drain and moved towards the terrified Johnny T.

Johnny slammed the door shut, knocking the clown back with the force of the slam, and ran upstairs, terrified.

Luke spat blood onto the carpet and chased him, furious at himself for not seeing the gun until it was almost too late.

It was lucky Johnny T wasn't thinking straight, or he would've pulled the trigger and taken out him and the clown.

Luke kicked the bathroom door, splintering the lock away from the frame.

The door bounced back as it hit the makeshift barricade that Johnny T had created.

Johnny T let out a cry of terror and continued digging around behind the bath panel for the box of shotgun shells that he had hidden there. He cursed, realising he was shit out of luck as he saw that there were only two shells remaining. If only he and Otis hadn't wasted them shooting at squirrels down the park last weekend.

He swung the bathroom window open and ducked under it. The door behind him again brayed against the cabinet he had used to brace the doorway.

As he moved out of the bathroom, he saw the grinning clown running across the flat roof towards the open window. A blood-stained cleaver glinted in his hand. He let out a maniacal laugh as he saw Johnny T.

Johnny T was too scared to even pull the trigger. He stood for a second, too terrified to move, as the clown raced towards him.

Chapter 123

Whimpering with fear, Johnny T hauled himself back through the window, landing in a heap on the bathroom floor.

The door slammed against the cabinet again, making him scream.

'Hey, Johnny,' Luke laughed. 'We're gonna cut your fucking face off like we did to Otis.'

Johnny T whimpered again. He managed to slam the window shut just as the clown reached it.

The clown's face appeared at the window, his black grin contorted and enlarged by the frosted glass. He let out a high cackle that chilled Johnny T's blood.

The clown's fists slammed against the window, leaving slick trails of blood down the glass.

Johnny T wanted to curl up and die. He knew he had two shells, one chance to take out each of the leering madmen who were intent on slaying him. He snacked the shotgun and aimed it at the window.

The clown loomed large, filling the whole window. Johnny T smiled, reckoning it was damn near impossible to miss.

The shotgun discharged, shattering the glass and letting the cold night air flood in.

'Have that, ya fucker,' Johnny T roared, his sense of triumph momentarily taking over his blind terror.

The door shoved open behind him. Johnny T screamed at the sight of Luke's sinister death mask. Up close, it was even more disturbing than he had thought.

Johnny T turned from the horrid apparition forcing its way through the open door and ran to the window.

The clown couldn't possibly have survived a blast at such close range. He peered out of the window and almost jumped out of his skin when the clown popped up in front of him.

'Missed me,' he laughed.

Johnny T ducked back inside the bathroom.

Luke was almost through the door.

The clown was most of the way through the window.

Johnny T had only one shell and after that he had to fight off one or both of the hellish freaks unarmed.

Deep down, he knew he'd never survive. He'd heard every second of what they had done to Otis and wanted no part in that. No, better to go out quick and painless. He tripped back over the edge of the bath as he stepped away from the clown.

'Fuck you both,' he screamed, jamming the barrel of the shotgun into his mouth.

Chapter 124

Luke saw his intent and cried out in frustration. He wanted Johnny T to suffer. This was far too painless for him.

The roar of the shotgun filled the tiny bathroom then the top of Johnny T's head hit the ceiling in a raging torrent of blood and chunks of brain and skull. The blood pissed out of the remains of his head. His eyes glazed over instantly, then he slumped back, spilling blood down behind him into the bath.

'Well, you can't win 'em all,' Alfred said. 'But still, that was pretty fucking impressive.'

Luke glowered – he'd wanted the pleasure of cutting Johnny T up and feeding him the pieces – but he couldn't help but appreciate the gore that dripped down from the ceiling and the seemingly never-ending crimson deluge that gushed from Johnny T's shattered skull.

'We'd best get out of here,' Alfred said. 'They'll have heard those gunshots for miles around.'

Luke nodded, but his eyes were fixed to the river of red that flooded into the bath and swirled down the plughole.

Alfred climbed out of the window and disappeared across the roof.

Luke watched for a few seconds more, relishing the bloody gaping hole in his enemy's skull, then he turned and ran downstairs.

He left Johnny T's corpse in the bath. There was only Tommy left from the Marshton Eight. The chances of him getting caught now were slim.

Chapter 125

Louie's eyes were dazzled by the sudden brightness. He had lost track of the amount of time he had spent trapped in the darkness in the boot of Hirst's car.

Blinking his eyes, he tried to adjust them to the glare. When he managed to focus, Hirst was standing over him.

'I think your friend Johnny T has finally got what was coming to him,' Hirst said. 'There was a call to the emergency services to say that gunshots were fired at his address.'

Louie groaned beneath his gag.

'It's ok, Louie, this is almost over with. It's nearly time for you to play your part.'

Hirst slammed the boot shut on Louie and picked up his radio.

'I am proceeding to the address. Do not send anyone in, I shall handle this alone.'

He got in his car, pressed the button to open his garage door and drove to Johnny T's address.

Chapter 126

Tommy watched the masked man who had killed most of his friends leave Johnny T's house.

He knew that Johnny T was dead. Had heard the struggles and screams and gunshots.

A very small part of him had wanted to charge the killer and make him regret killing seven of the infamous Marshton Eight.

But Tommy's mother didn't raise no fool.

He knew self-preservation was the best way forward. So he hid in Johnny T's back yard, round the side of the house. From this position he had not seen the clown running along the roof.

The lunatic who had butchered his friends walked right by him, seemingly in a trance.

He didn't notice Tommy, which was good, as even with the advantage of surprise Tommy doubted he could have moved to fight the killer.

Tommy couldn't make out the features very well, but the killer's face looked wrong. Kinda dead.

He remembered Otis's words. *Looked like a fucking zombie.* Shuddered. They'd all laughed at Otis and now he was dead, mutilated, just like the rest of the gang.

Well, not Tommy.

He still hadn't decided on a course of action, but he knew he'd either pluck up the courage to kill Luke, or he'd flee Marshton and never return.

One way or the other, he'd end this.

He flinched as the psychopath glanced over his shoulder, seeming to stare right at him. Tommy shrank back, willing himself to disappear into the wall on which he leant.

After a long couple of seconds (and at least ten heartbeats) Tommy watched the masked man turn away and leave the yard.

Tommy held his breath, fearing his sigh of relief was going to be loud enough to wake the dead.

He decided to follow Luke and think about his plan of action on the way.

As Tommy left the sanctuary of the shadows, he heard footsteps in the alley.

He flinched and ducked back into the gloom, certain that the killer was coming back for him.

Chapter 127

Hirst reversed his car into the back alley outside Johnny T's and dragged Louie out of the boot. He undid the handcuffs around Louie's legs and marched him into the house.

It didn't take him long to find Johnny T's body still bleeding in the bath tub.

'You're going to get the blame for that,' he said, uncuffing Louie's hands. 'Grab hold of that gun. I want your prints on it.'

Louie hesitated but the cold hard tip of Hirst's gun jabbed him in the back and stirred him to action.

He grabbed the shotgun cautiously, as if it was red hot to the touch. The clammy warm feel of his friend's blood made his stomach churn.

'Good lad, I might let you live after all,' Hirst smiled.

He called the station on his radio. 'I have apprehended a suspect at Johnny Taylor's house. He was in the act of removing evidence from the scene after he'd blown Johnny's head off with a shotgun. He was trying to make it look like a suicide. I'm bringing him in for questioning.'

'I would say I'm sorry for this, but I'm not going to lie,' Hirst said, shooting Louie in the knee, sending splatters of blood flying onto the wall and the floor.

Louie screamed and collapsed to the floor, holding his bleeding knee.

'Any shit from you and your head will look like Johnny T's,' Hirst said. 'Now get up. I'm taking you in.'

Nodding to show his understanding, Louie inhaled short, panicked breaths as he struggled to his feet.

Hirst cuffed him again and hauled him out to the car. He radioed ahead, to say that he had deemed it necessary to shoot Louie, as he was resisting arrest.

After a brief second of thought, he added that Louie had managed to escape and bundled him back into the boot.

Chapter 128

It hadn't been the killer, Tommy was pleased to note. It was Louie, along with the cop who they had thought was killing their gang.

So the bastard had captured Louie before he could complete the kill.

The cop was probably letting the killer get away with murdering them, some twisted streak in him getting revenge for the crippling of his son.

Again, self-preservation triumphed over morality. He'd remained hidden in the shadows until the cop left with Louie, flinching at the gunshot which tore through the still night.

His mind reeling, he took deep breaths of the cold night air and tried to figure out his next move.

Chapter 129

Luke had left the house, still savouring the memory of Johnny T's gushing blood, and went home.

He sat on his bed, staring at Bryony's head, wondering if he had made the right decision. Soon he knew that he had.

The room was starting to smell as Bryony's body decayed. Luke found the scent intoxicating.

He crawled into bed, enjoying the feel of the dried blood on his skin, and went to sleep.

That night he had an extremely vivid dream about Bryony. She appeared as an angel in a beautiful black dress.

He woke with a start, still seeing her floating above his bed, her pale wings appearing bleached in comparison to the darkness of the room and the dress she wore. She told him that she couldn't wait any longer for him to finish his killing spree.

'One more day,' he screamed. 'Just one more day.' The phrase echoed around in his mind for what seemed like forever.

He fell into a fitful sleep.

Chapter 130

Tommy had been there when the gang had put Bryony's windows through, so he knew where their killer lived.

He didn't want to break in – as that had been Otis's forte, and also he knew it was not wise to face the killer on his home turf.

Instead, he waited outside the house for Luke to leave. He was cold, terrified, and on the verge of giving up and going home when Luke finally left the house.

He tailed Luke, giving him a good head start. With dread, he realised that they were heading to Peth Vale. He knew never to go there, had heard the stories from when he was a kid.

Only someone with a death wish would go there.

Or perhaps a masked psychopath taking out anyone who had ever screwed him over.

Tommy waited in the dying bushes at the side of the house, not daring to set foot in the grounds of the notorious Murder House.

He started as the gates creaked open. The noise was like the tines of a fork being scraped across a plate and made him want to cover his ears, but he was loath to move and risk making a sound.

The masked man fully opened the gates and got into the car, taking a cursory glance around him.

Tommy got a quick view of the sinister mask he wore, but thankfully the car's courtesy light went out after a second, hiding the obscenity from him.

The car pulled away.

Tommy decided to wait. If the gates were open, that probably meant the killer was coming back. Besides, he could hardly follow the car on foot, could he?

Chapter 131

Roughly ten minutes later, Tommy watched the car pull into the grounds of the nightmare house again. He felt a twinge of fear, heightened by the sound of the gates slamming shut.

Luke seemed to be carrying a bundle of rags. Judging by the shape of the bundle and the way it was being carried, the rags contained a body. By the way Luke moved, Tommy could tell it was someone dear to him, a friend, or possibly a lover.

He watched Luke go up to the house and decided to leave.

No way was he setting foot in the grounds of the Murder House.

Fuck that.

Chapter 132

Luke knocked on the door. Alfred answered, looking pleased to see him until he saw the blood-soaked, body-shaped burden that Luke held in his arms.

'My girl,' Luke explained.

Alfred didn't want to know. The kid was seriously fucked up.

The sooner they killed the last one of the asshole gang the better. He'd happily claim the pretty blonde girl and leave town, go somewhere the crazy freak couldn't find him.

Luke moved past Alfred and laid Bryony's body on the bed in Peth Vale's main bedroom.

The sun was just starting to peek out from behind the clouds. He would wait with her remains until dark then head to the house of Tommy, his last tormentor.

While he waited, he and Alfred discussed their plan.

Chapter 133

Tommy knew that Luke would come for him, but he was forewarned.

He'd be ready.

A few phone calls later, Tommy's backup was arranged. A few of the Marshton Eight's hangers-on were up to sorting out the problem.

Maybe Tommy would let them join the gang, rebuild with him as leader.

Yeah, that'd be good.

Don't jump the gun, his mind warned him. *This guy will bury you if he gets chance.*

There was no room for error.

He knew Luke would make a home visit to take him out and hoped he'd be tired and careless, given that after Tommy his rampage would be done.

The three lads he'd called – Charlie, Ivan and Stan – were all tough lads. He knew they'd put up a good fight. They were due any minute.

Chapter 134

Hirst also knew that Luke would be visiting Tommy to complete his slaying of the Marshton Eight.

He was parked across the street, hunched low in his seat, watching Tommy's house. He figured Luke would show up when darkness descended upon the town.

A car pulled up a few hundred yards in front of him, its headlights low to draw as little attention as possible.

He recognised the driver as Charlie, a known associate of the Marshton Eight, who Hirst had personally put away on more than one occasion. So Tommy was getting backup, was he?

Naughty, naughty.

'Time for a reunion,' Hirst muttered, getting out of the car.

His hand ready on the butt of his gun, he sauntered over to Charlie's car. Charlie groaned as he spotted the man who had put him behind bars.

'Well, my old friend,' Hirst smiled. 'How are we tonight?'

Charlie said nothing.

'We ain't done nothing wrong, cop,' said Stan, Charlie's accomplice.

'Really?' Hirst beamed. 'Then I suppose you've had your license re-instated, Charlie?'

Charlie grimaced.

'And I'm assuming you've got insurance for this bucket of shit?'

Charlie said nothing.

'What are you doing here?' Hirst said.

'Helping Tommy,' Stan piped up.

'Shut up, Stan,' Charlie spat.

Hirst nodded. Just as he'd thought. 'Well, I'm willing to overlook the fact that you're driving without a license and insurance. And I'll even turn a blind eye to the baseball bat and kitchen knife in the floor well there, if you piss off out of here and don't come back.'

'We can't let Tommy down,' Stan said.

Charlie looked up at Hirst's unflinching gaze. Nodded.

'Good lad,' Hirst said. 'You don't want another five years inside, do you? Just get this heap of rust out of here.'

Charlie put the car in gear.

'What are you doing?' Stan asked, incredulous.

'I ain't going back inside,' Charlie said. 'Not even for Tommy.'

'There's a good lad,' Hirst beamed.

Stan opened his door.

'Get back in the car or I'll do you for carrying an offensive weapon,' Hirst said.

Stan stared at him for a second then looked away. He shut the door and settled back in his seat. His eyes locked on the dash, not wanting to look at Hirst again.

'Now, get out of here,' Hirst said.

Charlie pulled away.

Hirst smiled and rubbed his hands together. 'Come on, Luke. Where are you?'

Chapter 135

Luke and Alfred had watched Hirst chase away the hired hands that Tommy had called.

Alfred said he'd follow Charlie's car for a while, to make sure they were leaving town.

Luke nodded at the plan. He couldn't think straight, so eager was he to get his hands on Tommy and finish the final member of the Marshton Eight.

'I'll see you back at Peth Vale if I miss you here,' Luke said.

'Yeah, don't kill him without me this time.'

Luke nodded but he didn't hear what the clown had said.

Alfred hung back a few hundred yards, so they didn't realise he was following them, although he doubted they would notice if he crashed into them – they both seemed as thick as pigshit. He followed as the car made its way towards the edge of town.

Chapter 136

The nerves were getting to Hirst.

Cursing his nervous bladder, he got out of the car to relieve it in the untended garden across the road from Tommy's place. The thick bushes hid his view of the house.

While Hirst was emptying his bladder, Ivan showed up. Ivan was middle of the three guys Tommy had called – tougher than Stan, but softer than Charlie. He was armed with a lump of scrap metal and a jagged broken bottle.

'Let's sort this fucker out,' he grinned as Tommy opened the door.

'No sign of the other two yet,' Tommy said.

'They'll turn up, probably just scoring one last line of gear.'

'Aye.' Tommy tried a laugh, but he was too nervous.

It died in his throat.

Chapter 137

Hirst got back in the car and resumed his watch on Tommy's house.

He was sure he saw an extra body in Tommy's front room, but he was certain Luke could handle two. Still, he'd wait and see if Charlie came back for more.

Luke stretched away his sleepless night, then strolled onto Tommy's street.

He looked around, noticing Hirst sitting in his car. He nodded a greeting to the policeman – who shuddered at the brief glance he had of the grisly face beneath Luke's hood – then he started slashing the tyres of the cars in the street.

Stopping them from running, Hirst thought with a smile.

Luke knocked on Tommy's door, his foot tapping an excited beat on the floor.

Tommy answered with a sleepy look on his face. Luke grabbed him and pushed him back through the door.

'Remember me? I've come back for you, like I did with all of your friends,' Luke shouted in Tommy's face.

'Whatever happened, it was nothing to do with me,' Tommy pleaded.

'You kicked me in the head while I was on the floor. You waited till I was down, you fucking worm.'

Tommy's hand fumbled in his pocket.

Luke saw a flash of light, then felt a sharp pain as the knife slashed across his face. Bryony's skin tore, so Luke peeled it back.

'Remember me now, you fucking coward? Remember me now?' Luke's rage-contorted face screamed, visible through the split in the death-mask.

Luke didn't wait for an answer; he smashed a head butt into Tommy's face.

Tommy shrank away from him, minus two splintered teeth. His broken nose oozed blood and snot.

Luke advanced, fists clenched, his true face showing from beneath Bryony's lifeless features. His face was a blood-soaked vision of insanity. His eyes looked dead as they stared out from behind the mask.

Tommy was scared for his life; this madman was like something out of a violent, death-filled nightmare.

He was doubtful he and Ivan would survive. What the hell had he been thinking? He should have just run.

He clutched the knife to his chest, then swung it at Luke.

As Tommy slashed at him, Luke thrust his knife, sticking it through Tommy's forearm. He twisted it, so the blade wedged against the bone, then pulled it free.

Tommy screamed and dropped his knife.

Luke caught movement out of the corner of his eye and turned to see a man flailing a metal bar at him.

He moved enough to make it hit his shoulder instead of his head. Pain flared in his shoulder, making his hand tingle.

The lad was still off balance, so Luke kicked him in the back of the legs, sweeping his feet from under him. He landed hard, making the pictures on the walls vibrate.

Tommy scrabbled to his feet, clutching his bleeding arm. He saw Luke climb onto Ivan's chest and start pummelling him. Heard the crack as the first blow broke something in Ivan's face.

Ivan spat blood and swung a punch back at Luke. It landed hard, but Luke ignored it. Tommy ran to the door, kicking Luke in the back as he passed.

'No, man, don't run,' Ivan cried. 'We can beat him if there are two of us.' He screamed as Luke stuck Tommy's knife through his wrist, pinning him to the floor.

Tommy was struggling with the front door, in his state of terror unaware that it had locked itself after slamming shut. He pulled it hard, but to no avail.

Luke was starting to get up from on top of Ivan.

He stared at Tommy, a grin visible beneath the torn features of his mask. Then he slammed the knife into Ivan's gut and pulled it across. Steaming loops of intestine flopped out amid a stream of blood.

Tommy ran past Luke, now not daring to even try to attack him. He headed upstairs.

Luke slashed the knife at him. It missed, but a spray of gore from the blade hit him in the face. The feel of the blood on his skin sickened him. He let out a cry of dismay as he hurried to wipe it off his face with his sleeve.

Luke finished his disembowelling of Ivan and followed Tommy upstairs. Ivan twitched, his blood spreading around him on the laminate flooring.

Chapter 138

Tommy heard Luke pursuing him up the stairs. Every footstep slammed into his head like a punch.

He struggled to think.

There were no weapons upstairs.

He had to get out.

The door to his bedroom slammed. He pushed his bed in front of it, but he knew that it would take the furious Luke a matter of minutes to get in.

The impact made the bed move back a few inches. He let out a cry and looked around, seeing the window. It was a ten-foot drop, but better that than risk being caught by the masked psychopath.

The door slammed again, cracks appearing in the wood.

Covering his face, he ran at the window.

He seemed to fall for an age, then he landed with a thud on the floor.

One of his legs was hurt, and he was hugely grateful it wasn't broken. It felt like the king of all dead legs, but he hauled himself to his feet, knowing that if he could get into one of the cars on the street he could get away.

Chapter 139

Luke had heard the breaking glass and knew what it meant. He shoved aside the splintered remains of the door and rushed to the window.

Below him, he saw Tommy struggling to his feet and shuffling towards one of the cars. He smiled at his foresight to slash the tyres of most of the cars on the street.

Tommy smashed the window of his car, then cursed as he looked down to see the ragged wound in the tyre.

He rushed to the next car.

Tyres slashed here, too.

Ditto the next car.

Terror overwhelmed him as he realised that the killer had disabled all of the cars.

He couldn't drive away.

Couldn't run.

He was fucked.

With a grin, he remembered Ivan's car. His friend had just turned up, so it'd be unlikely to be damaged. It was just a case of finding it now.

Shuffling into the back alley, he saw the gleaming crimson paintwork of Ivan's car at the far end. A grin lit his face. There was no sign of the killer.

He was home free.

He got to within three feet of the car before he saw a shadow detach itself from the wall.

Shit, it's him!

Chapter 140

Tommy's legs felt numb, but he turned and tried to run.

Luke caught him with a punch that splattered his nose across his face.

He let out a wet sob. *He's going to kill me if I don't do anything,* he thought. The idea made him charge at Luke, catching him with a hard head-butt to the gut.

They flew backwards, Luke landing on his back, stunned by the impact. Tommy slammed punch after punch into Luke's face, determined that he wasn't going to die without a fight.

Luke laughed as he took the punches. Blood streaked down his face. He spat it up at Tommy.

'That the best you got, Tommy?' he mocked.

Tommy slammed a few more punches into his face and got up to run. Luke swung his leg round, catching Tommy's legs even though he jumped to avoid the collision.

The jump only served to give him further to fall. He fell at an awkward angle, catching his head on the side of the car.

Luke got up, spitting blood into Tommy's face. 'You're in for it now,' he laughed.

Tommy lay on his side and groaned.

Luke rolled Tommy onto his back then sat on his chest, raining blows onto his head.

Tommy instinctively threw his arms up to protect his head, but Luke stuck a finger into the wound in his forearm and used this to move his arms out of the way while he landed a few hard punches.

Tommy floundered as the powerful blows took their toll on him. Luke pulled the knife and stabbed it through Tommy's knee.

He laughed as yet another 'Hard man' turned into a gibbering wreck.

Tommy pleaded for his life, his voice ragged and choked with tears.

Luke pulled the knife free, stood up and stomped on Tommy's ribs. As Tommy bent double, Luke slammed his foot into his face, making him slump back to the floor.

Luke dragged him to the rear of the car, leaving twin trails of blood from his punctured forearm and knee.

He went inside for Ivan's car keys then picked up Tommy's limp body and dropped it into the boot.

Chapter 141

Once inside Peth Vale's grounds, he lifted Tommy out of the boot and dragged him along the flagstone floor to the poolside.

Tommy cried out when he saw Otis's rotting, fingerless hand on the corner of the patio.

'What is this place? It looks like an abattoir,' Tommy sobbed.

'This is the final resting place of most of your gang,' Luke snarled. 'When I first came here, the pool was just covered in scum. Now it's filled with it too.'

Tommy looked at him in disbelief.

Luke walked over to the pool and dangled a spade in the water until it snagged a rope on one of the tarpaulins.

He bent his legs then stood up forcefully, pulling the spade up to lift the tarpaulin out of the water. He set it down on the side of the pool and cut the rope with his knife.

Inside the tarpaulin were Scotty's decaying remains. He dragged the body over to Tommy, who screamed when he saw it.

'See?' Luke said. 'All of them are in there. Except Johnny T. He's still in the bath where he blew his own head off. Oh, and Dave. He got burnt to cinders at Otis's house. Your gang will soon be re-united in hell.'

'You don't have to do this. I'll give you anything you want. Money? Drugs?'

Luke shook his head sadly. 'None of that matters. The only thing that matters is that you die.'

Chapter 142

He then stood over Tommy and beat him frenziedly until he stopped defending himself and lay, sobbing, on the blood-soaked floor.

Luke stood back, then kicked him hard a couple of times. Tommy visibly stiffened every time Luke struck him.

'You can die right now,' Luke said. 'But you have to do it yourself.'

Tommy tried to crawl away.

Luke followed him and stamped on his injured knee.

'OK,' Tommy cried, 'I'll do it. I've had enough.'

Luke took one of the chairs out of the house and stood it under a thick branch of one of the trees in the garden.

He tied the rope around the branch and fashioned the other end into a crude noose.

Dragged Tommy over to the tree and lifted him onto the chair.

'End it now,' he told Tommy. 'End your own suffering.'

Tommy hesitated for a second, then put his head in the noose. His breathing laboured as Luke tightened the rope.

'Now look me in the eye and kick the chair over.'

Tommy broke down, tears pouring down his bleeding face.

'Please,' Tommy pleaded, his voice wheezing. 'It doesn't have to be like this.'

'You were all dead the moment the first one of you laid a finger on me. Make it easy on yourself.'

Tommy closed his eyes, trying to summon the courage to kick the chair over.

Luke became sick of waiting, cut the rope and dragged him down from the chair, throwing the loop of rope into the grass.

'Since you don't have the guts, I'm going to have to hurt you some more.'

Chapter 143

Luke dragged Tommy to the patio and drew his knife.

As the blade sunk into his side, Tommy recoiled in agony, blood gushing from his open mouth.

'Kneel,' Luke said.

He grabbed hold of Tommy's head and held it tight then stuck the blade into his left eye. A thick black jelly oozed out of the wound.

Tommy fell facefirst into the pool, his scream muffled by the filthy water.

Beneath the mask, Luke grinned as he beheld Tommy's suffering.

'Kneel and look at me,' Luke said.

Lifting his head from the water, Tommy writhed in agony, his bleeding eye leaving thick smears of gore on the dirty white tiles on the edge of the pool.

'I said fucking look at me,' Luke said.

Tommy saw the way he was thrusting the knife at him and took heed.

'I'm enjoying this,' he told Tommy. 'Are you?'

Tommy shook his head, whimpering. Terror had drained all the colour out of him, leaving him as pale as the tiles on which he knelt.

'I thought you were supposed to be hard?' Luke mocked him, grinning widely beneath the mask.

Tommy didn't get to reply. Luke, still laughing, ran the blade across his throat, opening a huge, gaping wound. Tommy's head lolled back on his neck.

He slumped forward into the pool, sending stagnant water flying through the still night air.

Luke watched as the blood gushing out of his slit throat gradually dyed the water red. He relished the sight of the blood spraying into the pool, slowly spreading in a crimson halo around Tommy's convulsing body.

'Well that was something special,' the clown's voice said from behind him. In his trance-like state Luke had not realised that he was even there. 'But I'm going to go in now. I'm fucking freezing. You coming?'

Luke shook his head, his eyes glued to the blood that still seeped out of the savage red smile in Tommy's throat.

When the bleeding stopped and the steam no longer rose from the pool, he exhaled hard, savouring the scene one last time.

Then he went inside.

It was almost time to finish the vile clown.

Chapter 144

Alfred had had plenty of time to think about his course of action and had decided he'd let the freak bring up the subject of the pretty blonde girl.

If she wasn't mentioned he'd not push it.

She was an absolute stunner, but he just wanted to be away from the freak.

As twisted as Alfred was, he couldn't cope with the extremity of Luke's psychosis.

The masked man brought up the subject, letting Alfred relax a little, though he remained wary of his strange acquaintance.

'I'm a man of my word,' Luke said. 'So I will bring you the blonde girl and the body of the bouncer's girl, like I promised.'

'Thanks, man. I appreciate it. It's been a blast.'

'Yeah.' The masked man moved awkwardly, as though something was on his mind.

'You ok?'

'Yeah, just trying to remember where the blonde bitch lives.'

Alfred nodded. He knew he was being lied to but didn't press it. All he cared about was getting the blonde girl and getting the hell out of here.

'I'll not be long,' Luke said.

Alfred nodded. 'Hey, let me have first go on her,' he smiled.

His attempt at lightening the mood failed. Luke stared at him blankly and turned away.

Chapter 145

Luke found Kate's house and put his fist through the window. The noise didn't carry far despite the silence of her sleeping street.

He hauled himself through the window, the knife cold against his belly.

Beneath Bryony's skin, he smiled.

This revenge was a long time coming. Kate and the clown were the two people who had caused the most misery in his life.

He had buried the gang and now the real fun could start.

Alfred wouldn't be prepared for his betrayal, indeed he sensed the clown's fear of him.

The fat bastard would be easy prey.

Luke's smile widened, making the sides of his mouth and eyes ache, further reminding him of the reason he was here.

Kate would be lucky to survive until the clown got hold of her.

He found her asleep on the settee. Her duvet was rucked up, revealing a perfect tanned thigh.

Tearing his eyes away from it, he pulled the knife from beneath the folds of Bryony's skin.

Her confused face stared up at him when he pressed the cold steel against her neck.

'Wha the?' she muttered.

'You probably don't remember me,' Luke began, speaking slowly as he figured out what to say. He'd fantasised about this day for years, but now it was here he found he was tongue tied.

Pulling the mask apart to reveal his blood-stained, scarred face, he said, 'I blame you for this. You lied to me, led me on. And they made me do this to myself.' His finger traced the thick bands of scar tissue around his eyes and mouth.

She gasped as she saw the damage that he had inflicted. 'But I thought you were dead,' she said.

He shook his head slowly. 'Sadly not.'

With that he lunged at her. His fingers clamped around her throat and squeezed.

Already, she felt herself weakening, felt the numbing darkness overwhelming her.

Then, mercifully, the fingers relinquished their grip. She wheezed in, the air like sandpaper on her throat.

Her relief faded when she realised that Luke was already binding her wrists with cable ties.

'We're finally going to the Murder House,' he said, smiling.

Then he slung her over his shoulder. He was strong, much stronger than she would have thought. She knew she'd be lucky to get out of this alive.

Chapter 146

In Peth Vale's dank basement, Luke laid Kate on the floor.

The concrete chilled her bare skin, but the trembling of her body was more from fear than the biting cold.

Her eyes moved from the clown to Luke and back again.

Somehow the clown was the least scary of the two.

Alfred eyed the prone girl, his eyes on stalks, his black painted grin seeming to stretch forever. The front of his pants bulged. Drool glistened on his grease-painted chin.

'There ya go,' Luke grinned.

Alfred nodded his thanks. He seemed wary of Luke, like he was waiting for something to happen.

'Well, it's been a fucking blast,' Luke smiled.

Alfred saw the ribbons of scar tissue around his mouth and hurriedly looked away.

Luke held his hand out. Alfred looked at it like it was a loaded gun, but took it anyway.

As he did so, Luke pulled him in hard. Light winked off the knife in Luke's left hand.

Alfred somehow managed to deflect the blow, which seemed as fast as a snake strike. The knife skidded down his right side, tearing a hole in his shirt.

Without thinking, he thrust his head at Luke, catching him unawares and bursting his nose. Blood poured down the back of his throat.

He didn't seem hurt, but the angle of the attack made it easy for Alfred to grab his knife hand and twist it.

Stunned, Luke let go of the knife. Alfred caught it as it slid down his side, and, moving with a speed he didn't know he had, thrust the blade at Luke's stomach. The knife sunk into his belly a few inches.

Luke bellowed with rage and thrust his fingers at the clown's eyes.

Alfred quickly slammed the rest of the blade in. His hand collided with the dead skin covering Luke's gut.

Luke fell back, blood already flowing from the wound and pouring through the ragged hole in Bryony's dead flesh onto the floor.

Kate watched all of this with wide eyes.

Luke cupped his hand to the wound and tried to stand.

The clown whistled. Luke watched the open cellar door.

Down the stairs came three figures. He recognised all of them.

Two were Stan and Charlie, the men that Hirst had turned away from Tommy's house.

The third was Dave.

Chapter 147

Through the split in Bryony's dead face, Alfred saw Luke's confused expression.

'You may be hard as nails with a psychotic temper,' he said. 'And you may be wearing one creepy-ass mask, but when I look in your eyes I still see that frightened kid I orphaned all those years ago.'

Luke gasped as he realised how much of his blood was pooling on the concrete floor.

'So, I took out a little insurance. Dave here was most appreciative of my revelation of who was killing his friends. And he and his mates are eager to make you suffer for what you did to the others.'

'You're all fucking dead,' Luke spat, blood-flecked spittle flying from his jaws.

Alfred shook his head, the painted grin widening ever further. 'Afraid not, my friend. These lads are going to bury you while I find a new place for me and the blonde girl to live. It's a shame I'm not going to see you die, but the memory of what I did to your sister will more than make up for it.'

Alfred moved in, heading for a thick chain which was connected to a metal ring on the wall.

Luke kicked out at him as he fastened the chain around his ankle.

Alfred grunted in pain as Luke's foot slammed his fingers up against the heavy metal chain. He sunk his foot into the damaged part of Luke's stomach, then, as Luke writhed in agony, quickly looped the chain through the ring and fastened a heavy padlock onto it.

Luke sat up, blood seeping through the fingers of the hand that clutched his stomach. He pulled forward, but the chain clanked and stopped his progress towards the clown.

Alfred tutted.

'Say hello to your sister for me,' the clown said, laughing. He turned to Dave, said, 'The money is in an envelope in the garage. Remember to burn the fucking place down when you're through with him. And make sure it hurts.'

Chapter 148

Dave nodded to the other two lads and they all stepped closer. Dave held a baseball bat. Charlie had a length of thick chain and Stan held a kitchen knife.

Luke staggered to his feet and lunged at the clown. Again the chain prevented his progress.

Stan moved in, but Luke's fist caught him flush on the jaw and separated him from consciousness.

Luke's other fist came round towards Charlie's face, but Dave intercepted with a swing of the baseball bat.

The bat shattered Luke's left cheek in a sickening wave of pain. One of Luke's teeth came out with a rush of blood.

His legs wobbled.

The metal chain clashed against the back of his head. It was more annoying than painful but he was still disoriented as a result of the blow from the bat.

In slow motion he saw the bat fly towards his head again. It caught him on the side of the neck and made him stumble.

He felt like he had just stepped off a waltzer.

His legs betrayed him, dropping him on the floor. He fought to get back to his feet, but his coordination was shot to shit and he stumbled and landed on his back.

Through his blurred vision he saw the clown waiting at the foot of the stairs, watching the proceedings with fascination. Kate was draped over his shoulder. He grinned as Dave moved towards Luke, the bloody baseball bat in his hands.

'Nice to see you again, freak,' Dave beamed.

Luke squirmed, but Charlie pinned him by planting a foot on his chest.

Dave raised the bat above his head. Luke tried to roll out from under Charlie's foot, but his energy was leaving his body with his blood.

The bat blotted out the light as it began its descent.

Chapter 149

A sudden roar flashed through Luke's ravaged ears. Through the haze of pain and adrenaline he failed to realise what it was until Dave pitched forwards, a growing red patch on the chest of his white hoody.

Dave hit the deck, already beginning his journey towards death.

The roaring sound came again and again. Charlie fell, a number of bleeding holes in his torso and legs.

Luke looked to the source of the sounds and saw Hirst at the bottom of the stairs, a gun in his hands, his face etched in a sickly grin.

He reloaded the gun in one smooth motion then fired another burst.

The clown fell, the back of his head a crater that vomited gore. His mouth poured with blood, adding crimson to the unsettling black grin painted onto his features. His eyes had already taken on the glaze that Luke recognised from his many victims.

Kate screamed, doubly taken aback by this fresh carnage. Being abducted by the masked man and taken to the clown was one thing, but seeing three men gunned down in vivid gory detail was quite another.

She curled up in a ball, her hands clamped to her ears, her eyes tightly closed.

Hirst ignored the terrified girl and ran to Luke.

'I've been watching out for you,' he said. 'So you could punish the bastards who ruined our lives.'

Luke nodded, his face contorted with the pain from his wounds.

'Who's the girl? Is she part of this?'

'The bitch who set me up.'

Hirst's face darkened. 'The one who caused all of this?'

Luke nodded.

Hirst moved over to her. She still sobbed, her face covered by her knees which she had drawn up to her chest. He pressed the gun barrel against the crown of her head.

'You caused all of this,' he said, his voice so quiet that Luke could barely hear it. The roar of the gun blast was deafening in contrast.

A huge bleeding hole appeared in her head. Luke marvelled at the sight of all the blood.

Hirst watched her bleed out, similarly captivated. Then, his face grave, he sighed and approached Luke.

'I'm so sorry to have to do this, Luke. I know you've been through hell. And I'm grateful for your part in bringing my son's attackers the justice they deserved. But I can't help feeling that you're to blame for all of this.'

Luke stared at him, incredulous.

'After all,' Hirst continued. 'If you hadn't been attacked by the gang, my son wouldn't have gotten involved and would never have been crippled. He'd still be alive if it wasn't for what happened that night.' He wiped a tear from his eye. 'I thought I could come to terms with your part in all of this, but I can't. I'm sorry. I can't.'

He pressed the barrel against Luke's temple. 'Please forgive me.' Luke tried to struggle, but the desertion of his blood had left him weak. Hirst's grip on him was too tight. He repeated, 'Please forgive me,' and pulled the trigger.

Chapter 150

The gun issued a dry click that seemed pathetic compared to the roar of the gunshot that both men were expecting.

While Hirst spent a moment figuring out what had happened, Luke gulped in air, desperately trying to summon the energy to defend himself.

'You know what,' Hirst said after an eternity. 'I'm glad the gun is empty. You don't deserve to die like that. You deserve to choose your own fate. You're probably bleeding to death and I'm going to burn this place to the ground just before I leave.' He handed Luke the gun and a single bullet and quickly demonstrated how to load the weapon. 'If you want to put yourself out of your misery, then go ahead. I won't have your blood on my hands.'

Hirst stood up, back-handing tears from his eyes, and made his way to the stairs.

There were a few cans of petrol in the corridor just above the stairs, supplies brought by the gang so they could obey Alfred's instructions.

He knew it wouldn't be long until the gunshots were reported so he ran through the house, slinging petrol around like a wedding guest going berserk with confetti.

He poured a good glug of it down the stairs into the basement, then lit it. The flames blossomed around him, casting everything in a hellish glow. The house was hell, no doubt about it. But he was on his way out.

He ran out of the house, hearing a solitary gunshot from the basement as he reached the car.

He said a brief prayer for Luke and, after pausing to admire the spectacular inferno for a second in his rear view mirror, pulled out of the grounds of the house.

Chapter 151

The police flooded into the grounds of Peth Vale, bringing our story full circle.

After extinguishing the blaze, the firemen went back into the house, finding more bodies in the basement. Though the corpses were charred and distorted, they were still recognisable.

Among the bodies, they found a gun, a shattered padlock and what looked like the skin of a female human being. The firemen blanched at the gruesome discovery.

In Hirst's absence, Brent was the officer in charge. He realised that the bodies in the pool were those of the Marshton Eight.

Remembering what had happened on the night that Luke's face had been tattooed, he identified Luke and Hirst as potential suspects. Either of them could have been responsible for the bloodbath.

He remembered that Hirst was the one who had broadcast the news of Luke Miller's death after the riot at the asylum and reasoned that his colleague must have been helping Luke, leading the police investigation away from him while he murdered the gang that had wronged the both of them.

He got into his car and raced to Hirst's place.

The house was in darkness, but he noticed an open window. Using his jacket sleeve to avoid getting his prints on the frame, he pried it open.

The house was quiet and had a deep, musty smell. He had an idea what the smell was, but didn't want to believe it.

A rustling sound came from upstairs, making him pull his gun.

He crept up the stairs, pleased that the floorboards didn't creak beneath his weight. The rustling continued.

At the top of the stairs, the smell intensified, becoming so strong that he gagged.

He moved cautiously into the room which had the open door.

A dim shape loomed out of the darkness.

He held his gun on it, waiting for it to move so he could send a round through its head.

The figure remained still.

'Show me your hands,' he commanded. The figure did not respond.

As he crept closer, he noticed that the figure was covered with a blood-soaked sheet.

He tore the sheet away to find himself staring at the rotting remains of Tom Hirst.

Chapter 152

Pieces of brain still clung to the kid's face, while streaks of dried crimson indicated where the blood had ran down from the bullet-hole in his skull.

After what seemed like forever he averted his eyes from the bloodied corpse and made his way down the corridor.

There was a closed door, from behind which the rustling sound was emanating. He turned the handle and inched the door open.

'You should never have set foot in here,' a voice said from inside the room.

His eyes not yet adjusted to the gloom, he jolted.

Sergeant Hirst was hurriedly shoving clothes into a suitcase that sat on the bed.

'Show me your hands, James,' Brent shouted, aiming the gun at his colleague's head.

'You know, you're partly to blame for all of this,' Hirst said as he turned to face Brent. 'If only you'd helped me when I asked for it, things may not have come to this.'

'What?'

'That fucking gang,' he spat. 'If you'd helped me to keep them off the streets then none of this would have happened. My son would still be a normal, happy teenager. And he'd still be alive.'

Brent didn't know what to say. He genuinely felt sorry for his colleague and friend, but he refused to accept responsibility for all of this.

He would not be blamed for the actions of psychopaths.

'I didn't kill all of them,' Hirst said. 'Luke took out the gang. I just made sure nothing got in his way. When it looked like they were going to kill him, I took them out. Then I killed him and the girl, because it's their fault this all happened.'

Brent was gobsmacked for a second. Hirst was right out of his fucking mind. 'James, we need to get you some help,' he began, trying to keep his tone sympathetic.

'No,' Hirst said, shaking his head vehemently. 'I ain't going to the nuthouse. You saw what they did to Luke in there. I ain't ending up like that.'

'You're already in need of help, James,' Brent said, taking proper note of his friend's dirty, dishevelled appearance for the first time.

'No, I've dealt with this the only way it could be dealt with. You can't lock up people like Johnny T and Dave. The only thing these fuckers understand is violence. You have to play them at their own game and take it further than they will.

Luke understood that. He was very astute that way.'

'Please, James, let me get you the help you need.'

Hirst paused as though he was thinking about his colleague's idea. In reality, he was edging his hand towards the gun that sat behind him on the bed.

Brent was occupied with Hirst's plight and hadn't noticed his hand sneaking behind his back.

'I don't need fucking help,' Hirst bellowed, his face taking on a beetroot colour.

Brent noticed the fact that Hirst's hand was behind him. 'I really don't want to shoot you, James,' he warned. 'But I will if you give me reason to believe you're going for a weapon.'

Hirst's eyes seemed to be staring into the corridor beyond him. Brent figured it was a trick to get him to turn away so that he could safely go for his gun.

A second later, Brent regretted his lack of awareness, as a blade plunged through his back, coming out of his stomach in a shower of blood.

The few inches of steel that poked through Brent's stomach glistened with dark blood.

The blade ripped up, opening Brent from navel to sternum. Blood and slick ropes of intestine cascaded down onto the carpet.

Brent pitched forward, his mouth moving silently as though protesting the unfairness of it all.

Chapter 153

Hirst was awestruck at the brutality of the murder he'd just witnessed.

He immediately thought of two people capable of such a bloodthirsty act and, to the best of his knowledge, both of them were dead.

He was further bewildered when a familiar, scarred face stepped into view.

'Shot the padlock off,' Luke explained, grinning.

Hirst was speechless.

'Before you put a hole in my head with the gun that you've got on the bed there, consider what I have to say. It's the least you can do after your spineless attempt at murdering me.'

Hirst blushed a little at this, despite his belief that Luke had been responsible for the state in which his son had ended up.

'Your son committed a heroic act trying to save me. Not many people would do that. And, in my opinion, he would be pissed off that he was damaged trying to save my life only for you to kill me. It seems an insult to him, like his suffering was all for nothing.'

'You're right,' Hirst sobbed. 'This wasn't your fault. And yes, he would be pissed off if I killed you.'

'And, let's not overlook the fact that we're both guilty of multiple murders.'

Hirst cocked his head to one side.

'So, really, the best thing for us to do is to get out of here. Two heads are better than one.'

Hirst nodded and closed the suitcase. 'You got a passport?' he asked Luke.

'Yeah, at Norma's.'

After stopping at Norma's for Luke's passport, Hirst drove just below the speed limit, wanting to look as unassuming as possible.

When he reached the edge of town without being stopped, he pulled over and they dumped Louie in a ditch by the roadside.

A few miles outside of Marshton, he called in Louie's location.

'That should give us a bit of breathing room, but it won't be long before they figure out what's happened,' he said.

Chapter 154

Louie groaned as he tried to drag himself to his feet. His damaged leg was still oozing blood and he felt sure he'd picked up some skin-rotting infection from the filthy water in the ditch.

He could already hear sirens in the distance which gave him the feeling that Hirst had set him up.

'Bastard,' he muttered. His breath came in ragged bursts with the effort of dragging himself out of the ditch and across the field that led towards home.

In the distance, a huge black column of smoke wound its way up to the heavens. Flames lit up the night sky around the house on the hill.

The sirens became deafening and a spotlight stung his eyes as it flooded the dark field with light.

'Turn around slowly,' a gruff voice told him.

He knew he was fucked. His leg was severely slowing him down.

He could see a large group of cops heading into the field after him.

With his reduced mobility there was no way he was outrunning anyone. He let out a cry of frustration and raised his hands as he turned.

The nearest cop slammed the butt of his gun into Louie's temple, sapping the meagre strength that remained in his legs. He collapsed in the wet grass.

The cop made him cry out in pain as he roughly bent his arm up his back. He read Louie his rights and started walking him back to one of the police cars.

'It wasn't me,' Louie insisted. 'It was Tom Hirst's father and some other guy.'

The cop scoffed at the idea of Hirst being a killer. 'Sergeant Hirst's a hero, son, don't you be talking shit about him, y'hear me?'

Louie continued his protests until the cop slammed a fist into the base of his skull and began dragging his limp body to the car.

Chapter 155

When Hirst and Luke were far away from Marshton, Hirst stopped and punched directions to the nearest airport into his sat nav.

He and Luke boarded the next plane, not caring where it went, only that it was far from England, far from the memories that plagued them.

In their new home in the Spanish sun, it was as though an immense weight had been lifted from their souls.

The past was behind them.

The guilty had paid for their crimes.

Hirst had photos of his son to remind him of all the good times they had shared.

Luke had photos of Bryony and his family.

The solution was ideal; Luke was in need of a father figure, Hirst in need of a son.

The future was a blank slate, ready for them to make their mark.

For both of them, the nightmare was over.

Bonus

Read on for a taster of *The Lazarus Contagion*,
the next Rayne of Terror release.

I: Integration

ONE

Nothing ever happens in Taunton, Mark thought with a grimace. The town was the kind of subdued dwelling hated by the young and sought by the old.

He groaned as he set off to meet his friend Rick for their weekly trek to the mall, a trip which was becoming as dull and pedestrian as every other aspect of life in Taunton.

The only thing that kept him going was Rick's razor-sharp putdowns and the hope that something exciting would happen.

'Fat chance,' he muttered, touching a flame to the tip of the cigarette that poked from between his lips.

He glanced around furtively as he inhaled the warm smoke. The last thing he needed was for one of his mother's friends to see him with a cigarette.

The only thing worse than the dull routine of going to the mall would be being grounded.

Mark pushed his shoulder-length blonde hair away from his forehead. His jacket was making him sweat in the heat of the day. He went hands-free on his smoke while he removed the garment.

'Whoa, gay t-shirt,' said a voice from his left.

'Fuck you, Rick,' he said, turning to see his friend grinning and flipping him the bird.

'Ready to go spend some of your rent boy money?' Rick beamed.

Mark punched him on the shoulder. Rick winced and his smile disappeared.

'Whoa, you hurt, man. No fair.'

Mark grinned and flicked his cigarette at his friend. It landed on his chest, sending sparks flying everywhere like a miniature Catherine wheel.

'Ok, message received,' Rick said.

They chatted as they walked.

The general consensus was that the day was going to be as mind-numbingly dull as any other.

But this would not be the case.

At the mall, they shoved their way through the crowds. For two fifteen year old boys, the jostling masses of semi-naked women were a godsend. Rick's eyes nearly popped out of his head as he saw a pink thong peaking from the back of a slim lady's jeans.

'Seen at least fifteen girls I'd fuck,' he grinned.

'Ditto.'

'So where you wanna go? Just get some shakes like normal and watch the chicks go by?'

'Maybe in a bit. I want to get some new trainers. These are practically falling off my feet.' He raised a shoe that was more air than material.

'If we have to,' Rick groaned. 'But don't be long.'

'Stop whinging. There's nothing else to do.'

Rick shrugged.

The bargain sports store where Mark bought his trainers was crammed with sweating, jostling punters.

The scene was a little overwhelming – a crowbar would probably be needed to get more people into the store.

The walls were ten feet high, covered in shoes and baseball boots and racks of clothing. The staff all wielded six foot long poles so they could reach the items on the higher shelves.

Mark shoved past a woman who clearly had dodged any sporting activity since he and Rick had been in diapers and headed for the men's trainers.

'It's fucking red hot in here,' Rick said, fanning air onto his face.

While Mark waited for a path to clear to the shoes, someone barged into him. He almost turned and planted him one but the fact that the man was built like a brick shithouse put him off.

He was bald and had a blue Lakers cap wedged on his skull. His entire face was contorted by an expression that was equal parts agony and crazy. He staggered as if heavily intoxicated.

'Whoa, he's loaded already,' Rick said. 'Not even twelve yet.'

Mark shushed him, not wanting the big guy to hear and become angry.

Mark cursed under his breath as the big man turned and looked right at him. It seemed he had heard the exchange and thought it was Mark who had insulted him.

'I didn't say that,' Mark said, his hands coming up instinctively in front of his face.

A strand of drool came from the right side of the man's grin. His eyes looked unfocussed and glazed over. He seemed to be looking through Mark.

His mouth moved but the words didn't make sense.

'Hee no. Come aaaa. Helmee.'

The man looked distressed and more uncoordinated than ever.

Mark opened his mouth to ask what he meant, but before he could, the man turned, taking out a young girl as he lunged forwards into the crowd.

'Noo,' he shouted, frantically looking over his shoulder as he shoved deeper into the crowd.

Voices of protest came from the other customers, but they were blotted out by the blaring of the store's alarm.

'Think someone's holding the place up?' Rick said. 'That'd be pretty cool.'

A few dozen people managed to shove their way out through the crowd before the store's shutters began to come down.

Mark heard a scream over the siren and looked back to see a huge man in a black uniform appear. His face was obscured by a large, ominous-looking gas mask.

His beefy hands clutched a submachine gun.

Acknowledgements

I'd like to keep this as brief as possible, as it might end up longer than the story if I get carried away...

First of all, I need to thank my frankly awesome wife and daughter for their support and belief in me. You have no idea how much it means to me that you dream big too. I love you both more than I could ever put into words. Thank you both.

Mez, Pez and Chuckles – you are the best family a guy could ask for. Thanks for supporting me in everything I do.

Bev, Chunk, Ren, Mike 'O'Popolous' Kell, Conk, Klunk, Keithy Boy (flying in the sky so fancy free!) and all the Bishop morons – you're the best friends I could have ever hoped to find. Cheers! \m/ \m/

The Baron – for being the craziest man in any room at any given time. They broke the mould when they made you, mate. Just keep away from that window...

Ian – for all the feedback and crack and music recommendations. Cholera does indeed bounce. The next gateaux's on me, my friend.

Stephen Bryant of SRB Productions, who created this kickass cover. Awesome work! Thank you.

I'd like to thank Rod Glenn, awesome writer and head honcho at Wild Wolf, for giving me a foot in the door with *Twisted Tails* and for all the advice and help you've provided. *Pipe Dreams* is gonna be cracking!

Reggie – the metal is strong in you! *House in Wales* rules. Cheers for the advice and feedback. Keep it metal. And I promise I'll review *Division of the Damned* soon... \m/ \m/

Poppet – thanks for all the advice on the business side of things. It's nice to have someone to help me muddle through it. Thanks for all the freebies too. Sequel to *Quislings* on the cards?

John Holt – thank you so much for helping me negotiate my way through the minefield of the EIN and tax situation. It is hugely appreciated.

Fiona McVie – For giving me the opportunity to take part in my very first interview. Thank you!

Jim McLeod – Thanks for allowing me to take part in my second interview and featuring me on the excellent Gingernuts of Horror site.

Last but certainly not least, Chuck W Lovatt, the man with the funniest Facebook page in history. Thanks for your support, mate, I know I can always look forward to some encouragement and wise words from you. Chuffed!

Thank you to everyone else who has supported me in any way, especially the people who have shared links and those who have taken the time

to read my work. I am also hugely appreciative
of all of the readers who have left reviews.
Cheers!

About Jacob

Repeated viewings of *The Shining* as a child have left Jacob with a love of the dark and the disturbing that really comes to life in his writing.

He works to a soundtrack of blisteringly heavy music, and, like his beloved metal, his writing is brutal, uncompromising and intense.

Jacob's work includes: *Sunshine* – A relentless horror novella in which holiday-makers transform into violent psychopaths;

Flesh Harvest – An action-packed horror novella involving a number of grisly deaths in a sleepy town in the North East of England;

Digital Children – A horror novella which has been described as '*Pet Sematary* on steroids';

Walk in the Park – A pulse-pounding horror novella in which a young mother is dragged into a living nightmare;

Karma Personified – A hitman's confessional;

Dying Breed – A series of terrifying apocalyptic horror novels; and many others.

Manufactured by Amazon.ca
Bolton, ON